WITCH

MARK BROWNLESS

Published by SpellBound Books

ISBN-13: 978-1-8384252-9-6

the Shadow Man

MARK BROWNLESS

Life is the sun and love is the moon
and neither the sun nor the moon can pull us apart

Victoria Hooper

CHAPTER 1

MOVING IN

November, 2019.

Rain hammered down on the roof of the car, sounding like thousands of tiny elves hitting the metalwork in a rhythm. *It's funny what you think about when you are driving.* Or so Gabe Hooper thought.

'Shouldn't we be there by now?' Victoria Hooper asked from the passenger seat.

'I think it's just up ahead,' he replied, thinking that it had been just up ahead for a mile or two. It hadn't been the easiest of days – moving house never was. So many memories to leave behind, and theirs were particularly difficult. 'There!' Gabe exclaimed seeing a small sign for their house, up ahead.

The orange indicator light blinked on and off, illuminating the turning and the rain droplets pouring down. The car turned off the main road, onto the downward slope of the gravel drive, which Gabe had almost missed, such was the ferocity of the weather, reducing his visibility to almost nothing. The driveway dropped gradually away from where it had been built up to meet the road, with steep drops either side, disappearing down into the trees. If this rain continued, he thought, it might wash the whole lane away. The road turned sharply left, before the first of the large trees. More tall pines were in front, forming an impenetrable fence in the rain. The track snaked right and left, down through the arboreal avenue. Emerging out of the gloom ahead, a myriad of white lights lit up a large building, illuminating a removal van backed up to almost kiss the gable end, with men scurrying back and forth like rats in an alley. The lane opened out as they approached their new house, sideways on to them, off to the right, with the old barn looming like a dark shadow in the trees to the left. From the glow of the house lights, he could just about make out the blackness of the lake beyond. He pulled the car in as close as he could to the removal van, the rain still lashing down.

'It looks different,' Tor said, from the passenger seat.

'It's bound to, we've only seen the place in the day and in pictures.'

'I hope those guys know what they're doing.'

'It's what we're paying them for,' he said, getting out and stretching himself up to his full six foot one, the last inch being the hardest, after the three-hour drive. Previously of athletic build, that had gone a little baggy in recent years, he brushed his wavy, shoulder length hair back from his face. 'Stay put, I'll see if we can get in,' he said leaning in, before closing the door and running across to the back of the van, beginning a conversation that Tor could barely see through the illuminated raindrops.

He ran back to her side of the car, hunching his head down between his shoulders in that way people do, as if that will make them smaller and less susceptible to getting wet. As far as he knew, there were no scientific studies to back this up. He pulled open the door.

'Come on, Tor, we can just about squeeze in by the tail-gate while the guys are unloading.' Guiding her by her elbow, they ran toward the house, bounding up the steps onto the decking that spanned the front of the house and that the removal van was currently overhanging. The house was built in the style of a Victorian boat house, with imposing stonework on this gable end and the roof protruding out over the deck with ornate wooden supports. The ground floor was all stone walls, but the upstairs was built into the triangular roof with more modern Velux windows and lightboxes. Running across the deck, they nodded at the removal men piling boxes up on the tailgate of the van, and, to help, they grabbed a box each and squeezed between the platform and the house, disappearing in through the front door. Inside, they took a few steps into the short hallway which opened out into the large open plan kitchen diner leading into the living space at the far end of the house. Looking at each other, they couldn't stop smiling. It was everything they'd ever wanted in a house – by a lake, in the countryside, open and airy.

They were home.

'Love you, Gabriel Hooper.'

'Love you, Victoria Hooper.' Putting their boxes down they embraced and stole a brief kiss. His arms wrapping around his tall, slim wife, reaching down to cup her bottom through her bright blue jeans. 'I think I better find the kettle though to keep these lads going.'

'Good idea. The box is labelled 'Kitchen – kettle.''

'Why? That makes no sense.' Gabe grinned and looked at the boxes that were scattered around the kitchen worktops, the central island and piled up on the floor. 'We don't own this much stuff. There's been some sort of mistake and they've moved somebody else's stuff in with us as well.'

'You'd be surprised, babe.'

'We didn't pack anywhere near this many boxes.'

'Well, you didn't, no.' Tor raised an eyebrow.

'Ouch.' Gabe moved several boxes out of the way on the worktop and quickly found the kettle box. Whilst it boiled, the sound slowly growing in the room like a small jet engine, he searched for tea bags. He almost expected to see them listed on the inventory written on the cardboard, but it only took two guesses to pick the right one. With tea stewing, he turned his attention to the nearest box to him and began to unpack the contents. Tor stood in the middle of the kitchen directing traffic, as it came in through the door, like a police officer at a road accident. He watched her, pretty with high cheek bones and brown hair tumbling in waves down onto her shoulders, loving her organisation, her control within the chaos – one of her great strengths. In what seemed like no time at all, the last few boxes and pieces of furniture came in from the van and the sodden workers had hot drinks and some biscuits that Tor managed to locate. Gabe chatted briefly with the owner. They'd gone with a small company so they'd get a more personal service and been less like a number than with a big remover. They were also half the price. With handshakes all round and a final wave from the decking as the huge behemoth of the removal van pulled away from the house, brushing the undergrowth at the edge of the trees before disappearing up the lane, they could shut the door to leave the house empty and silent. Gabe stood in the middle of the kitchen, appearing distracted.

'What's wrong?' Tor asked, touching his arm. He held up his hand to ask her to wait for a moment.

'Just listening to them going up the lane – you can hear them all the way to the road, so we'll be able to hear any visitors we get,' he smiled.

'So that's it then, we're in.' Tor raised her eyebrows as she looked around the room. 'Let's get the duvet on the bed and washbags out for later – then go to the pub for some food,' she said decisively, brushing some hair back from her face and tucking it behind an ear.

'Good shout. You remember where the pub was you Googled?'

'No. But I was getting 3G on the road, so I'll look it up again when we get there. When are we getting wi-fi?'

'Early next week they said.'

'Okay. Well at least we've got a phone signal, which I'm a bit surprised about. Come on Hooper, let's get to the pub.'

∞ ∞ ∞

The rain seemed to gather itself, as if it was disappointed by its efforts earlier in the day, and its dad had told it to buck its ideas up. Now it really meant business. Even with the wipers on double speed the visibility was appalling and Gabe found himself driving at twenty miles-an-hour along the winding road. They'd left all the outside lights on at the house as a beacon for when they returned – it wouldn't do to miss the turning and drive halfway around the lake looking for it. Their lane sloped steeply up to the main road, and he wondered what it would be like in the dead of winter with frost and snow – would they have any chance of getting out? Still, being snowbound with a roaring fire by the lakeside did have a certain romance. As long as they didn't run out of loo roll or pasta. The main road was wide and well-maintained, with crash barriers on the sharper bends and solid white lines down the middle for most of it to stop overtaking. There were no streetlights, nor even cats eyes to mark their way, so the full-beam headlights were the only guide they had and they were busy having a running battle with the rain. Gabe's lack of familiarity didn't help – *what was coming after this hump in the road, is this a left or right hander up ahead?* Headlights appeared in the rear-view mirror, coming up so close behind that the other driver might as well have been sitting in their back seat. It's easier to follow someone of course – you just do what they do when they turn left or right, and if they get round a bend at the speed they're going, then you will too. Solidarity with one's fellow motorist in testing conditions is one thing – being right up someone's arse, isn't.

'Any idea where this pub is?' Gabe said, squinting hard, as if it would make the headlights pierce further into the night, he changed from fourth down to third coming out of a right-hander as the engine started to complain.

'Google said it was about two miles down the road, after the end of the lake and before the village.'

'What's it say, now?'

'Dunno – no signal.' She held up the glowing screen of her phone to reinforce the point, adding to the faint glow from the dashboard lights to cut through the darkness.

'I wish this guy behind would back off.' The other driver surely couldn't be comfortable with being that close in these conditions –

stopping distances would be out of the window. Tor stole a quick glance behind her and just saw headlights tailgating them.

'There!' she said after turning back, and despite being somewhat dazzled, she saw lights ahead, set back from the road into the hill.

'Sure it's not a house?' Gabe stole a glance to the left and saw the place.

'Don't think it's a house – too well lit.' Gabe slowed the car, indicating left, the car behind deciding enough was enough, roaring past with over-revved engines.

'I've made a friend,' he said, turning onto a lane sloping uphill toward the welcome lights of what was very obviously the local pub. Next to the turning was a sign in Welsh welcoming them to the village of Cwm Cysgod. There were a few cars parked on the gravel at the front of the pub, huddled together while their owners warmed themselves inside. Gabe parked as close to the entrance as he could before they made a dash for it. Before he'd even closed his car door he was soaked and he looked across at Tor, who had sensibly put her coat over her head, so at least she'd stay dry somewhere. Pulling the door open they almost fell inside to get out of the rain, straight into a scene from *An American Werewolf in London*, where the patrons of the *Slaughtered Lamb* all stop and turn to look at the young backpackers. Silence greeted them. The only movement was the publican polishing a glass. Gabe imagined he could hear it squeaking.

'Evenin',' said the man from behind the bar, attempting a smile. Gabe realised this place probably wasn't on the tourist maps.

'Hi,' Gabe replied, embarrassed that he gave a small wave in accompaniment, which faded as quickly as it had begun.

'Oh. English is it?' An elderly woman sitting at the bar responded, nursing a small glass – maybe a port and lemon. Her hair tightly permed and salt and pepper grey, she was so thin she looked like she might break if she went outside in the wind.

'Yes, I'm afraid so.'

'Don't get many English around here,' she said, looking him up and down with fiery eyes, carefully made up with sky blue eye shadow.

'Steady on now Carol, let them get in and have a drink,' chided the barman.

'What? Well, we don't. I'm only stating a fact, isn't it?' Gabe got the impression that this conversation might've normally been conducted in Welsh but was all being done in the Mother tongue for their benefit.

'What can I get you?' Once again, an attempted smile, but in comparison with the old woman, it was a positively glowing welcome.

Gabe looked at Tor, who simply nodded. 'Pint of cider and a gin and tonic, please.' He stood at the bar next to Carol, being careful not to drip on her and cause further bad feeling. 'We've just moved in at–'

'Ty Llyn?' said an old man sat in a rocking chair in the corner of the room by a roaring log fire. The hearth was set in an inglenook and it was the first time Gabe had noticed it or him for that matter. The logs crackled and spat and he wondered if the rocking chair was in danger of being set alight, as close as it was to the flames.

'Yes, the Lake House.'

'Don't get a lot of new residents so we knew you were coming. You're a writer, aren't you, Hooper?' said the old man, gently rocking back and forth, his eyes staring at Gabe while he sipped at his pint. He looked every inch a farmer, brown tweed trousers, stretched across a beer belly and pulled almost up to his chest by braces, covering a shirt of thin checks, unbuttoned hallway revealing a white vest that was probably in-situ year-round. His hair was clipped to a number two at the back and sides with a wild combover attempting to hide most of his scalp. It failed miserably.

'Yes, yes, I am.' Gabe was more than a little flattered that these locals had done their research on him, and obviously knew his work. 'As is my wife, Victoria. Tor. She writes children's books.' *Well, one children's book that sold millions*, he thought.

'I thought your last book was rubbish,' Carol chimed in. 'Totally unbelievable. Like you'd just made everything up.' She raised her eyes to the ceiling as if asking for divine help to explain the ridiculousness of Gabe's novel.

'It is fiction though, Carol. May I call you Carol?' He gave her a questioning look and she nodded. 'I do tend to write more fantastical stories in my fiction, as a way of the reader gaining some escapism from their daily lives.' He smiled at her.

'Right. Well, I didn't understand any of what you just said, but like I said, I thought it was shit.' Carol wrapped her long green cardigan around her, some of the larger holes offering a view of her pink jumper beneath, and nodded, as if that was the end to the matter – a thousand reviews on *Amazon* had been blown out of the water now that Carol had made her decision.

'I thought it was alright,' said the man in the rocking chair.

'You would Idris, just to be different to me.'

'You could start an argument in an empty room Carol Jones, it doesn't need to be about a book.'

'Well, whether you liked it or not, I'm very flattered that you took the time to read my work.' Gabe smiled sheepishly as the barman made eye contact and put their drinks onto coasters.

'Why did you move?' he asked, before adding with a nod. 'Mal Jenkins, by the way.'

'Writer's block, eh love?' Tor interjected. 'It's hard to write living in the city with lots of distractions, so we thought we'd move and get Gabe a fresh start and fresh inspiration.'

'I wish I had a job where I could just sit there and not do anything if the mood took me. Cleaner's block it'd be called,' Carol smiled, amused at her own joke.

'Cleaner's blockage more like,' said Idris with a cackle, which was rewarded by a scowl from Carol. 'You couldn't write so you thought you'd come down here?'

'Something like that.'

'Iawn,' Idris nodded. *Good.* Then drained his pint, setting it down on the little round table next to him.

'We'd like to get some food, please?' Tor leaned across the bar to ask Mal.

'We don't do food. Sorry,' said Carol, evidently more involved in the running of the place than your average customer. Tor looked around at the small number of tables, and saw empty plates and bowls where the patrons clearly had been 'doing' food.

'Sorry, but haven't all these people eaten?' she smiled sweetly.

'Ah but that's different. Tonight's Mal's curry night. Just for the locals to get together. Like a community thing.' Carol looked stern – fierce even – as if 'locals' was a closed shop, something that would take a long time – if ever – for them to be regarded as.

'Please. We've been on the go all day and haven't got anything in. If you've got something left, we'd really appreciate it.' Carol was staring straight ahead, unmoved, but in front of her Mal gave the smallest of nods and the tiny, slight woman slid off her barstool to walk back behind the bar.

'We don't advertise food,' explained Mal. 'It gets complicated with inspections and licensing. We're not on the 'map' as a pub, don't get a lot of tourists, just everyone here.'

'Don't mind Carol. Her bark is worse than her bite,' Idris joined in. 'She doesn't like anybody.' A fresh pint had materialised on his little table. His loose lips pursed to sip at the full glass – it was impossible to tell if he had teeth or not. 'So, you got in alright then?'

'Yes thanks. Gonna take a while to unpack, but everything's in.'

'Nice day for it.'

'It's been launching down all day. When they were unloading it was like something from a horror film, as if the place was haunted or something.'

'Course the place is haunted,' Idris said, setting down his glass, his eyes intense.

'Oh Idris, not now, they've just got here,' chided Mal. Carol came through the two-way kitchen door behind the bar, carrying two steaming bowls of green curry and rice. There was one naan bread between them. She sat them down on the bar where the Hooper's had taken up seats. They thanked her and tucked ravenously into classic pub curry – sweet, sour and just a bit spicy, just what they needed. The bar fell almost completely silent, as if they were the sole focus of the place for that evening – the entertainment, or the freakshow. It was disconcerting to have everyone watching them eat.

'Haunted you say?' Gabe said at last, bringing the conversation back to Idris' earlier comment. 'Really?' Gabe was more playing along with the old man, as if Carol and him were a double act, first one putting them off, then the other.

'Yep.'

'Idris? May I call you that?'

'It's my name.'

'Right. What makes you say the house is haunted? Is that well known or just some local stories to scare the kids – that any old place is haunted?'

'They're not stories. The lake is haunted by an old witch. Doesn't like anyone being around.'

'Anyone seen this witch? Have you?'

'No. But I know plenty about her. She's real enough.'

'But has anyone seen her? Anyone here?' Gabe raised his voice and looked around at the people in the pub. Nobody answered.

'Not a believer then, Mr Hooper.' It wasn't a question. 'In'trestin', you being a writer of fantasy stuff and all. Fine by me. You enjoy your house on the lake.' The old man looked away and rocked gently back and forth in his chair.

'What does *that* mean?'

'It means whether you believe in her or not, she'll still come after you. She won't leave you alone just because you're a sceptic.'

'That's quite a fanciful claim, Idris. That this ghost-witch will come after us,' Tor said, leaning on the bar now she'd finished her meal.

'Fanciful. You wouldn't say that if you've been round here for long enough.' It was his turn now for his eyes to grow fierce, looking annoyed that he was having to explain something as obvious as witches. Like he was explaining gravity.

'Because you haven't got an explanation for things that happen?' Tor smiled kindly.

'Oh, I do. It's the witch. Perfectly reasonable explanation if you ask me.' He folded his arms across his belly.

'I think we can bat this argument back and forth all night and still not agree on anything.'

'We just did.'

'Look we're gonna make a move – want to make sure that the witch hasn't broken in and made herself at home while we've been out.' Gabe paid Mal the barman.

'You take this seriously, now.'

'Well, I tell you what, Idris. We'll keep an eye out for any weird things that might happen and we won't just dismiss them if they do. How does that sound?' Gabe shrugged then smiled at the old man.

'It sounds like you'll be believing me in a weeks' time.'

'Maybe we will. Idris, it's been a pleasure talking to you. Carol.' The Hooper's nodded at both old stagers and with a wave of the hand to everyone else in the bar, pushed out through the door, into the night.

CHAPTER 2

-\/-

A GOOD NIGHT'S SLEEP

Taking Tor's lead from earlier, Gabe already had his jacket hooded over his head when they went outside, fingers tightening on the material to prevent it being blown away. Tor followed, similarly ready to brave the deluge. But the night was clear. The rain had stopped and the wind had blown most of the cloud away. An almost full moon shone down, illuminating the sky in a brilliant blue-grey, only occasionally hiding behind cotton wool clouds as they raced across the heavens on the wind. Stopping at the car, they took in the view in the moonlight. Rolling hills covered in coniferous forest, small valleys and hollows cutting through the canopy with streams or roads. The hills further back, tall and overseeing all before, with only the occasional windblown trunk on their slopes. From the car park, the hill sloped down to the main road, and they could trace it, a gap in the trees like a gash in the foliage, winding its way along the valley, seeing the light of the village of Cwm Cysgod twinkling in the bottom and up onto a low hill. The road became a black line, twisting and turning through the woods, and beyond, in the distance, over the tops of the trees, they could see the lake. Their lake. The moonlight glinting off the surface.

'It's not a bad spot, is it?' Gabe said, Tor leaning her head against him.

'No, it's not. We could've picked worse places.'

'Well, *you* could.'

'Hey don't blame me.' Her eyes widened, playfully.

'It *was* a pin in a map though, wasn't it?'

'No. How on earth could you think such a thing? Meticulous research found this place.' She rolled her eyes.

'Ah yes. So, a pin in a map then.' They climbed into the car and slowly rolled back down the hill to join the main road – a different place to drive now, in the moonlight, and without the rain. At the junction, Gabe looked both ways, the road lit up by the moonlight glinting through the trees, reflecting like jewels off the wet road surface. There were no cars at this time of night. He turned the wheel to the right and gunned the engine, tyres losing traction for a moment, screeching and slipping, before gripping the soaking tarmac, the car shooting off down the road. Tor shot him a disapproving glance.

'What?' He smiled back at her.

'You,' she stifled her own smile and folded her arms.

Gabe enjoyed the sweeping turns, the contours and humps and hollows of the road, not pushing too hard on the unfamiliar bends, or burying his foot on the straights, but he looked forward to driving along in the daytime even more. The car responded immediately to the slightest movement on the wheel, hugging the road surface.

'Shit! What the fuck?' Gabe exclaimed as they rounded a left-hand bend and dropped into a hollow, a split second before there was a loud bang and a screech of brakes as the car came to a juddering halt in a cloud of smoke from the tyres.

'What the hell was that,' asked Tor, her eyes wide, fingernails digging into the armrest and central console.

'We hit something,' Gabe said, wiping a shaking hand down his face, before getting out of the car, smelling the brakes. He looked around but there was no traffic, and he could see no debris around the car. Thirty yards further back there was a dark shape in the road, however. Convinced it was a body, that he'd hit someone, he walked slowly toward it, nervous, not sure what it was and desperately hoping he hadn't hit a person – maybe a small child.

And why would a child be out walking the roads, in the middle of nowhere, at this time of night? He thought to himself – eyes unwavering from the shape in the road.

The body, not the shape. It's a body.

The moonlight was enough only to show the outline but no detail. It was only when he got up close that Gabe realised what it was, and he squatted down by the side of the large tree limb lying in the road. Looking up at the overhanging trees above, he could see a freshly broken part of the trunk of one – it was either the wind, being saturated with rain or both that had brought it down, and he just hadn't seen it in time rounding the bend.

Lessons learned.

Squatting in the middle of the road, he slid his hands under the smaller end of the trunk, lifting it upright, so it stood side-by-side with him like an old friend in a hunting photo, then he turned and pushed it off the side of the road, it tumbling end over end, crashing down into the gulley below, sliding its way down toward the stream he could hear bubbling toward the lake at the bottom of the banking.

'Haven't you had enough excitement for one night?' Tor asked him as he got back into the car, having watched him clear the road of the log in the wing mirror.

'Why, what did you have in mind?' He grinned as he started the engine again and pulled away.

'Oh, and by the way.' She paused for effect, and he took his eyes off the road to look at her. 'You're never allowed to play with Idris ever again.'

'Yeah, you're probably right.'

Beyond the outskirts of Cwm Cysgod, the trees became somewhat thinner to the left, the land sloping gradually down to the lake, moonlight shimmering on the surface. Although they were looking for it, the turning was obvious, headlights even picking up the sign for Lake House. The car turned onto the gravel and meandered its way through the trees, twisting and turning along the lane down to the house, parking in the same place as earlier, which would no doubt become the place where they always parked from now on. Arm in arm they walked around the decking to the side of their new home, and stood looking out over the water, the fresh breeze creating a chill as it blew in their faces.

'Let's get inside,' Tor said, shivering, the romantic moment unable to keep out the cold. Gabe opened the front door and nearly fell over the box he'd left by the side of it. Bending, he opened the cardboard flaps that had been carefully tucked under one another, and pulled out the doormat – the 'unwelcome' mat as they called it – and put it in place in front of the door. Sliding the box to the side with his foot, he heard a tinkling sound of metal on metal from inside and bent to lift out their windchimes. 'Don't start messing about with them now love,' said Tor, thinking of several hundred things he could be doing that were more of a priority than putting those up. Or going to bed.

'Won't take a sec, there's a hook,' Gabe replied with a smile. A thick beam ran horizontally the width of the house, supporting the overhanging eaves. Previous owners had clearly used it to hang things from as there were a number of hooks and brackets along the length, maybe from hanging baskets or outside lights. Gabe reached up onto his tiptoes and slid the metal loop of the chimes over the nearest hook, a thick, mean looking thing that he thought would be at home with half a pig hanging from it, untwisting the chain and each of the chimes so they were hanging properly, immediately singing out their tune in the breeze. 'Feels more like home, now,' he said.

'And at least we haven't got neighbours here that we can piss off with the noise.' Tor kicked off her shoes by the mat and went in search of wine.

∞ ∞ ∞

The moon rose higher in the sky, a sentry watching over the whole horizon, scaring off any clouds from wanting to come out to play. The wind whistled down from the hills, rolling into the valley, sweeping over the trees, causing them to whisper and sigh in response. There was a moment of silence as it jumped off the treetops, like a child who'd made a ramp from some bricks and a piece of wood and was racing along on their bike to make the big leap – suddenly, silently airborne for a split second – before crashing to the surface of the lake as the child crashed to the floor, both screaming as they landed. Ripples were whipped up on the water, disturbing the otherwise mirror-like surface, making water flow and a current where there had previously been none.

At the edge of the trees, in that moment of silence, was a hollow. A fold in the ground, a shadow between shadows, between the tree roots. A nothing. It was as black as black and as cold as the water lapping up to it. A place where everything was absorbed – light, sound, heat, hope, maybe even time itself. It was overgrown and unnoticed, somewhere you could be standing right next to and not know it was there.

The tinkling of the wind chimes at Lake House was lifted by the swirling wind and taken up over the trees and back around the lake, jingling like festive sleigh bells. A last cloud dared to race across the sky, running from the disapproving gaze of the moon, whilst joyfully chasing the sounds of the chimes. They were carried across the lake to the far side, tossed around by the breeze, bouncing along the shore, and sweeping into the silent place, into the shadows, the dark where no joy ever visited. The wind, whispering through the early autumn leaves, brought a chill to the air. The whispers grew louder as they dropped into the hollow, almost coalescing into words. Words that swirled and circled around the cold blackness, chanting, taunting, insisting – circling around and not taking *no* for an answer. Deep within the hollow, beneath the rotting layers of leaf mold and ancient tree roots, something stirred. The darkness moved like a blanket, raised from its slumber by the bells and whispers. The air moved, distorted – curving around the shape – the temperature dropping further causing moisture in the air to freeze and form a frosty lip to the cave. The wind grew and clouds now gathered overhead, rolling in from nowhere like school children at lunchtime, ignoring the displeasure of the moon. The whispers swirled around and around almost giving solid form to that which had risen, as it slowly emerged from the darkness into the dappled moonlight at the lake shore. The wind chimes tinkled their pretty refrain – vague and disjointed on the breeze – but a definite sound nonetheless. Then the whispers faded and died, disappearing on the breath of the wind, like a sigh. The thing that remained shrieked, screaming a shrill noise across the water surface, then took to the air, rising above the trees, climbing vertically as the storm clouds covered the moon like a shroud. It rose and banked, turning toward the sound of the chimes, toward the house at the far end of the lake. Toward Ty Llyn.

And it flew like the wind.

∞ ∞ ∞

Tor sat cradling her wine glass with her feet tucked under her in familiar fashion, Gabe sitting at the opposite end of the sofa as if they'd had a row. Normally the most straightforward of tasks; locating a bottle of wine, corkscrew and two glasses, had become particularly onerous and she admonished herself for not putting the opener at the top of a box. And labelling it so. Still, if that was the biggest mistake she'd make in this whole move, she would've done okay. The cool evening brought a chill to the house and a feeling of dampness from both the rain and the place being empty for so long. She knew it would resolve itself by throwing all the windows open tomorrow morning to get some air flowing. In the absence of heating – Gabe was going to look at the boiler tomorrow – he'd gone looking for fuel for the large log burner in the corner of the sitting room, re-appearing with an armful of weathered logs he'd found under the eaves, just as Tor popped the cork from the Malbec. Soon, and to her pleasant surprise, Gabe got the logs roaring, with, in the absence of tinder and kindling, the help of the blowtorch from his toolbox. Slowly, the cast iron of the stove started to warm the space. Tor wasn't sure about the open plan design of the ground floor – the large kitchen diner carefully 'divided' from the living area by the kitchen units and breakfast bar. She was already thinking about movable room dividers to separate things off.

They'd spent the last few days talking whilst packing – reliving memories, exchanging wistful glances – and in the car driving here. It was the first time they'd sat down and talked for some time, not from any lack of a desire to communicate but simply because of time, and, because they just… didn't. It was like a skill, something that you had to practice to be able to do well, and it seemed that neither of them worked hard enough at their relationship to do that. Besides, there were some things that were there to be talked about, the elephant in the room of the conversation, that they needed to and never properly had. So, it was easier to just not talk at all. They'd talked in the pub too, and whilst doing the cursory unpacking since getting home. Now, when they could sit and chew the fat, they seemed to have little to say, as if they'd exhausted all topics, apart from *that* one. The removal men had almost thrown the sofas in an 'L' shape into the sitting room, facing the log burner in the corner with its impressive cast iron flue going straight up through a plate in the ceiling at the junction with the blank end wall. The room was oddly unbalanced, crying out for a book shelf in the other corner and, no doubt, the TV occupying the big wall space in the middle. She worried that, like their car parking 'space', they would unpack in a hurry and just put things where they were and that would become their permanent home without thinking best how to use the space they had.

'Let's just take our time with the unpacking,' she said, resin from one of the logs spitting its agreement from inside the stove.

'You don't have to tell me twice. But neither of us are gonna want boxes hanging around for weeks on end.' Gabe shrugged.

'No, God no. I just mean, let's think about where everything is gonna go – the best place for it – rather than put it somewhere and it's still there ten years later. I know what you're like.'

'I strongly predict one Sunday afternoon, not so long from now, I'll be moving furniture around each room in this house like musical chairs with you pulling the strings, my love, trying every conceivable combination of positions for them, because *I* know what *you're* like.' He toasted her.

'I don't want to just dump stuff. Let's get it right.'

'Okay, fine. Agreed. But can we agree that that bloody great big wall is where I'm gonna hang the telly? Just before I start drilling holes.'

'Yeah okay,' she laughed. 'Don't do it now, though, eh? Neighbours might complain about the noise.'

'The neighbours, eh?'

They sat and stared at the orange flames licking slowly around the glowing logs in the stove, taking in the smell of the heat from the cast iron and burning wood, the room having become warm and the wine starting to take hold. Tor looked at the picture of Mikey on the windowsill – not it's final position, no doubt, but certainly the first thing to be unpacked, so he was with them in their new home.

'We did do the right thing, didn't we?' she asked, sliding down the sofa to rest her head on the arm and her feet in his lap. He put his glass down and began to play with them, strong hands and fingers sliding up and down her arches with familiarity, gently loosening each tiny joint in her foot before moving on to the next one, then soothing the band of fascia in the soles – loosening the tightness.

'I think so.' He had been tempted to say *sure, course we did.* But this wasn't the kind of *sure, course we did* kind of conversation. It wasn't the kind of *sure, course we did* kind of lifestyle change that they'd opted for in moving, either. It was meant to bring them closer together, to talk, to share, to rebuild parts of themselves. To fill a Mikey-sized hole in them both. It was meant to save them – and *sure, course we did* really ought to have got left behind in the move. 'We weren't going anywhere in the old house. We needed a fresh start, to get away. Too many memories, too many–'

Ghosts? Was he going to say ghosts?

'Things from the past that we couldn't get over. I couldn't write – neither could you. Here will be different. The memories we want. Us living again. You know all this – this came from you.' He nodded to her.

'I hope I don't get the blame.' Her eyes blazed for a second as she wondered where this was going.

'Hey, no, it's okay. It was a good idea – a great one, and, honestly, one I would probably have never had. So, good on you. I'll just hump the furniture where you tell me.' He smiled, as the tension that had just sprung up in her legs at the thought of him accusing her of something, her getting ready for a fight – fight or flight she supposed – that tension eased, like that in her feet.

Tor's eyes started to get heavy and she put her glass down – didn't want a spillage on their first night. She looked at her watch. It was just before ten. 'Well, it's been some day. So much to think about. Leaving the old place was so hard. There was a point…' she paused, eyes suddenly brimming with tears, and her voice catching in her throat. 'There was a point where I didn't think I could. Like someone else shouldn't be allowed to live there, in our… home.' She sniffed as tears rolled freely down her cheeks, Gabe wrapped his arms around her legs, his eyes never leaving hers. 'But you just have to. It either goes on or it doesn't, right?' And now she looked afraid, as she asked the same question again, about whether they did the right thing in moving.

'Life has gotta go on, babe, yeah.' He nodded and kissed each kneecap, resting his chin in the gap between them.

'Yeah.' Tor blew out a big sigh and sniffed hard. 'I think I'll get ready for bed.' She peeled herself away from his grip, slowly levering herself up from the sofa, in that moment feeling a lot older than her thirty-eight years.

'Yeah. Me too.'

∞ ∞ ∞

Gabe drained his glass and picked up Tor's, tidying bottle and glasses away before turning the fire down to give them some late evening heat. He wondered if the stove would help heat the first floor, from the warm air rising up the stairs and the flue radiating into the spare bedroom. He hadn't even noticed it in the end room and resolved to get to know the detailed layout and properties of the house more in the next few days. It was one of those things – spend weeks pouring over details of a place on the internet, then visit it and pick apart everything about it to make sure it's right for you before you buy – and then, and only then, do you really start to get to know the place.

Letting the cold tap run for a good long time to clear the pipes, he filled two glasses of water for them for bed. He knew the water came from a bore hole, but in his imagination, it had been drawn from the icy coldness of the bottom of the lake – confounding mermaids and lake gods as the water disappeared – some ancient pumping system taking the crystal-clear liquid along a series of pipes and in through the cellar somewhere, straight to this tap. At the top of the stairs, he almost bumped into Tor wandering between bathroom and bedroom cleaning her teeth. She'd put her hair up in a clip so she could wash her face and had changed into her sleeveless, white, *John McClane* vest top that did little to hide the movement of her firm breasts as she walked around, and blue-checked pyjama bottoms. Tor always walked around when she cleaned her teeth – in this case, moving toiletries into the chest of drawers in the bedroom (*but don't think for a minute that it'll be staying where it is*), with bobbles and shower gel moving in the opposite direction.

'Fanks,' she nodded at the glasses, mumbling around her toothbrush, foaming at the mouth and having to make a sudden run for the bathroom to spit before she spilled any.

Gabe set their drinks down on their respective bedside cabinets. Their wooden bed frame was in the spare room along with all its bolts, waiting to be assembled – the mattress on the floor would do for tonight. After completing his own ablutions for the night and settling into bed, he noticed how weird it felt, reaching up for their drinks, and he knew he was at risk of knocking things flying in the night when he was at his most clumsy. But that was only half of how strange it felt as he looked around at the plain four walls of their new bedroom, boxes and half-unpacked items scattered across the floor under the large corner window overlooking the lake, covered by thin almost gossamer curtains, letting the moonlight stream in. The bedside lamps had no shades – they were in a box somewhere, and Gabe thought that might be a mantra for the next few days; *they're in a box somewhere.* Settling down in their own bed, in crisp sheets, pillows propped behind them, it felt a little more like home than if they were staying at a rented cottage or something. He opened Stephen King, and Tor had CJ Tudor. Odd how, here, in this community, they were as much *The Outsider* or *The Other People* as in their books. Yet, as good as they were, after the physical and emotional trials of the day, the fictional prose couldn't sustain their interest for long and, eyes heavy, they turned off their lights. The glow of the moon through the giant corner window diminished somewhat as cloud gathered in a swirling mass over the water at the far end of the lake.

'Good night, babe,' he said, kissing her.

'Good night yourself,' she touched his cheek as she kissed him back.

'We did make the right decision. Moving. Whatever happens.' He kissed her again, feeling her lips respond.

'Let's hope so.' She wrapped an arm around his back and opened her mouth to his, their tongues meeting like strangers on a railway platform – politely exchanging a handshake and a token flower. He couldn't remember the last time they had kissed like this, let alone anything else, and his arousal against her thigh betrayed just how interested his libido was.

'Not quite ready to go to sleep just yet, are we love?' she smiled, resting her forehead against his and taking his bottom lip between hers, before reaching down, under the waistband of his shorts. He groaned at her touch and gasped as her fingers encircled him, silencing himself by crushing his mouth to hers. Urgency gripped them both, and Gabe rolled on top of her, pushing aside *John McClane* and exposing her breasts to his mouth and hands. She arched her back as he kissed down from her neck, wrapping her free hand around his back as she stroked his hardness with the other. His mouth closed around a nipple and she gasped, digging her nails into him through his t-shirt. They both heard the loud bang and clatter like the sound of glass shattering.

'What the fuck was that?' she asked, rudely snatched back to reality.

'I dunno, I'll go take a look.' Gabe levered himself up from the low bed and went to the door. 'Stay put.'

'Like hell I will,' Tor replied, pulling her vest back down and reaching for her hoody that she used instead of a robe.

They raced down the curving stairs to the front hall, expecting to see glass broken and a dead bird perhaps. But there was nothing. The noise had been loud, loud for them in the bedroom – enough to distract them from what they were doing – so what the hell had made it? They exchanged a glance, Gabe looking through to the kitchen to see if anything appeared amiss.

'It was at the front, I'm sure,' said Tor, gesturing towards the door. Gabe turned away from her and peered through the glass panels.

'What the hell?' he said. Turning the key that he'd left in the lock, as was his want, he pulled the door open. There at his feet lay the mangled remains of their wind chimes, the delicate metal pipes bent or broken in a twisted mess on the decking. He looked up at the hook in the overhead beam. The curved piece of solid metal that had struck Gabe as far too big and chunky for the job at hand had been pulled straight by something. 'What the fuck was this?' he asked, looking from hook to chimes and back again.

'Didn't you hang it up properly?' asked Tor in her slightly irritating way of implying just about anything was Gabe's fault.

'Well of course,' he replied, suitably irritated. 'It doesn't come with instructions. You either successfully hang something from a hook or Isaac Newton calls you a twat. And look at the hook – it was bent and…' he shook his head.

'Hook shaped?'

'Yes. Alright, yes it was like a hook, and now look at it.'

'And how do you propose that this hook pulled itself out straight?'

'I guess someone didn't like the chimes.'

'Someone?'

'Well, I don't know. It was just something to say. I've got no idea. Very odd.'

Gabe went out onto the deck, and down the steps, his t-shirt blowing furiously in the breeze that was roaring in from the lake. He peered up the lane, but his vision was limited by the darkness, making a mental note to investigate the lighting system tomorrow to see what they could light up outside and what they couldn't. Turning he jogged toward the lake, straining his eyes into the woods and looking for anything moving around the house, the wind pushing him back, trying to keep him away. For a moment he imagined the increasingly urgent beeping of the motion trackers they used in *Aliens*, and wondered what they'd show up in the darkness of the woods. Hopefully not angry xenomorphs. Tor stood with her arms folded across her chest in the doorway, shivering.

'Let's just go back inside. You can have a good look around tomorrow morning in the light,' she shouted against the noise of the wind.

'Yeah, okay. I think I will lock up, too. I did before coming up to bed the first time, regardless of what the locals might do.' Gabe pushed the mangled wind chimes to one side with his foot until it could be forensically examined in the morning and closed the door behind him, locking and bolting it. 'I'm just gonna do a sweep down here to see if I can see anything. You go back to bed.' Gabe turned and walked through the kitchen, looking out of the windows at the narrow perimeter of light produced by the house. Marching into the sitting room, he scanned around, looking through the patio doors and even turning on the outside lights to extend his view.

Nothing was amiss.

Switching off the lights in turn, Gabe took one last look around before going upstairs. Their welcoming new home suddenly feeling somewhat more sinister – every shadow a mystery and every noise a threat. It was silly of course. Something odd happened to the chimes and now their new home seemed more scary.

'Not the first evening I expected,' Tor said as Gabe came back into the bedroom, the bedside lights illuminating the room once again.

'Yeah, maybe we're gonna have to re-define 'normal', living around here.' Gabe slid into bed next to her. They turned their lamps off for a second time and spooned like they always did when they drifted off to sleep, both of them restless and fitful with dreams troubled with noises and dark, foreboding skies.

CHAPTER 3
-\/-
BARN

The sky was a uniform grey, clouds folded almost into fish scales, reflecting off the mirrored surface below – the lake as calm and still as the air. Wisps of mist hung in the trees on the far side, like cotton wool 'snow' stuck in a Christmas tree. Ducks took off noisily from the water, cleared for take-off on the runway this morning, then landing almost immediately, ready to dig in a fresh patch of mud for worms and other goodies for their breakfast. Staring out across the water, leaning against the balustrade of the decking, Gabe thought that there really should be a dock, extending from where he was standing, out over the water. Slurping some steaming coffee from the Homer Simpson mug at his lips, he mused about his new DIY project. It would take a bit of building, but it would be great to do a spot of fishing out there and walk straight into the kitchen with his catch without ever getting wet. There was a boat, half-pulled out of the water, down on the shore off to the right – a large rowing boat with a flat section at the back which might be a place for an outboard motor, Gabe thought, his expertise in boat construction expanding with every new thought.

'Aren't you bloody freezing?' Tor called to him from the kitchen, the sliding doors wide open.

'There is a certain chill in the air, yes,' he replied, shivering but not wanting to admit his fallibility.

'I know I am, now that some knob has left the doors open and let all our lovely warmth out.'

'You should come out, embrace the freshness of the air.' He reached his arms wide for effect, becoming *Outdoor Man* in his native environment.

'I hope there aren't any dogwalkers in those woods.' Her voice echoed through the kitchen and lounge, bouncing through the doors from all directions, demonstrating many aspects of Christian Doppler's work.

'Why?' he asked, half-turning back towards the house.

'Well, it's just, *you*, boxers, and a t-shirt. Is that really the first impression you want to make on some of the locals? And it would leave an impression, believe me.'

'Damn cheek. I'm lovely. Besides, you slept next to this all night.' He'd turned round to face the kitchen arms spread again to highlight his magnificence, and nodded down at his body.

'Yeah, about that… Thank goodness I had my eyes closed.' Tor laughed and bustled out into the hallway.

Gabe wandered along the decking to the front of the house, looking up at the overhanging timbers, and the straightened hook that had suspended the wind chimes for such a brief time. There was a scrape on the hook where, presumably, the hook of the chimes had been pulled along it, but no other marks to indicate a tool or machine had pulled the hook straight. But something must have – Gabe knew he couldn't have done it without some heavy leverage. He sipped the last dregs of his coffee and his gaze dropped, falling to the workshop across the driveway, and recessed some thirty yards back into the woods. His first thought was *workshop*, but was it, or a barn or a garage? He vaguely remembered seeing it when they'd first viewed the house with the Estate Agent, who, quite frankly, couldn't wait to get shot of the whole place. Their first, paltry offer, designed to make the agents think the house wasn't worth the amount they'd asked for and to drop their price, had been accepted immediately. It seemed they'd bagged a bargain. So far removed from the house, hidden away in the woods was an odd location to have an out-building, but maybe whomever had built it was wanting to get away from someone inside. Or maybe, perhaps, they were hiding, feeling like they were running away from something – even real life itself. He smiled to himself; *aren't we all*, he thought. He decided then and there that he was going to investigate the workshop today and see what was inside. Decision made and chilled more than he wanted to admit, Gabe came back inside and slid the heavy doors shut.

∞ ∞ ∞

The cloud and mist had soaked everywhere in dew. Ferns, starting to die back to brown statues were bent double under the weight of the water droplets. The air thick with the smell of moss and leaf mold. Gabe walked along the dirt track toward the workshop. Wide enough to take a car, it was becoming overgrown by brambles and nettles, with branches reaching out from the trees behind, it felt like the foliage had taken over and was closing in around him as he approached. Lichens grew on the trunks of trees and their fallen comrades in the damp atmosphere, tiny heads of growth in various colours, all clamouring for space and light. It reminded him of corals he'd grown years before in a marine fish tank. Looking up at the canopy above, he could imagine being in a kelp forest – the seaweed swaying in the current like trees in a breeze. The coral reef of Lake House.

Reaching the large double doors of the workshop, he recalled trying to get inside on their first viewing, but the overly keen Estate Agent said they didn't have the keys. Those keys still hadn't materialised, so Gabe, crowbar in hand, levered the padlock easily off the catch, it landing in the mud at his feet where the sun never shone. A tentative pull on the door did nothing, so he pulled harder, the door giving and then dropping on its hinges, the wooden frame catching in the mud. Annoyed, Gabe came in close to the door and lifted it clear of the ground, yanking it open, swinging outwards accompanied by cries of protest from the hinges that had been resting undisturbed all these years. Fully opened, the door swung free of the mud and Gabe stepped inside the dimly lit building, gloom filtering in through dirty windows. It seemed bigger inside – about the size of a double garage – with dustsheets and tarpaulins covering mysterious shapes of various sizes, ancient dust – pre-dating the discovery of gravity – stubbornly hung, suspended in the air, and low beams gave an increased feeling of claustrophobia. A home-made workbench, about six feet long, was in the corner to the right of the doors, the sturdy top made from what looked like timber roughly cut from the trees nearby – as rustic as it was solid. A vice was clamped onto the corner and it still held onto a piece of wood, a plane discarded next to it with wood-shavings and sawdust scattered all around. Gabe suspected he was the first person to set foot in here for some time. And that the last visitor had perhaps left rather hurriedly. This place was now the domain of the spider. Huge, dusty cobwebs were strung from beam to beam, and beam to dustsheet or workbench. A generous layer of dust covered everything, becoming dislodged in clouds whenever he moved anything or pulled a sheet off, huge eight-legged monsters skittering away to a new hiding spot in the shadows once discovered, ready to jump out on the unsuspecting once more. Pulling back another dustsheet, Gabe found a long portable bench with what he thought was a log splitter on it. Beyond it, in the far corner were some larger tree limbs stacked up against the wall and a chainsaw on a bench that looked old and rusted, with large piles of sawdust on the floor. Underneath the filthy window, doubled-glazed with so much dirt and grime it only allowed the slightest glow to seep in to illuminate the place, he pulled back another sheet. Beneath were dozens of sheets of glass all carefully lined up and leant against the wall – perhaps a greenhouse that still waited for someone to rebuild it, or a cold frame that would never grow tomatoes or courgettes. Leaning against the glass, out of place, was a picture frame about three feet square. Gabe picked it up, surprised by the weight and stood it on the work bench, leaning it against a chipboard tool rack, from which several axes were hanging. The wide frame had ornate gilding in the shape of leaves and trees, although was tarnished from neglect and damp. He blew on the top corner and a cloud of dust formed and slowly floated away. Having made a clean bit, he blew the fine covering away from the whole frame. The painting was unmistakeably of the lake – water rippling gently under the moonlight from a cloudless sky – it was so real he could almost see it moving. The view was familiar too, like it had been painted from the house, and Gabe hefted the frame and left the workshop to investigate further.

A gentle breeze had got up; whipping across the water, it was cold, cutting through his fleece. He held the picture up at the water's edge, and the view was similar, but the perspective was wrong – he needed to be higher. Backtracking toward the house, up the slope and onto the steps of the decking he looked out again, comparing picture to view. It was better this time, but again, the view wasn't right, the picture didn't look up to the trees like he did now. Turning to the house, Gabe looked up to their bedroom window on the corner. That was it. The artist must've painted the picture from there, looking out across the water, spending days in the room to capture the view exactly.

'What've you got there?' Tor looked up after pouring boiling water into the cafetiere as Gabe came into the kitchen.

'I found this picture in the workshop,' he said, setting the frame down on the counter.

'Oh, so it's a workshop now, is it?' she smiled at him.

'What?'

'Well, it was a shed this morning, or a barn, wasn't it? You'll be setting up a craft beer business by the end of the day.'

'There's a lot of stuff in there. Someone used it as a workshop.'

'To make what?'

'I dunno… stuff.'

'So, if I don't see you for hours on end, you'll be out there, making *stuff?*'

'Maybe. Anyway, I found this, just like it'd been discarded out there.'

'It's a nice picture. Horrible frame though.'

'I thought it was quite ornate.'

'Well, it is, but that doesn't make it any less ugly. Are you gonna hang it up in here?' Tor looked surprised.

'I was, but if you'd rather not…'

'No, it's fine. It is of the view I s'pose. Where are you thinking?'

'There's an old screw in the hall outside the spare room – been painted over a few times – so I thought I'd try there.'

'You can't beat on old screw.' She smiled to herself.

'That's what I'd heard.'

'Okay. See what it looks like.'

Upstairs, Gabe hooked the wire on the back of the picture over the wall-mounting in the hall. He didn't know why but he felt like this was where it had hung before – something must've hung here for there to be the screw, but it could be anything that the previous owners took with them – yet somehow, this felt right. The picture had come home. He stepped back and admired it, watched the movement on the water, felt the breath of the breeze on his face. The frame was fine, *what was Tor on about*, would probably cost a fortune these days for that level of work.

With one last look he turned to head back down the stairs but stopped suddenly, a shrill noise chilled him to his core, the hair on the back of his neck standing up. He turned back to the painting, which hung there innocently, like the naughty schoolboy with a *who, me?* expression on his face. Nothing had changed, the frame hadn't slipped on the wall, which might've explained the sound. The picture was still – more lifeless, almost, than when he'd looked at it before. He wasn't sure what he'd expected to find – anything that would've fitted into the category of explanation would've been good – because this wasn't it, and his pulse was racing, his heart in his mouth. The noise had been right behind him, not bouncing off walls and echoing around corners after coming from somewhere outside. The sound had come from the picture – the painting itself – a shrill noise, almost a scream.

It had been the shriek of a fox.

CHAPTER 4

-\/-

PIPES

'I can't believe that I left it behind,' Gabe snorted from the bedroom.

'Done what now?' Tor called from the spare room as she was unpacking a box. 'Tell me exactly what you can't believe you did? I bet I can.' Boxes were piled high all around her, like giant Duplo blocks, containing lamps and pictures, ornaments and books. There were plastic underbed boxes containing bed linen and duvets, holdalls and cases with spare clothes. It had made sense to just dump them in one room upstairs when they were unloading the van the evening before. Gabe was screwing together the wooden frame of their bed. Tor carefully pulled a lamp from a box as she called out to him, peeling away the scrunched-up newspaper from around it and checking that it was no worse for its journey.

'The bed spanner.'

'What bed spanner?'

'The specialist spanner that came with the bed.' Gabe sounded frustrated, as if everyone would instinctively know the full history of the bed spanner.

'What about it.'

'It isn't here.'

'Here where?'

'You know you really should've been a psychiatrist, because all you do is turn everything I say into a question.'

'Everything you say?'

'Funny. The bed spanner isn't here.'

'Did you have it at the old place?'

'Yes. Yes of course.'

'But you could use your tools – spanners and what-not – if you needed to?'

'Yeah. I'd need to find the right size and it would be a bit on the cumbersome side, but–'

'But you didn't when you took it apart?'

'No, I used the bed spanner.' Gabe's frustration mounted, as if he was having to explain to a five-year-old, without 'mansplaining' as Tor called it.

'So, you used a spanner to unscrew some bolts on the bed, a spanner that only has one purpose and no other, and you didn't put it with said bolts that you tied in a plastic bag and taped to the bed so you knew where they'd be?'

'Well now you say it like that it sounds faintly ridiculous.' Gabe was tired of shouting between rooms, so he'd come to her and was stood leaning his head against the doorframe.

'Only faintly?' She looked up at him and smiled sweetly, brushing her fringe out of her eyes and tucking a few wisps behind her ear.

'There was obviously a very good reason for me not putting it in that bag.'

'Which was?' She raised an eyebrow in a more than passing imitation of Roger Moore's, *Bond.*

'Well, I don't know now, do I? But think of it like this, why would I choose to do something that is obviously ridiculous?'

'You really want me to answer that, after twelve years of marriage?'

'No. The correct answer is that it wasn't ridiculous at the time.' He held his hands out to her, palms up, as if he had perfectly explained a mathematical problem.

'That's not helping much. Okay then, is there anywhere else you might've put it?' Tor asked.

'Well, the toolbox I suppose.'

'There you go,' she said, having just helped a five-year-old understand adding.

'But I didn't put it in there.'

'And you know this..?'

'Yes. Wouldn't have put it in there.'

'So where is it?'

'That's what I'm trying to work out… I should go and look in the toolbox, shouldn't I?'

'I would.'

'Back in a mo,' he smiled sheepishly at her and rolled away from the doorframe. His head appeared back a split second later. 'Cuppa?'

'Love one.'

Gabe boiled the Boeing kettle and found the teabags in their jar on the worktop – at least they had found their place. With tea stewing, he turned his attention to his toolbox, sat next to the kitchen units, the black plastic lid open and screwdrivers, pliers and the hammer all tossed loosely on top. He rummaged around in the second layer down, which contained all his spanners, and almost immediately found the one for the bed.

'Mate you are proper losing it – you gotta sort yourself out,' he said to himself. 'Found it!' he shouted up the stairs, sliding the little tool into his pocket. He returned to the more important job of making his wife some tea – after all, it wouldn't be too out of character to forget to make it and go back upstairs empty handed, he thought. He squeezed each teabag out against the side of its mug with a spoon, the dark liquid trickling back down the side, before dropping the bags into the food waste bin. With a final stir, he picked up the two mugs, and Tor screamed. Not the blood-curling scream of the terrified in mortal danger, but more the scream of someone having a close encounter with a very big spider or something. Gabe still ran up the stairs to see what was wrong, mounting the steps two at a time.

'Tor?' he said as he reached the upstairs hallway and saw his wife looking up at the ceiling. 'Is everything okay?' He slowly walked towards her, one hand reaching out to clasp hers. She screamed again, surprised by the touch, aware of him now for the first time. Then he heard it, a long low moaning sound, coming from somewhere above the ceiling – as if a zombie had taken up residence in the loft space. It lasted for a few seconds then died away. Their eyes met, then both looked up as they heard it again

– like a low pitched pre-orgasmic groan. Then there was an answering cry, a higher pitched wail, like both man and woman were coming together.

'What the hell?' Gabe said, but Tor shushed him with her fingers to her lips, then beckoned him to follow. She walked on tip-toes into the spare room where there was another groan, followed by a staccato chattering, like finger nails typing on a keyboard or the arrival of the distress call at the start of *Alien*, this time coming from the walls.

'I can almost hear words… chanting, maybe,' Tor said, hair falling across one side of her face. Her eyes were shining, alive with fear and excitement, and she left the bedroom to rush into the hallway again. Then a scream. A shrill, high-pitched wail, different to before. The scream a baby might make in it's pushchair to get some attention when all around are busy.

'Bathroom,' Gabe said and followed Tor as she chased the sound. The chattering noise was back and more amplified in the tile and stone of the big bathroom. 'It's the pipes, it's gotta be,' he said.

'Ever hear pipes wailing like that?' As if in response, the chattering became a scratching sound, like dozens of rats were trying to get out of the wall cavity. Gabe looked at her and back at the wall. He quickly went to the radiator and turned it off, then in turn went into every upstairs room to do the same.

'What are you doing?'

'If it is the pipes, I've closed off all the flow up here, and I'm gonna do the same downstairs, too. Then I'll increase the pressure in the boiler, and then open up each rad in turn.'

'I thought you hadn't got to grips with the boiler?'

'No time like the present, is there?' He grinned at her.

'Are you thinking it's air in there?'

'It's what I always used to do at home, the first time we used the heating in the autumn.'

'This is home,' she corrected. 'Besides, our pipes never used to make that sound.'

'It's a much older house, more rooms, bigger boiler. Lot's more places for air to build up, and who the fuck knows.'

∞ ∞ ∞

The only really narrow part of the downstairs was where the wide front entrance foyer of the house narrowed into a short hallway leading to the open plan kitchen and rest of the ground floor, and it contained several doors. On one side was a large utility room in the centre of which sat their washing machine, waiting to be plumbed in, the outlet pipe hooked over the back, allowing the occasional drip to make a puddle on the bare concrete floor. This room had been a big selling point for Tor to get the laundry out of the kitchen. Next to this was a long narrow boot room leading to an outside door, with a simple sink and some cheap kitchen units. Opposite was a small box room, that they'd occasionally referred to as the study, and a cellar door. Gabe had only been through this door once before when they'd first looked around the house. Now, he opened it, the hinges dutifully creaking in the style of a creepy film, and pulled the cord to switch on the bare lightbulb overhead with a click. The steps going straight down in front of him were wooden, he went down each of the five slowly, every step producing new creaks and cracks like he was wandering around the deck of an old ship. At the bottom was a small landing, turning ninety degrees to the next set of five steps – these were stone and covered in a layer of dust, then a further landing and bare lightbulb before a final five steps led into the cellar itself. Fifteen steps wasn't a huge amount but it did make Gabe think of the descent into the *Mines of Moria* under the *Misty Mountains.* Having turned back on himself, he couldn't see the door to the hallway, and a chill went through him as he tried to remember if the door had a handle on the inside, and if it could close by itself leaving him trapped down here. Shaking himself from any further *Scooby Doo* scare stories he looked around the cellar, with yet another bare lightbulb hanging from the low ceiling, meaning he would need to avoid banging his head against it as he moved around. The walls were made of stone that had been simply painted white and Gabe wondered if it had been tanked in any way to stop damp coming through, particularly this close to the lake. He did think that even the lowest level of the house was still above the lake water level.

But he wasn't an engineer.

From just about any American novel or movie, it seemed most houses had a basement, but they seemed to be a very rare and old-fashioned thing in the UK. In this one, the boiler dominated the room. Situated against what Gabe assumed to be an external wall, it was a big modern-looking system, about the size of a large fridge freezer and almost twice the size of their previous one. There were no lights illuminated on the front console, but there was power to the red light on the small master unit on the wall. Next to it was a large red power switch in the 'off' position. He knew there was oil in the tank after checking when he had a wander round the house with his first coffee of the morning earlier. Shrugging he flicked the switch, which was stiff and felt like it wouldn't go, but then clunked over, lighting up in a satisfying green. The boiler hummed and whirred into life, the sound of a pump and then a muffled *whump* as the oil ignited, a small roar of flame coming from low down as it started to heat the water in the sump. He knew the boiler would need to warm up – maybe even heating the hot water before he could switch it across to the central heating. Either way, he had a wait on his hands.

The rest of the room was as typical an indoor dumping ground as you could get. Free-standing wooden shelves sat in the middle, bedecked with old boots, a home brewing bucket and plastic barrel – both wrapped carefully in blue recycling bags, a pair of wooden tennis racquets that may only have spiders webs in the middle of them anymore. An old jacket hung from a rusty nail sticking out from the wall. These were sad unwanted items that, even when moving out, previous occupants couldn't be bothered to throw out – or maybe they were even forgotten about. In the corner sat a filing cabinet, and although covered in dust, looked relatively new. On top was a poly-pocket containing the manual and warranty for the boiler, which Gabe could see was installed just five years before. Opening the top drawer, there were a number of house receipts from over the years, helpfully left behind by those who had come before. It did seem a little odd that they weren't left in a folder in a kitchen draw, but perhaps they had been and the last owners decided to store them down here. Maybe they even wanted to convert this basement into something but never got around to it – the estate agent said they hadn't lived here long. At the far end of the room, on the external wall next to the boiler was an alcove with a strange pair of doors on top. Gabe only knew what it was because he'd seen the doors from outside on his reccy, and although overgrown with brambles and nettles, it looked like the kind of doors that would open up in a coal store. It made sense that it wasn't a cellar at all, but fuel storage for whatever large solid fuel burning cooker/boiler had run this place in days gone by.

The boiler switched itself off, and, for a second, Gabe wondered if there was a problem, but he realised it had just come up to temperature. Taking the manual out of its pouch on the filing cabinet, he looked at the dials on the front – one each for hot water and central heating, with settings for temperature and timing.

'Here goes nothing,' he muttered, and pressed the button above the central heating dial, turning it all the way up and setting the timer to come on continuously. There was a pause, a gurgle and another *whump* as the burner kicked in again. This time the gurgling churned around the boiler, and then up and out of the large diameter copper pipes coming out of the top of it, up the wall and across the ceiling before diverging, disappearing into various holes drilled into the concrete. Following, like a child, as it chased the air bubbles through the pipes, Gabe raced up the steps, his foot slipping on the dusty stone steps just before the first landing and narrowly avoiding falling up the stairs. Taking his time after this warning, he steadily climbed the other flights of steps. Mercifully relieved that the cellar door hadn't somehow closed on itself, but also noting that there was a handle on the inside – c*ourse there was* – he was happy to leave the cellar behind. Racing into the kitchen, he made eye contact with a bemused looking Tor.

'Any joy?' she asked warily, looking down at her dust and cobweb covered husband, then back up again.

'Yep, fired up straight away. Just got to force the air around now,' he said, bending to open the thermostatic valve on the kitchen radiator. The pipes gurgled instantly, transmitting sounds of bubbling and belching air through the pressurised water, filling the tubes with hot water. 'Ow, bastard!'

'You okay?'

'Yeah, the rad is really hot.'

'Almost like a… radiator?'

'Didn't expect it to get this hot, this quickly. Very pleasantly surprised.' He moved on to the two radiators in the sitting room, and opened them fully in turn. Once again, the scalding, noisy water filled them just as quickly. He looked at Tor.

'Now what?'

'Two minutes, just to make sure these have forced their air out somewhere else, then we'll close them down and head upstairs. In fact, better still, do you want to head up to the spare room and see if you hear anything similar to before?'

'But I don't see how it will be – the boiler wasn't on before – how could it be the pipes?'

'I'm not sure either, but in the absence of a better explanation, any chance you could humour me?' he pursed his lips and shrugged.

'Okay. Fair enough.' Tor headed up the stairs, her feet landing almost silently as she disappeared around the spiral. Gabe closed down the valves once more and headed for the stairs, already hearing gurgling from within the walls where the pipes must be buried.

'Anything?' he called up ahead of him as he climbed the stairs. Nothing. 'Tor?' He reached the upstairs hallway and went into the spare room to find his wife sat slumped on the bed. 'Tor?' he asked.

'I'm okay,' she sniffed, cuffing a tear away from her cheek.

'What's wrong?'

'Nothing. *Everything*. Oh, I don't fucking know.' He sat by her side and gathered her into his arms, pulling her head onto his chest.

'It's okay. It's okay.'

'I just had this horrible feeling that we've left him behind. Left his memory or something,' she sobbed.

'But we haven't. That's why we've come, so we just have the memories that we want.'

'But you can't just pick and choose the good from the bad – shouldn't we remember everything?'

'Not if it's going to break us, love, no. We need him, with us, making us stronger, living with us forever.' His fingers entwined in her hair. 'What made you think of him, anyway?'

She laughed, a long string of snot dripping from her nose. 'Running up the stairs – like one of the silly games we used to play when he was tiny.'

'Yeah. Course.' Gabe nodded with a smile, his eyes red and filling with tears. 'So, did you listen to my pipes?' he asked in mock annoyance.

'I didn't hear anything, sorry.'

'Let's start in here then.' Gabe opened the valve on the radiator underneath the window. Once more, pipes gurgled and bubbled as water and air tumbled and fell over themselves dashing around the bend and the corners, racing along the straights. But these weren't the moaning chattering noises of earlier. These were very different. Normal sounds. He went into each room and opened valves. Returning to close some and opening others with the aim of pushing any air in the system back to the boiler. After twenty minutes of this he happily declared. 'All the rads are hot, and the system is working really well. I just need to open the downstairs ones back up.'

'But we haven't solved the problem, and it's not the pipes.' Tor shrugged.

'Well, just because I couldn't simulate it now doesn't mean it's *not* the pipes, but I do take your point.' He let out a sigh that whistled between his teeth. 'I better check the boiler.'

Gabe left the room and Tor heard him creak and rattle down the stairs, then creak through the cellar door. A low moan came from the far wall, away from the radiator and the pipes. The moan of a ghost from a Scooby Doo episode. It came and it went three times, before being replaced by chattering – *I can almost hear words* – she'd said earlier. This grew and grew to fill the room, like she was suddenly in the presence of a couple of dozen foreign nationals, speaking all around her in different unintelligible tongues. Tor was in a room filled with words she didn't understand. Chanting and wailing, reciting rites and incantations. They surrounded and enveloped her, enclosing her like she was being rolled up in a duvet, the sound acquiring form and substance, suffocating and dragging her in, so all she could hear were the words – the chanting that meant nothing. This was very wrong, she was becoming hypnotised or enchanted or something – pulled in at any rate – and she had to do something, had to get out. Dragging herself away from the pull of the voices, she slowly levered herself upright, her feet unsteady as her legs had gone to sleep, the room spinning as she stood, the emotions of the last few minutes and the fear of right now almost overwhelming. Even the air had changed – it was thick and viscous – Tor felt like she was trying to breathe water. Staggering to the door, leaning on the wooden frame she managed to take a breath before grasping the handle and turning. The door didn't move. She turned the handle again and pulled hard on it, leaning her body backwards, but again the door was stuck. Not stuck like it had become swollen following a lot of rain which had made it tight in its frame, but stuck like it was nailed shut – like there was no door there anymore. Her chest tightened and she realised she couldn't breathe, her airway as tight as the door in the frame. Grasping the handle again, she took a step backwards, one foot in front of the other, ready to use all her weight to pull against the door. Twisting the handle again, she quickly transferred her weight backwards and yanked for all she was worth, arms straightening and shoulders jerking seemingly almost out of their sockets. With the sound of tearing on a door painted shut, finally it released, flying open and Tor fell backwards, landing heavily, before bounding back up and rushing out of the room into the hallway. To safety. All was silent. As normal as the bedroom had been strange. The air was normal, and fresh, and she leant against the wall next to the picture of the lake, her shoulders slumped and head leaning back against the plaster, taking several large deep breaths.

Had she had some kind of panic attack?

She'd had a few in the early days after Mikey, but not like this. This was a hallucination, or something else, on top of whatever happened to her chest.

Her breathing rate slowly started to ease and she felt calmer. Deciding that she needed some tea, Tor slowly walked down the spiral stairs, not wanting to hear another groaning pipe for a very long time.

∞ ∞ ∞

'All pleased with your little self, aren't you?' Tor said, raising her wine glass toward him in mock toast then sipping at the red liquid.

'One shouldn't limit oneself to one vocation my love, one never knows what other skills or even gifts one might discover within oneself.'

'One will be getting smacked round the head by this saucepan if one doesn't shut up.' Tor put the large pan on the stove and waited for the kettle to boil for water for their pasta. After the incident with the pipes that afternoon she had stayed very much in the vicinity of Gabe for the last couple of hours, not wanting to be by herself, firstly putting the shades on their bedside lamps as Gabe put the bed together and then bringing some semblance of order in the kitchen. Gabe had continued to fuss with the radiators like he was the lead engineer on the Thames barrier – moving water here, bleeding air there – and finally all was well, stable and, she had to admit, very toasty. Years ago, her dad had said something about Gabe that had stuck with them like a family saying. The two men had been laying a patio together, and her ex-builder father, Bill, had been impressed by Gabe's skills. So, he told him that, if the writing 'didn't work out' he could lay patios for a living – getting himself a van and writing that on the side of it. After that, any job he'd done, or skill he'd demonstrated around the house was something that could be 'written on the side of the van.' As she was cooking, she thought of that, thought of her dad and his jokey ways. 'Hey, you know what?' she asked, turning to face Gabe.

'It's very unlikely that I will, given the vagary of the statement.' He nodded sagely at the great wisdom of his comment.

'What did we say about being a twat?' She raised an eyebrow at him. 'Anyway, after today's performance you could put 'plumbing and heating engineer' on the side of your van now.'

'I think we're gonna need a bigger van.'

'For all your tools?'

'No, for all the stuff that I've got to advertise along the side of it, that I now do.'

'Oh. Very high opinion of oneself, one has, eh? I didn't think there were that many things. 'Never finishing a job' should be in big letters on there, obvs.'

'Touché,' he added appreciatively at the banter, this round clearly won by his wife – as most of them were. 'Let's just hope there aren't any more hiccups with it, and the pipes stay quiet.' He nodded and turned to put some tools away in the big toolbox that seemed to have taken up residence in the kitchen.

∞ ∞ ∞

Tor shot him a glance – no smile or irony. He knew the boiler was off when they first heard the sounds, so it can't be the pipes, and so the problem can't be fixed. She let it go. There was no sense in starting an argument over something they couldn't do anything about, particularly when they had been getting on so well together. Really it was just being pedantic – they didn't know what this afternoon's noises were, and they couldn't therefore have been fixed.

She sliced some chorizo with Gabe's large sharp knife and remembered, years ago, how she'd cut herself when using it and had shouted for Gabe to come and help her. Not realising how bad the cut was he'd muttered something back, until she shouted again that she'd cut herself on 'the sharpest knife in England.' That had definitely brought him running to stem the blood.

Tor mused on this as she finished making dinner, her thoughts coming back around once again to the events of the day, to not being convinced with Gabe's explanation, and knowing that part of her was remembering Idris' warning about the witch.

∞ ∞ ∞

Gabe cleared away the dinner dishes while Tor went upstairs to put on her pyjamas in their usual 'you cooked so I'll clear away' arrangement. Tor had a certain economy with her cooking – two pans maximum and meticulous tidying as she went along meant that she was a pleasure to clean up after. Gabe on the other hand believed that there was no point in having a great many pans and plates if one never used them, so tended to cause carnage when he cooked. It occurred to him, for the first time ever, that he'd got by far the better deal with not having to clean up his own mess.

The scraping sound painfully pierced his forehead and reached in to jar him from his thoughts. The sound of something hard scratching across glass. He looked up in the direction of the sound to the patio doors, but saw nothing untoward. Wiping his wet hands on a tea towel, he absently tossed it back onto the worktop as he walked over to the glass, seeing his own reflection against the darkness of the night beyond. And there it was again – a fountain pen scratching against the paper it was writing on. But still he saw nothing. Taking a step back, he glanced along each panel of the sliding doors, expecting to see something. The scrape of fingernails on a blackboard came again, right in front of him this time. Laughing at him. It was like a childhood prank. The spooky equivalent of knocking on a door and running away. He walked right up to the glass, right where the sound had come from – or had been transmitted from – right where he should be able to see something.

Through the glass, from the glow of the house lights, he could see the decking out to the handrail. There was darkness beyond as he scanned what must be the beach, but the darkness got even darker when he was looking in the direction of the lake itself. There was black and there was black. Other than that, he couldn't see anything.

Nothing to report.

Then, there was movement. Not out toward the lake or over at the beach – a blur or vagary that might suggest something was there – no this was right next to the glass, the large spider you've not noticed that was next to your foot which suddenly moves and becomes the scariest thing ever. It was a shadow, a darkness within the dark, a shape not six-feet from him which was there, like the spider, but then faded when he noticed it. With shaking hands, he managed to unclip the lock of the sliding door and glided it smoothly open, the chill of the night air and the breeze galvanising his senses. He stepped outside, wind ruffling his hair, looking to where he'd seen whatever it had been, but there was nothing. The decking, the vents and windows, the railings, the harsh glow from the security light above.

Nothing to report.

The hair on the back of his neck stood up – children in assembly when the head teacher walks in – standing to attention. He had that moment of thinking, *it's behind you.* The hairs doing their best pantomime chant to get him to realise. Fear gripped him, as if turning around would legitimise whatever it was, making it real, and by ignoring it it would go away. Like he did with his overdraft. Taking a deep breath, he spun on his heels, turning quickly, trying to be quicker on the draw than the shape. But if it had been there, if the unruly pupils below his hairline had been right, it was gone now, and the decking was empty.

Shivering, he realised just how cold he was and stepped back inside, closing the door once again.

'Bloody hell, am I paying you by the hour?' Tor said as she came back down the stairs, dressed in check lounge trousers and long sleeved t-shirt, which she'd change before bed. *Pre-bed pyjamas.*

Gabe was too distracted to think of a clever response, scuttling back to his clean-up duties as if she'd caught him on *Pornhub.*

'Is everything okay?' Tor frowned as she watched him.

'Er, yeah. Great thanks.' He looked up from the dishwasher and forced a smile. Years ago, Tor would've pushed him, but not these days. Their relationship had taken the heaviest of batterings and so anything that might push it in that direction again was to be avoided.

'Okay. I'll give you a hand – you finish with the dishwasher and I'll wipe down the worktops.' She picked up the dishcloth and rinsed it out under hot water in the sink. Working together, the kitchen was clean and tidy, with the extractor fan sounding like it was competing with the kettle in readying itself for take-off in the background. 'Want to watch something?' Tor asked as she hung tea towels from the rails on the cooker.

'Do you know what? I think I might have an early night.' Gabe nodded.

'Okay, me too. Might have the chance to read a bit before falling asleep this time.' She smiled as she got two glasses out to fill with water for bed.

As he waited for Tor to finish in the bathroom, Gabe stripped out of his clothes and slid on some shorts and a t-shirt. The room glowing a soft yellow from the two bedside lamps, now demurely wearing their shades, feeling cosy with the curtains drawn. Throwing his laundry in the linen basket, he turned back to the bed. The scratching sound stopped him in his tracks. Looking up at the window, the curtains blocking his view, something scraped over the glass again. For a moment he imagined that one of the trees had grown across from the woods, a long finger like branch extending out and scratching away at the window. Heart thumping hard in his chest, he flung the curtains open, the material swishing on its rail, swinging open dramatically, revealing the expanse of glass like a theatre stage on which the following scene would play out.

'Nothing to report,' he said to the empty space beyond. The trees hadn't grown – of course they hadn't – but then, it they hadn't, what had scraped along his window on the first floor?

His window.

Something had made that sound – he wasn't imagining it. It had come from across the room, drilling into him in that sharp shrill way that some sounds do when they go right through you. Making you shiver. Yes, something had. But what?

'Gabe?' Tor asked as she walked back into the room, to find her husband staring out of the window.

He looked back to her, shaken from his thoughts, and quickly flicked the curtains closed again. 'Thought I heard something.'

'At the upstairs window?'

'Yeah, might've been a giraffe, maybe.'

'Nutter. Go clean your teeth.'

∞ ∞ ∞

The curtains closing was very much like a light being switched off outside the window. The shape floating outside the glass thrown into darkness. She paused for a moment, head tilted to one side, waiting to see if they would open again. Wondering what they would do, smiling to herself – having her fun. She hovered, slight up and down movements maintaining her position, like a helicopter having to work against the wind.

The curtains remained resolutely closed and so she slowly drifted back from the house, drifting away twenty feet off the ground, taking in the view of the place. *Her house.* With one last look, she turned away, and, with another smile, flew off into the night.

CHAPTER 5
–\/–
WALK BY THE LAKE

The kitchen smelled of fresh coffee and freshly cooked croissants. Gabe was beating eggs in a bowl when Tor came down the stairs.

'Did we go on holiday and I forgot or something?' She yawned and accepted the mug of freshly brewed Kenyan that he handed to her, in her *Queen of Fucking Everything* mug, sipping carefully at the scalding liquid. She perched on a stool at the breakfast bar. 'So, go on. Who did you shag that warrants making me breakfast?' She smiled sweetly over the rim of the mug.

'Whom.' He poured the eggs into some melted butter in their heavy frying pan, giving them a minute to start to set before stirring.

'Ooh, twat alarm going off this early. It's not becoming, dear. Why all this?' She waved her hand in the direction of the carnage in the kitchen.

'Well, it's hardly 'all this', some croissants from the freezer and scrambled eggs. Gordon Ramsay's not shitting himself just yet, babe.' He stood facing her, arms lifted out to the side, his self-deprecating look spoiled by the wooden spoon in his hand which contained some partially cooked eggs that were threatening to jump off and freefall to the floor.

'Yeah, but you don't ever cook breakfast. Not never, not no how.' She shrugged and sipped more of the scalding brew.

'Yep, you're right. I'll stop. There's bread in the bin and you can toast some if you want…' He made a big play of leaving the mess in the kitchen, tossing the utensil into the pan before throwing his hands in the air as he flounced off in mock indignation.

'Okay, okay. You need to work on your acting skills. It really isn't like living with Matt Damon. What are you cooking up – and don't say eggs.'

'Well, nothing really. I just thought we've been flat out in the couple of days since we've been here and had a years-worth of weird–'

'Just a year?'

'Maybe. So, let's do normal things today. Let's have a nice breakfast and go for a walk around the lake – it'll be nice. Let's remember why we bought this place, and the spot we fell in love with.' Gabe resumed working on his precious eggs.

'Sounds good. Think I'll be needing a good breakfast before that little lot, chef.' She smiled up at him and raised her mug in a toast.

∞ ∞ ∞

The sun glinted on the water, and looked like a summer day. As they walked hand in hand across the shingle beach, the gentle breeze rolling in across the cool water had developed a real chill by the time it kissed their cheeks, and they were glad they'd put fleeces on. Striding out faster now, in the mood for a brisk walk, their breathing coming hard and fast, they gulped lungfuls of clean, crisp, air. Wispy high cloud was enough to water down the power of the sun and keep it a jacket day. Stones skittered and rolled as they were launched along by a boot, and pebbles, smoothed by the rippling of the water, shone in a myriad of colours at the water's edge. The far bank rose slowly, reflected off the mirrored water surface. Some of the tall pine trees on this bank had collapsed in places, making the forest less dark and dense, light penetrating within and allowing more undergrowth to sprout and flourish. As they climbed up the loose sand and soil of the bank, they had to clamber over several fallen trees on their way to the top. It was as if they had become too tall for the damp soil to hold and the wind had done the rest. One particularly wide trunk barred their way from climbing higher, so they turned back down and walked along the beach for a while instead, schools of small fish darting this way and that in the shallows.

'He would've loved this. The space to run around, the beach, the water,' Tor said as they scrambled along the shore, Gabe holding her hand for balance.

'Yes. Yes, he would. We'd have needed more than one pair of red wellies.' Gabe smiled and slipped himself, making one knee of his trousers wet and muddy.

'There's still not a day goes by…' Tor stopped and looked wistfully across the water, back toward the house, brushing a strand of hair back from her face, eyes full of tears.

'Me neither,' he said, stepping up to her side, putting his arm around her waist, pulling her in close to him. Her head flopped sideways onto his shoulder, the tension in her body evaporated and she sagged against him. The tears flowed freely – there had been a time when she couldn't grieve, where she'd admonished herself for doing so as if it were a sign of weakness, or where she thought that she should just pull herself together, to snap out of it. It had made her angry. Not the loss, not the questions and the heartbreak, but the lack of control. Now she knew it was okay, that it wasn't a show of weakness or a failure to move on, but something that she might always do. 'I don't think there ever will be – and why should there?' Gabe echoed her thoughts and they stood in silence, lost in thought, and memory and shared grief.

'We did do everything, didn't we..?' she looked up at him, pleading, needing affirmation, her cheeks wet from her tears, her eyes red, and saw he was the same.

'Yes of course we did – you know that – nobody could've done any more. You, in particular, tried everything known to man and then some. But it just wasn't enough. Sometimes there's just nothing you can do.'

Her jaw hardened and she bit her lip. 'Maybe,' she said through her teeth as she looked away from him and back across the water to the house, which looked magnificent – almost as if it rose straight out of the lake, like it and its perfect reflection were one. The road up and behind was a narrow stripe framing the view. The sunlight piercing the gaps between the trees, meant that this bank was much more open than around the house, where it felt like they were hidden away from the outside world.

∞ ∞ ∞

The soil was loose, boots sliding down the bank as the substrate raced down alongside like a child running to take a jump into the lake. They kicked the sides of their boots into the slope, digging them in, slowly traversing backwards and forwards, ascending in the least direct fashion, toward the firmer ground at the top, away from the water. Gabe clambered over another fallen trunk, sliding off it on the upper side, his knees absorbing the impact as he landed, boots sinking into the leaf mold. Up ahead he saw a flash of white between the trees, a glimpse of something, then it was gone. He stared, frozen in place, looking through the trees, unsure of what he'd seen, but determined not to miss it if it appeared again.

'It's ok love, I'll manage, you just carry on,' Tor said, sarcastically, behind him, as she struggled to climb over and slide down the big fallen tree, landing at his side.

'Did you see that?' he asked, flicking a quick glance at her, oblivious to her exasperation.

'See what?' she gave her head a shake.

'Up ahead, in the distance between those two trees, behind the one that's snapped off.' He pointed, drawing her eye with him. 'About sixty yards or so.'

'What did you see?' she looked from 'x'-marks-the-spot to Gabe and then back again. Then he moved off, pulling on her hand, walking in that direction.

'I don't know, it was something white and it moved between the trees.' His eyes were fixed on where he'd seen… whatever he'd seen.

'Something white and moving? Was it a polar bear? Abominable Snowman, maybe?'

'There's no need to take the piss.'

'If I couldn't take the piss, I might as well be dead.' She smiled, then stumbled slightly on an exposed root.

'There. See it now?' he pointed, beyond where he'd had the first sighting.

'Yes. Looks like a person..?' Tor looked up from her trip to see a flash of white, taking a second to process what she'd seen.

'Someone up ahead, walking.'

'Anyone you recognise from the pub?'

'No,' Gabe replied, taking longer strides, rushing now, crunching more heavily through the undergrowth, scaring some birds noisily into flight that had been hiding down by the water. 'It looked like a girl – a woman – in a white dress.'

'Very practical,' Tor said, having to hurry to keep up with her husband. 'Maybe she's done a runner from a wedding.'

'What?' Gabe said, distracted from his scanning of the trees for movement.

'A white outfit, as you do, for tramping round the woods? Not the smartest idea.'

'Oh.' He looked ahead again. 'There! Look.' He pointed about a hundred yards ahead as the unmistakeable figure of a woman in a flowing white dress appeared from behind a pine tree, moving quickly, diagonally away from them, before disappearing behind another large trunk. They paused, watching and waiting, expecting to see her coming out from the other side, but there was nothing. As if she'd gone, disappeared – *poof* – in a cloud of smoke with a magician shouting 'ta-da!' They exchanged a glance, both breaking into a grin, and seemed to make a decision without words, setting off at an increased pace, striding along, bouncing through the layer of pine needles and hurdling over fallen limbs.

'Hello!' Gabe called as he breathed hard with his exertion.

'You seem awfully keen to catch up to a young woman in a frock, darling.' Tor smiled sweetly. 'Offended, much.'

'Sorry? Oh. No, it was just the surprise at seeing someone out here, and dressed... unusually. And, they might be a neighbour.'

'Didn't get a look at her boobs then?' That same sweet smile, like *just playing with you, or am I*? 'And a neighbour. How nice. On top of seeing ghosts, we've got a fruit loop living near us rampaging round in a tablecloth.'

'That's a bit harsh. Hello!' Gabe said again as the woman appeared up ahead. She turned at the sound of his voice and looked back at them, standing with arms and legs akimbo, her dark red curls blowing around her face in the breeze. She was motionless like that for a moment, Gabe imagining that she was staring right at him, before turning and disappearing once again behind a tree.

'She seems a bit odd.'

'Hmmm?' Gabe was distracted, looking between the trees in the distance.

'You know. Walking alone out here, white dress, looks at us and then blanks us. Not seem a touch odd to you? When you go for a walk, don't you nod and say 'good morning' to people you see?' Tor was frowning as she spoke.

'Yeah, I suppose so. Maybe.' Gabe, by contrast, was miles away.

They reached the trees where she'd last appeared, but there was no sign of her. No footprints on the soft soil. Beyond was a clearing where the track dropped down to the water's edge, twisting round a soft muddy inlet where more trees had fallen over the years in the unstable ground.

'Where'd she go?' asked Gabe, kicking the pine needles in frustration.

'She walked off into the trees like she has been doing. Could be anywhere.'

'But these are the trees where we last saw her, and there aren't any now for a hundred yards. She'd be halfway across the clearing if she'd carried on. And it's a bog, she'd be up to her waist.'

'She must've doubled back up the slope,' Tor pointed higher up the hill, above the track where the ground rose and disappeared into the forest as it became deep and dense.

'But we'd have seen her between the trees - it's how we've been seeing her all morning.'

'Hardly *all* morning.' Tor pulled a face – *really?*

'You know what I mean.' Gabe turned away to look again.

'You fancy her, don't you?' Tor snapped in a strange voice.

'What? Don't be silly.' Gabe turned back to see the look of venom on her face.

'You do, don't you?' She sneered, face contorting. 'You want to fuck her.'

'What the hell has got into you?' Gabe was taken aback by his wife's reaction.

'What? What did I say?' She replied, voice softened again.

'That I fancied the girl,' he said diplomatically.

'No, why would I say that? Why would you - you hardly saw her through the trees. And besides, you've got me.' She beamed at him, twirling around and performing a curtsey. 'I'm sure I can keep you busy enough to not need the ginger chick in the dress.' She grabbed his hand and they walked up the hill around the clearing. Frowning, Gabe kept looking sideways at his wife, who was chatting happily about things she could see or the light glinting off the water below. Gabe wasn't sure what was more strange - her outburst, or the fact that she was now, seemingly, oblivious to it.

Looking further along the shore, more muddy inlets abounded, and there was no easy way to keep walking through the trees, without traversing the ever-steepening slope. This whole section of the lake was a series of slippery banks that would be impossible to walk along. Beyond these banks the ground sloped steeply upwards, the beginnings of the hillside that demarcated the edge of the valley. It was a more solid substrate for trees and fewer had fallen here. Following the slope upwards Gabe saw it wasn't continuous just above them, it looked like there might be a road or a track interrupting it, a dark slash in the trees above.

'Let's head up there, it'll be an easier way back,' he said to his wife, and turned into the loamy-smelling gradient, covered in tree roots, and began to climb.

CHAPTER 6

-\/-

IDRIS

The rising fart had become something of a regular occurrence in the last few years, Idris Dawson thought, as he let one go halfway up from his threadbare armchair. Pausing for a moment when upright, steadying himself, he bent to pick up his plate – the remains of a tin of beef curry and a bag of rice that went in the 'ding' – before heading for the kitchen. Further flatulent aftershocks accompanied him as he shuffled along. The cottage was small – seemingly even smaller when his wife was alive – and dark and dusty. A grandmother clock, rhythmically denoting the passing of time with its stern ticking, counting down the time he had left before he could join her, the only sound in the lounge once his intestines had had their say. Ellie had never liked noise in the house – no music or a radio playing in the background. The clock had been the metronome to her day – the pace of her life dictated by the sound of its mechanism, echoing through the house. Setting his plate and cup down on the brown Formica work surface by the stainless-steel sink, immaculately clean but tarnished with age and use, he opened the hot tap and poured a squirt of Fairy Liquid into the bottom. She'd been gone for six years now, leaving a hole much bigger than her small form, and one that could never be filled. The emptiness of the house without her was the same as inside him. He tried to fill it with Strongbow and his other pastime. But nothing fulfilled him. He could drink enough to forget and serve others as a duty, but the chasm inside him was massive and almost unbearable.

He bent at the sink to wash the dishes, his arms filled with soap bubbles – the squirt of washing-up liquid into the scalding water had clearly been overly-enthusiastic. He looked across and saw Ellie watching as he scrubbed. She nodded, smiling in that tight-lipped way, grey hair pulled severely back in a bun. Supervising. Pleased in her own way that he was doing some kind of house work.

You need new trousers… and a shirt.

Her ethereal voice echoed around the room. Idris had never been clothes shopping on his own in his life. Ellie had always insisted that he dress smartly to go out – whether it was to the pub or anywhere else. Several years on, those same clothes had seen better days, and he was starting to look like an elderly farmer in threadbare tweed.

'It doesn't matter what I wear,' he said grumpily, wiping his plate vigorously before rinsing in hot water and setting it to drain.

It does. You must have standards. Have I not taught you anything?

'It's different now.' He shook his head, as if she wouldn't understand – she wasn't here.

Because I'm gone? Or because of her?

Idris didn't reply, pretending he hadn't heard or had misunderstood. Finishing the dishes, he pulled the plug out of the sink, rinsing the bubbles away with cold water as the water gurgled out down the plughole. Picking up a tea towel, he turned toward her and she faded as he walked past, reappearing at the other side of the room, Idris barely noticing the phenomenon these days.

And you need a haircut.

'Stop your nagging, woman, my hair is just fine.'

It's touching your shirt collar – what's left of it.

'Hardly flowing down my back though is it.'

Standards, Idris. Standards. You're letting yourself go.

'Aye, well standards can go to hell when there's just me, and who gives a shit what I look like?'

Ellie's arms folded across her chest, her expression stern, her image flickering as if the air that made her up was angry. *Idris Dawson, you will listen to me or there will be trouble.* He shook his head and snorted quietly, glancing up at the carpet beater that still hung on the wall, yet another thing that he hadn't removed after she'd gone.

'Maybe then there would've been, but not now.'

Answering to her all the time, now, are you? There always were three in this marriage.

'Don't be ridiculous, Ellie. How could there be, given what she is.'

I know exactly what she is. What you are. What you think. I always knew where I stood.

'You are seeing things that aren't there,' he said to his wife's ghost.

I see more than you think.

'I don't doubt it.' He turned and hung the tea towel over the rail on the oven door, then shuffled to the other side of the kitchen. Ellie had faded from the room. His heart felt particularly heavy today. Idris existed here. It had never been a 'home' filled with colour and life and joy. Just somewhere to rest your head. A working house that Ellie ran with military precision, a machine that Idris formed a part of. But don't disturb its workings.

His thoughts drifted to the new owners of Ty Llyn. For English people, he didn't think they seemed too bad. The kitchen cupboard doors had very gradually dropped with age, so now hung at awkward angles to the jolly yellow drawers above them, the brown surfaces of the doors having faded with time. Idris reached up to one of the wall units, pulling down a bottle of Bells and a small glass, and poured a large measure. Ellie wasn't here to chide him about his drinking, he smiled grimly, and tossed the measure of dark liquid to the back of his throat, which burned, satisfyingly, all the way down to his stomach.

Ty Llyn.

Someone else to come and try their hand. Someone else to live in that idyllic spot and make a life for themselves in the valley.

We'll see.

And we'll see what she has to say for herself. She'll know. Know that someone has moved in, know that they are in her domain, in the house that she stands as guardian over. And Idris knew what her response would be. He shuffled back to the living room, walking across the room and over to the large captain's chest under the window. The dusty brown curtains – that Ellie would've had him beating clean, hung over the washing line every few months, and which hadn't been done at all in her absence (*You're letting the house go to wrack and ruin*) were half open, letting in a glow of light muted by the equally dusty net curtains. He tapped the chest, then flicked the latch aside so he could lift the lid. The papers and journals were all there as they should be, some yellowing with time, some encased in plastic to protect their delicacy, some carefully preserved under the plastic wrap of a photo album, such was their age. It was all there. The full story. Everything anyone would need to know about Cwmgwrach. Witch's valley.

CHAPTER 7

-\/-

FOX IN A WHITE DRESS

On hands and knees, they slowly scrambled to the top of the slope, until it levelled out onto a farm track, curving round on the firmer, higher ground on this side of the lake. Tor was first to arrive on the lane, her hand sinking into some slime on an old tree stump, making her slip, Gabe, below her, giving her a boost from behind.

'Thanks! Saucy,' she said as she struggled to her feet, looking down at her palm which was covered in green. 'Should bottle this, could make a fortune.' Gabe, huffing and puffing, got to his feet by her side, brushing his trousers down with his hands at first, but giving up when none of the dirt was moving. They looked down the track, in the direction of home. A dense planting of trees was lined up along the path and no more than a narrow central strip of light penetrated from above. Moss and slime grew on any exposed surface and the atmosphere was cold and damp. They peered as far as they could along the lane before the gloom took over.

'Let's leg-it back to the house. I could do with a beer,' Gabe suggested.

'You could always do with a beer, but yeah, this place can't be in the tourist brochure.' Tor turned on the path and they were both glad to fall into a rapid march. The lane was ramrod straight initially, but then it meandered along, turning sharply at times to follow the relief of the hillside that it was dug into, wheel ruts from a 4x4 or tractor had been made in the soft substrate and were now full of foul-smelling water.

'Don't imagine this is the busiest road,' she said.

'No. Hardly the M5 is it? And is it me, or is it getting chillier?' Gabe looked up to the tops of the trees, the canopy slashed apart by the road, a narrow strip of brightness above, hinting at warmth, but not providing any. And it definitely seemed like it was getting colder – a chill in the air, with small pockets of mist collecting in clearings and behind bushes, ethereal sentries appearing from behind tree trunks to silently monitor their walking.

'Yeah, temperature's definitely dropping.' Tor agreed – their breath visible in front of them, clouds of water vapour dissipating into the air. A shrill cry came from behind and they spun around looking back from where they'd come. The path was empty.

'What the fuck was that?' Tor asked.

'I dunno, but it was really close. Like, right behind us. A fox maybe?' Gabe shrugged it away as an everyday occurrence, managing to convince neither of them.

'A fox? Making that noise?'

'Yeah, they do make a shrieking noise.'

'Do they now? Aren't they nocturnal?' Tor knew she had the upper hand.

'Yes, but if we've disturbed their den...'

'Thank you, Attenborough. Let's get home. I've suddenly got a craving for Prosecco.'

'Yeah, let's go.' Hand in hand they set off again. After a few steps Gabe had an urge to look behind him. It popped into his head and stood there waving, looking for attention, like a playful dog holding its lead in its mouth and wagging its tail to persuade you to take it for a walk. He ignored it. They marched on, striding through puddles and patches of moss, their boots slipping in mud and catching again on gravel, steadying each other to avoid a fall.

Look behind you, look behind you.

The urge was growing inside him, pushing away anything else in his mind, dominating his thoughts – becoming compelling. He didn't know why he just didn't look – he hated being ordered around, being told what to do, even if it was his own sub-conscious. They never went on package holidays because being herded like cattle from airport to coach to hotel to 'welcome drinks' was his idea of hell. Nevertheless, this was gnawing away at him, like the need for a cigarette – going from being no big deal, to the biggest deal, to the most all-encompassing deal in his life. It became a 'must do.' To placate the id, he turned to take a quick look over his shoulder.

The girl was stood in the middle of the track facing them a hundred yards back, her dress shining white. She was motionless, not even her red hair moving in the still air. Gabe stopped, his mouth agape, staring back at her. Continuing on, oblivious to Gabe, Tor found his hand pulled from her grasp. She too turned to look back, about to ask why he'd stopped, but thought better of it when it became abundantly clear. In the distance, the girl lifted her chin, staring at them, and although she was a long way away, they both later thought she had a particular expression on her face.

It was a sneer.

It was as if she was looking down on them or pitied them. She was superior – a predator regarding her prey – her head tilted to one side as if curious. She raised her hand to point to them and opened her mouth to shriek again, like Donald Sutherland at the end of *Invasion of the Body Snatchers*. The noise came, starting and finishing sharply, shrill and painful to the ears, echoing around the trees, coming at them from in front, from the sides and even behind. It echoed away into the canopy, seeming to take wings and fly, leaving them behind.

And then she came at them.

∞ ∞ ∞

Running down the track as fast as they could, holding hands again but this time in a grip so hard that it would leave marks – holding on for dear life – they splashed and slid, always hoping to get more traction to move faster. Gabe grabbed Tor's elbow to prevent her slipping. Without discussion and following the briefest of glances, they'd turned and fled from the pointing girl, not daring to look back.

'It wasn't the fucking wildlife then.' Tor panted.

'No, probably not.' Gabe splashed down into a stagnant puddle, his knee giving forwards, almost causing him to fall. This time it was Tor's turn to help him up, shooting a glance over her shoulder when she slowed – but saw nothing.

'Fucking wildlife,' she cried.

'I've just realised something. She wasn't wearing any shoes.'

'What? She must have. You can't go walking out here barefoot.' Tor said, incredulously.

'She did.'

'You're sure?'

'Yes!' Gabe snapped. 'I'm not making it up. She was barefoot on the track.' *And her dress was clean, despite it looking muddy at the bottom when we first saw her.* But he kept this thought to himself, as if it would've turned this encounter from strange into full-on crazy.

They hurried along the lane, looking left and right and stealing regular glances behind as it slowly climbed and curved round to the right, presumably meandering its way back to the main road about a mile or so away. The bank sloped down to the right, dropping away to the beach at the bottom of the lake and they could see their house through the trees, the daylight filtering through – almost seeming too bright, as if they were emerging from a Grimm fairy tale, back into the real world. Glad to be leaving the more defined path, despite the distance they had made on it, they crashed down through the undergrowth and pine needles beneath the dense canopy, sliding over fallen trees, hurdling old stumps, regardless of the risk to their ankles. Finally, they ran out onto the loose shale on the shore. Only now did they slow their pace. Only now did they look back along the shore to look up at the path they'd ran along. The inlet with the fallen trees was in the distance, a low mist hanging around the tops of the remaining pines. Gabe looked back into the trees but couldn't see any sign of the track, but he imagined where it must be and traced their route – they had been running for at least a mile, and his t-shirt was drenched in sweat under his jacket.

Emerging from the trees into the sunlight by the water, the air temperature was much warmer than in the lane. Gabe had been convincing himself that something supernatural was at work; the barefoot girl in the self-cleaning dress and the temperature dropping when she arrived. But it was probably just the cold, dampness of the trees, and the lake along with the lack of direct sunlight. They really shouldn't be looking any further than, what was, a simple enough explanation. They walked away from the beach and climbed onto the rocky platform on which the house stood. Despite their only being in residence for a couple of days, nowhere had ever felt quite as welcoming as when Tor unlocked the door and they went inside – regardless of the packing boxes, regardless of not quite knowing which cupboard housed what and where everything would eventually come to rest. Right now, here felt a lot more like home than out there.

'A nutter,' Tor said, not even bothering to take off her boots as she pulled the bottle of Hendricks out of the cupboard.

'Excuse me?' Gabe said, wondering if gin before lunch was the best idea, but then headed for the fridge to liberate the beer he'd been promising himself.

'She must be a local nutter. Escaped from somewhere, or stopped taking her meds or something.' Tor shrugged as she filled her glass, unconcerned how much room there might be for a mixer.

'We don't know that.' Gabe flipped the lid off his beer and dropped it into the pedal bin.

'And *your* explanation is..? A bride lost on the way to the church? Someone separated from their school field trip? Nobody in their right mind is going to willingly go for a stroll by a lake in the autumn in a lacy white frock and nothing else. Including shoes, by the way, as you said.' She raised her glass in mock toast to the craziness of it all.

'Looks like there's a talking point for us in the pub. Wonder what Idris will make of it?'

'You're not thinking about what he said, are you?' Tor stared at him.

'Which bit,' Gabe asked innocently, taking a pull on the Corona, knowing full well which bit, now that it was underlined three times in his memory of the conversation.

'When he was talking about ghosts and witches.'

'He was quite compelling,' he replied, shrugging to evade the question.

'Compelling? You're talking about ghosts. You're about as far away from believing in ghosts as anyone could be.'

'I *am* a writer though.'

'Moving into paranormal werewolf romance, are we?'

'Using the '*are we*' are we?' Gabe smiled. 'Look I dunno. Yeah, he's an old local who'd had a few ciders, wanted to put the wind up the English and hold court in front of his cronies. I get all that.'

'But?' Tor took a large gulp from her gin, enjoying the burning in the back of her throat and the immediate calming effect it had on her heart rate. The hell with the tonic.

'I don't know, love. Let's not think about it. Let's not *overthink* it, either.'

'Not guilty. *You're* the writer, as you said.' She raised her hands in front of her. 'It was a nutjob. End of.' She made a motion to pull her hands apart to emphasise the point.

'Yes. You're probably right.'

∞ ∞ ∞

Tor was finishing tidying up after dinner and Gabe snuck out to 'bring more wood in', but really just wanting to check outside. The wind chimes, pipes and scratching at the windows had been bad enough, but today had been very disturbing. He wanted to make sure there was no sign of her now. The breeze lazily flew down the valley, pushing his hair back from his face, the chill reminding him of the time of year. Leaning on the balustrade of the decking, his face pointing out across the water, he imagined himself a ship's captain, waiting for the tide, ready to set sail. He saw the movement out of the corner of his eye. He scanned across – something down by the water, a shadow, almost an *idea* of movement, barely a distortion of the air around. He immediately thought of the girl in the dress – a ridiculous notion that she would still be there – unless she was the witch of course, spying on him, climbing into and out of the murky depths. But he could see no flicker of light-coloured material – no white dress in evidence.

Not her then.

But what? It could easily be an animal – he swore he'd heard a fox before, and so maybe it was one of those, going back and forth to the water's edge to drink or maybe fish. If that was a thing when you were a fox.

The twig snapped over to his left. Loud and clear, just twenty or thirty yards away, across the parking area at the edge of the woods. Gabe's head spun round so quickly he thought it might twist off. The gloomy movement on the far bank now forgotten. The lights from the house preventing his eyes adjusting to the darkness, he marched quickly across the decking and off onto the gravel, landing with a crunch. He paused, listening, eyes scanning the trees and bushes illuminated by the house lights.

'Hello?' *Great, you're talking to a fucking badger or something.* 'Hello-oh.' Taking baby steps he walked past his car and over to the edge of the woods, squinting to see anything – not sure what he was looking for or what he would find, but whilst the movement on the far side of the lake might not have been anything at all – a trick of the light or something – there was no mistaking a snapping twig. 'Is anyone there?' He tried one last time – as if someone would just stand up, compelled to reveal themselves after he insisted a third time. Slowly stepping sideways, eyes penetrating little by little, further into the foliage, he still saw nothing. Pausing, being as still and quiet as he could, apart from the persistent thump that he realised was his heart hammering in his chest, he heard nothing further. Taking one last look up the drive and down toward the water, he snorted a chuckle and turned back to the house, leaping up the steps onto the decking, disappearing around to the patio doors, where the eyes that had been watching him from the undergrowth could no longer follow.

CHAPTER 8
EGG ON YOUR FACE

'I'm going to the pub,' Gabe announced, out of the blue. He'd spent the morning storing away packing boxes in the barn, and putting together two flat-pack shelving units they'd brought with them for the lounge. It was high time all their books were on display and not in boxes in a spare room. They'd just finished eating bacon and egg sandwiches, Gabe still with some dried egg yolk that had dribbled onto his chin.

'You know I love you – just not right now,' said Tor, smiling sweetly at her husband who looked about five.

'Really?' he asked.

'No. Sometimes I wonder why we got married in the first place.'

'You coming?' Gabe persisted with his previous subject.

'Wasn't thinking of doing. Is this going to be a thing, now?'

'What do you mean?'

'Well, we never used to have a pub we went to. So, is this going to be different?'

'Might be. Might like to have a local, to go and have a pint with the boys.' Gabe smiled.

'The boys?'

'Yep. Them.'

'The boys you don't know yet.'

'The very same. Every single one of them.'

'What if there aren't any boys?'

'Well, the girls, then.'

'I should be jealous.' She nodded.

'You should be.'

'Mhm. The only one of the girls I've seen was about seventy-five and with only half her own teeth. Crazy jealous, me.' Tor nodded before changing tack. 'Why are you really going?' She interlaced her fingers on the table, her sandwich having been delicately and sensibly consumed using a knife and fork.

'Just want to follow-up on what was said the other night. To see if anyone else has got anything to say.'

'About what the other night?' Tor frowned at him.

'Well, it isn't about the weather. What do you think?' Gabe rolled his eyes then made them go very crossed, something which grossed her out and made her smile at the same time.

'Good luck. You sure they aren't gonna say 'y'all ain't from round here now are ya boy, but in a Welsh accent?'

'I think I'll be okay. Last chance.'

'Gotta paint my toenails, dear. A girl has to do these things.' Tor got up from the table and started to clear the plates, ready to go into the dishwasher. Gabe carried their glasses over. 'Why don't you head off? We'll only just get in each other's way here,' she said in a common mantra for them in the kitchen.

'Sure?' he said, about to go and wipe the placemats down.

'Yep, bugger off out from under my feet.'

'You're the boss.' He made a mock salute.

'Don't you forget it, mister.' She smiled broadly at him then opened the dishwasher to resume her tidying.

∞ ∞ ∞

The road was slick with the rain from earlier, but the air was clear, the sky blue and cloudless with a light breeze vainly attempting to dry things out. Gabe could see the pub up on the left – a much easier proposition than when they came here on that first night. *Was that only a few days ago?* Time was definitely going at a different rate here. He turned the car off the main road and pulled slowly up the hill. There were a few cars parked outside for the early afternoon session. Gabe parked and got out, opening the now more familiar door and went in.

As welcoming as the pub had felt the other night after their journey in the pouring rain – despite the initial frostiness over ordering food – it felt like he'd stepped back into the seventies today. The décor inside, that they hadn't noticed before, was dated – flower patterned carpets, mahogany cladding on the bar, and red velour seats sat opposite from wooden benches padded with 'lounge' cushions. Mal Jenkins was standing behind the bar, once again polishing some glasses dry that had presumably just come out of the dishwasher. He raised one in mock toast on recognising Gabe. Glancing at the movement to his right, he saw Idris rocking gently back and forth in his chair, in the corner under the dart board.

The old man didn't acknowledge him, but seemed to stir as the door slammed shut again, slowly levering himself to his feet, as if he was unfolding. He swayed slightly as he reached his full height, and toppled forward as he bent to pick up the remains of his pint, steadying himself on the table with his other hand to stop him pitching onto the floor. Draining the glass, he thumped it down onto the table a little too hard. His fingers wrapped around something next to the glass and he turned to leave. Gabe realised, wide-eyed, that they were a set of car keys. He glanced at Mal, to Idris and back again. Mal gave an embarrassed shrug. 'Five and drive round here,' he said by way of explanation.

'And ten for men,' cackled the old man as he passed Gabe, swaying from side to side. He turned as he reached the door and said. 'Look for the dead tree.' Then pushed his way out into the sunshine.

Glaring after him, Mal said. 'He's harmless enough.' As if justifying his serving the old man when he knew he was driving.

'Not in a car he's not.' Gabe shook his head.

'That car's almost as old as him – practically drives itself. You know he's lived here most of his life. Got no phone, no wi-fi, nothing. All he does is come here.' Mal shrugged as he continued with his polishing. 'It's different round here. I came from a town as well, and you have to get used to the way they do things.'

'That would seem apparent.' Gabe slid onto a stool by the bar.

'It just takes time – that's all.' Mal held a glass up to the light, checking for marks then slid it onto a shelf above the bar. 'Can I get you anything?' He asked, focusing on Gabe, seemingly for the first time since he'd walked in.

'Bottle of Peroni, please,' he asked, and accepted the cold bottle from the barman, after he'd flicked the lid off into a waste bin beneath the counter. Condensation ran down the green glass, making the paper label soggy and Gabe's fingers absently peeled away at a corner. He took a pull on the beer, enjoying the feeling of the ice-cold liquid sliding down his throat. Pursing his lips, he set the bottle carefully onto a coaster on the bar. 'What did he mean when he left just now?' Gabe asked, still staring at the bottle.

'I didn't catch it – what did he say?' Mal had found himself another glass to polish within an inch of its life.

'He said, 'beware the dead tree.'' Gabe repeated for the barman's benefit. 'Do you know what that means?'

'He's talking about a tree that's dead – that's about all I know.' Gabe wasn't sure if the man was being deliberately facetious or not.

'Well, I know that, it's just, what is the significance of it – what does it *mean*?' Gabe was becoming a little exasperated with these people and the way they did things.

'I don't know, Mr Hooper, but I'd guess it wasn't far from your place if Idris is mentioning it. It must be a tree in the forest that he knows or thinks holds some meaning.' Mal shrugged, what can I say?

'But why tell me. Why say that and not something else?' Gabe was searching for an answer, searching in Mal's eyes for something that wasn't there.

'Like I say, I can't help you. Idris does come out with some stuff, you know.'

'I'll just bet he does.' Gabe sipped his beer, fingernails now peeling the wet label off the glass.

'He's been even more… Idris-like, since his wife died.'

'Idris-like.' Gabe couldn't help but smile, but then it faded quickly. 'So, he's on his own?'

'Yes,' Mal nodded.

'Do you think he's… not as strong mentally as he was?' Gabe skirted around the question he wanted to ask.

'I don't think he's barmy,' Mal didn't skirt around anything. 'But all he's got up there are his thoughts and two dead women in his life. I'm quite glad he spends as much time down here as he does, otherwise I think he would go doolally.'

Gabe nodded. 'Yes, I think you might be right. Thank you. Thanks for your time.' Finishing the beer, he set the bottle down on the bar, the last remaining froth clinging to the inside of the glass, trying to stop itself sliding to the bottom with the dregs of the bottle.

Two dead women in his life. That's what Mal said.

Gabe got up and left.

∞ ∞ ∞

'He's been asking around,' Mal said into the phone.

'Was there today?'

'Yes.'

'And Idris?'

'A bit drunk. Said something then left.'

'Well at least he didn't stay around. It's too early.'

'I would say so.' Mal shrugged.

'We don't want to arouse suspicion. We needed it quiet for a while.'

'But there's no telling Idris. You don't see him every night.'

'Thanks be to God. He's like the spokesman.'

'What now?'

'Ball's not in our court, is it?'

'No.'

CHAPTER 9

JUST PASSING THROUGH

The place certainly felt a lot more like home now that the TV was up on the wall. Tor still had doubts about it being placed centrally like that – it was the first thing you saw when you came into the house through the front door and she didn't really want a television to dominate such an old place like this, with all its history. Gabe had been able to use the same 'floating' bracket they'd used in the old house to hide all the cables behind and had wired their home cinema and satellite box into their fifties-style unit sitting beneath – wide and squat like a slim brown toad. The satellite guy had come when Gabe was in the pub and so they were fully connected with the outside world. Now, sharing the sofa and a glass of wine, streaming *Stranger Things* on Netflix, Tor had to admit that it was, gradually, becoming more like home. The episode they were watching finished – it was getting a bit too supernatural for her with giant tentacle creatures made up of dead bodies – and the familiar 80s electronic theme music started playing.

'Watch another?' Gabe asked, the leather seat cushion farting as he stood up. 'Back in a mo,' he said over his shoulder as he headed through to the kitchen. She didn't watch him leave, staring into the middle ground as the theme music played, thoughts bouncing from something to nothing and back again. The room felt big and empty without him – not that he was a particularly big guy, or with a huge 'room-filling' personality, but he was there.

And now he wasn't.

Suddenly, Tor was cold – the temperature in the room felt like it had dropped and she shivered, goose-pimples appearing on her arms. Maybe Gabe had been keeping her warm sat by her side, or maybe he'd just left a hole that had been filled with colder air, she smiled as she thought about a Gabe shaped blue hole in the air like in a cartoon, as she too got up to get her fleece. The cellar door creaked somewhere below as Gabe disappeared downstairs, and now she felt properly alone for a moment, which in itself was odd. As quickly as that feeling arrived, however, it disappeared, shoved out of the room by a presence. She could feel a disturbance in the room – someone was there – the ideas of a person moving, filling and warming the air that she'd just been having were suddenly more real. An icy chill gripped her that had nothing to do with the temperature. Gabe was downstairs banging around, no doubt fiddling with the boiler like it had become his midlife crisis equivalent of a trainset. She could definitely feel someone in the room, something that was certainly there but just happened to lack form and shape. So convinced was she of it, that she expected them to jump out from behind the curtain or from under the coffee table at any moment. *Surprise.*

'Hello?' she said, nervously – confused – partly foolish for talking to an empty room, part convinced she wasn't alone. She looked back around the lounge, walking across to the curtains, ruffling them to make the intruder drop out, and looking under the coffee table, perhaps a cat had somehow got into the house earlier and had been hiding away. But she saw nothing out of the ordinary. The TV guide fell off the table, landing on the floor right in front of her with a slap, making her jump. She stepped back and held her hands to her chest, realising how fast her heart was beating. Smiling, she felt relief for a second as if she'd just been aware of the thing slowly sliding off the table, and that had triggered her feeling of foreboding. Shaking her head, she looked up from the open copy of the *Radio Times* on the floor, and there was a shape right in front of her. A distention of the atmosphere, a change in density creating a fullness in the space, curving the very air she was looking at, but there was nothing tangible she could see or feel. It was like *The Predator* was standing there, noiseless, motionless, almost shimmering as the air bent around it and reflected the lights. About the same size, slight, and slim, they stood facing each other, or rather the thing was just there, whether it stood, floated or was the first sign of madness in her brain she wasn't sure, but their Mexican stand-off seemed very real. Who would be the first to draw? Tor's play was to run – to dart to the sliding doors off to the side, running along them into the kitchen, because she could easily outrun an apparition, obviously. Logic had packed its bags and left some minutes before. The distorted air hung there, tiny movements keeping it in one position in the room as if air currents would cause it to drift or distort.

‘Hello?’ Tor said again, not feeling at all strange about talking to this thing. It seemed to have no immediate effect, however, but then the movements, the small corrective oscillations grew larger, as if it were a tall grass swaying in the breeze, dancing to a silent tune. Back and forth it moved, like a pendulum, hypnotic in its way. Then the swaying stopped, as if it was hoping Tor would keep talking, so it could dance to the sound of her voice. And then it rushed forward at her, striking her hard, pushing into her and she screamed.

∞ ∞ ∞

The tracing on the computer monitor climbed again, reaching new peaks as the graph slowly crawled across the screen. The harsh white glow illuminated the man’s angular features as he hunched over his keyboard, leaving no room to hide for the lines and wrinkles, his round glasses perched toward the end of his nose, peering intently at the screen. He made a few adjustments to the output with the mouse and suddenly it split into two, the larger peak staying the same as before but now turning blue and labelled ‘EM’, the second, in red, much flatter – showing very little. In the top left-hand corner, there was a label on the graph which said ‘House’. The man shrugged at the new graph – the flat red line – it had been a long shot. He sipped from his mug of barely warm coffee, made before this hugely revelatory data came in with a loud ‘ding’ to announce itself on his computer. Cycling through the other sensors, there was nothing anywhere – all dark – and triangulating the externals confirmed that the energy signature was coming from the lounge. The graph continued to climb, and on two occasions he had to adjust the scale to keep it on the screen.

Interesting.

He shrugged. This peak was new – a major event. He checked for the fourth time that the output was recording in real time and that it was being uploaded to the main server. Later, he would look back through the logs for the last time there was such a peak, but he was fairly sure, from memory, that he hadn't seen one like this. Not since his records began. Why do people always say that? *Since records began.* Well, of course it's since records began, because if it was before there were records there wouldn't be any recording to go in the records. Otherwise, someone would say, *hey, let's start some records.*

Smiling, he took off his glasses and rubbed his hands over his cheeks, massaging under his eyes. He should probably tell someone. Looking up at the four other screens at his workstation, once again he saw nothing out of the ordinary anywhere else. Electromagnetic readings were off the scale at the house, and the lounge in particular. She might as well be phoning in her position. Reaching for his own phone he opened up a new text message.

`Recording large EM readings at house. Biggest I've seen. Recording and monitoring. Updates to follow.`

The response came almost immediately

`Duration?`

`Four minutes and counting.`

`Peaked?`

`Just, starting to drop.`

`Just EM?`

`Yes. All other sensors blank.`

Okay. Thanks for letting us know. Keep on it.

Levering himself up from the chair in front of the monitor screen, he walked across to the dresser and poured himself a glass of scotch, taking a sip of the golden liquid, the burning down his throat galvanising his thoughts. He found himself wandering across the room to the patio doors, with their high vantage point over the water, and looked across in the direction of Lake House, which was just a couple of lights in the distance, barely visible through the trees.

What was happening? He wondered.

∞ ∞ ∞

The boiler pressure was a little low where it had vented some air. Gabe had been monitoring it numerous times a day – usually when he'd heard a gurgle or glug of air rushing through the pipes as it was jostled and pushed along by the water, like a molecular rugby scrum. He'd found himself running through the house like a madman trying to trace the sound.

It wasn't like he was obsessed or anything.

Opening the valve a quarter turn, he gradually boosted the pressure, being careful not to put too much cold water into the hot system. Water under pressure rushed into the back of the boiler, but there was something else, it sounded higher pitched. Gabe closed the valve and heard the tail end of Tor's scream. With a final squeeze on the round valve, he turned and ran at the cellar steps, trying to take as many as he could in one leap in his haste to get to his wife and find out what was wrong, but he missed the third step and slammed his shin into the sharp stone lip. With a cry of his own, collapsing in a heap on the steps, he wrapped his arms around his leg, holding his shin, knee pulled into his chest and eyes closed at the sharpness of the pain. *Fuck that hurt.* Pulling the trouser leg up he saw that the top of the shin was swollen, with some bruising already appearing, but the skin wasn't broken. He rocked backwards and forwards for a minute or two, blowing out hard through his mouth as if he were trying to cool down some food, and the pain slowly started to subside. Knowing there wasn't time to dwell on the extent of the injury, he had to get to Tor and just hoped he could walk on the leg. Levering himself up into a standing position using the wall as a crutch, he winced in pain as he tentatively put some weight through his foot. Gabe wobbled for a moment, blackness encroaching on his vision and he thought he might faint, but it stopped, and steadily receded. Taking a step up with his good leg brought tears to his eyes, and he limped heavily up the step, repeating the motion on the next, trying to move as quickly as his bruised shin would let him. White hot, searing pain shot up his leg with every step, digging into the bone just below the knee itself and he was sweating profusely by the time he reached the top of the stairs, falling against the doorframe for a moments rest.

'Tor?' he called. 'You okay?' He paused, and heard nothing. Groaning he hobbled into the hall and saw his wife standing in front of the sofa, head down, hugging her arms across her chest, crying. 'What the hell happened?'

'It felt like something passed right through m,' she said, her chest shaking as she spoke between wracking sobs.

'What?' He walked toward her, the pain in his leg forgotten, but still causing him to limp. 'What are you talking about?'

'After you'd gone. It was like, as you left, the temperature got turned down, becoming really really cold. I got up to get a jumper, and something was in front of me.'

'Something?'

'Like a shape.'

'What shape? Like a person?'

'Yeah. I guess. *I* don't know.'

'But what did it look like?'

'It didn't look like anything, it was just the air.'

'I don't even know what that means – how can you see the air?'

'You can't see the wind but you know it's there, can't you,' she snapped – the last thing she needed was to justify herself to him right now. 'She distorted the air behind her, like in a heat haze. And then she passed through me.'

'How the hell can you know that? What would that feel like?' Gabe had heard the scream. *Fuck*, most of the village and the people in the pub had probably heard *that* scream.

'When the temperature dropped, it felt like I wasn't alone, like someone else came into the room.'

'What do you mean?'

'I don't know. It felt like there was another presence there, like when you know someone is there with you even if you can't see them, and you know when they've gone.'

'Yes, okay.'

'And someone *was* there.'

'Who did you think it was – you knew I was in the cellar?'

'I didn't even think like that, it was like it was either familiar or not, and it felt familiar. So as weird as it was, I wasn't scared.'

'Did you see it?'

'No. I didn't see anything. Just before… it did what it did, I thought I could see the air shimmer, like a heat haze in the summer, but it wasn't anything… tangible. Just a shape.'

'A shape of what?'

'It was a person – a bit smaller than me and slight.'

'And you've said 'she' a couple of times…'

'Look I don't know – I really don't know what I'm thinking or saying – pour me a brandy or something would you? I wanna calm down and warm up. And why the fuck are you limping?' Gabe took out two glasses and pulled the brandy out of the cupboard – for Christmas, usually, but they'd make an exception.

'Boring story. Continue with yours. What *did* it do?' He poured two generous measures and handed one to Tor.

'I was standing there and this thing was right in front of me like we were chin to chin. For just the briefest of seconds it felt like we were facing off against each other, like in a duel. Then it felt like something pushing against me, when someone bumps into you in a queue, then it pushed *inside* me passing through me. It was like…' she looked around, searching for an explanation. 'Like getting an internal examination with the doctor – it felt like my insides were being churned around by something as cold as ice. But all of them – not just my bits, but everywhere, inside my ribcage, the lot. And then it pushed out of my back, just as it had pushed in. It was as if my clothes resisted but my body didn't.'

'Jesus. I wanna say bullshit, but that's a very definitive description.'

'The room got really cold first.' Remembering her drink, she took a sip of the spirit, making her lips tingle.

'Well, that's why I got up, to check the heating.' He shrugged.

'You felt it too? Shit, I thought I was half imagining it… someone had opened the doors,' Tor finished the sentence absently, seeming far away.

'What?'

'The temperature had dropped, the draft, the chill. It's how it would've felt if someone had come in and left the doors open. But it's warm again now.'

'The boiler's fine – chugging away as normal.'

'The doors are shut.' She smiled and gulped down the rest of her drink, before taking the bottle off the worktop and pouring herself a bigger measure.

Gabe was struggling with her figurative explanation of something opening metaphysical doors to let a very real draft in, so brought the conversation back to the narrative. 'And when it had passed through you, that's when you screamed?'

'Yes.'

'Did you see it again?' Part of Gabe was disbelieving but part of him was fascinated as well.

'I felt really winded, but I did turn around. Couldn't see anything, though. The shimmery-thing had gone.'

'So, are you thinking what I think you're thinking?'

'What? Like it could be something else? It wasn't a cat that'd got in and passed right through me.'

'And you couldn't have shivered and felt a bit strange in your belly at the same time..?'

'What, and because I've had a couple of drinks, I'm imagining the rest? Are you really asking me that?' Tor was surprised about how angry his line of cross-examination was making her.

'I'm just trying to think through the scenarios is all.'

'You don't believe me and think I made it up.' She spat at him.

'Hey, hey, no.' He gathered her into his arms, Tor resisting at first but welcoming the comfort in the end, submitting to his embrace and sagging into it. 'I'm sorry, okay? It's not the most usual thing you expect to happen when you pop out for a second.'

'No. I suppose we'll need to see if she comes back or whether she was just sizing us up.'

'She?'

'It's got to be the witch that Idris told us about. Or do you think there might be more than one spirit flying about the place?'

'Yes, but they were talking about a witch, not a ghost.'

'And she never left because of what they did to her.' Tor was insistent. 'And witch, ghost, can a witch become a ghost? Do *you* know the exact definitions in terms of paranormal beings? Jesus, what the fuck have I just said…'

'Okay. Let's say a ghost passed through you.'

'Because it did.'

'I *know*. I'm not disputing it – let me finish. Let's say this ghost passed through you, and that ghost is the spirit of the witch that they executed. What did she want? Why was she here?'

'Well, obviously we don't know. All I know is that I *felt* her.' Tor was impassioned, talking with her hands like she never usually did.

'What does that mean?'

'It means she pushed inside me. And like when anyone is as intimate as that – when you push into me – there's a connection. There can't not be.'

'Tor, I–'

'And when she pushed inside me, I felt a lot of things.'

'Like what?'

'Like anger and rage. Fear as well. Being horny too. But the overriding feeling was that of pure evil – complete nastiness – and it felt as if she were trying to take me over.'

'And you fought her off?' *Horny?*

'Well, obviously, yes.'

'And when I came upstairs, she just went – pushed out the far side of you and disappeared.'

'Something like that, yes.' She shrugged, taking a drink from her brandy glass – but a sip this time, savouring the warmth of the spirit. 'I do know one thing, though.'

'What's that?'

'She wants you dead.'

CHAPTER 10
-\/-
CORRIDORS OF POWER

The footfalls of the black shoes, polished within an inch of their life, echoed down the corridor, reverberating off the marble tiles, statues on pillars and oversized paintings of long dead political figures. Clearly important people in the corridors of power preferred to gaze at themselves rendered in oils rather than in a mirror. The man rushed along, breathing hard as he neared his destination, briefcase swinging wildly back and forth. He paused at the large oak door, adjusted his lapel and took a deep breath, before turning the handle and pushing it open.

The office inside was tastefully decorated and equipped, oak panels and large paintings adorned the walls, several plants grew tall with fronds or blade-like leaves in ornate pots, and a large oak desk sat at ninety degrees to him as he entered. An attractive middle-aged woman sat there, typing on a keyboard.

'Is he in?'

'Yes, but he's on a call, and you don't have an appointment, sir.'

'He'll see me.' The man crossed the room in five strides, rapped on a door on the far side that was the twin of the one he'd just come through, and barged in without waiting for a response.

'Hey, you can't just…' The woman rose from her desk and had sidestepped round it in a flash, following the man into the rear office. 'I'm very sorry, sir, but he just barged in and I–'

Her boss was sitting at a large polished oak desk, twice the size of hers, two screens pointed at him from the left corner. He was taking a phone from his ear. 'It's alright, Lucy. It's okay,' he said, and then into the mouthpiece of the phone. 'I'll have to call you back.' Before setting it back down on its base unit with a firm click. The green light flashed, turned red, then went out. 'This is an unexpected surprise.'

'I have news.'

'Well, I didn't think you'd just brought me a fucking sandwich.' He smiled at the other man, standing awkwardly now, swinging his briefcase. 'Out with then. Haven't got all day.'

'There's been activity.'

'And that's it? I'm on the phone to the cabinet office and you expect that 'there's been activity' is going to give me a hard on?'

'This is big.'

'My hard on usually is.'

'The activity is off the scale.'

'Where?'

'The house. New owners. The operative says he can't remember this level of response.'

'This has been a joke operation for so long – something on the books that isn't – that everyone's forgotten about it. Why the interest? Why now?'

'Well, it's part of my portfolio–'

'Eric, I couldn't give a fuck about your SMART goals and your end of year bonus.'

'There's a buyer.'

'What?'

'A private organisation has taken an interest.'

'Where did they spring from?'

'A sustainable energy conference. One of their directors approached me. They seem to be very organised and have a viable model and plan.'

'They are aware of the difficulties and the history?'

'They seem very aware, yes.'

'And that doesn't put them off?' The man sat back in his chair, steepling his fingers.

'No.'

'What do they want?'

'Reassurances on profits, technology rights, that sort of thing…'

'And?' he was growing tired of the stalling.

'Army assistance.'

'Fucking hell – do they want an open top bus parade as well?'

'Sir?'

'They don't want much, Eric, do they?'

'It seems a viable plan. It's all in here.' Opening the briefcase on the desk, he slid out a manilla folder and handed it to his superior.

'What's the operative say?'

'He is supportive of the idea, but has voiced similar reservations to you.'

'And all you need me to do, is persuade the Brass.'

'Yes, sir.'

'Crafty little fucker aren't you, Eric?' He smiled knowing full well that Eric was probably on the board of the company involved. 'You realise I can't protect you if this goes tits up.'

'I understand, sir.'

'If you'd come to me before…' And cut me in. 'But the Defence Secretary would hang me out to dry, and I can't afford that. You understand?' His eyes bore into the man standing in front of him.

'Yes sir.'

'Leave me the file, I'll be in touch. Oh, and Eric?'

'Sir?'

'Don't ever come to my office again.'

CHAPTER 11
-\/-
THE DEAD TREE

Gabe finished stacking the now flattened cardboard packing crates in the workshop, piled up next to the rows of dusty glass. His work there done, he pushed the door open with his shoulder, catching the material of his old waterproof on a rusty nail sticking out from the inside of the frame – its life-story a mystery. Maybe it had held a set of keys, some barbecue tongs or something more fearsome or sinister. It had had a purpose and a role once, but here it was, alone, corroded and redundant, watching the dust settle in the barn over the decades from its lofty vantage point, with nothing to do. And yet now, after all the years of waiting, here was its chance. The chance to grab hold of something, to bring it close, something that it could bond with, that it would loyally suspend until someone needed it. The nail reached out and snagged the faded Gore-Tex, holding it for a second like a lover, in a grip that said it would never let go, but the shiny material slipped through its grasp and luckily wasn't damaged. Leaving the nail alone again.

Humming to himself, Gabe went around the back of the workshop, the aging timber on the corners giving in to the effects of the weather and time, beginning to rot back from their cut edges, leaving small fingers still intact as the rest crumbled away. Paint was peeling and flaking away like the wood beneath – once a teal green, he supposed, now faded and darkened to look khaki. A small gravel path ran along the side of the shed, neat and ordered, holding back the chaos of the forest as the brambles and wild grasses encroached, testing the boundaries of the gravel sentry. The path abruptly stopped at the end of the shed, with undergrowth beyond, and he walked around the back of the building on mud and leaf mold. No sun ever warmed the timbers here – it was dark and damp with a strong smell of rot and a thought popped into his head that he should start a mushroom farm. Reaching out to check the integrity of the barn, to give the timber planks a shove, his foot glided on a layer of mud and old leaves, turning over, twisting under itself with a pop, and he went down hard, landing in a patch of water at the edge of some brambles that were quietly extending their boundaries from the woods, minding their own business so nobody would notice, whilst liking the idea of overgrowing the shed and making it theirs. A hundred thorns stabbed into him, tiny little pinpricks of pain all over his body. A random thought entered his head, of going into the doctors for an injection and the nurse tells you that you'll just feel a little prick, which always makes everyone smile – this was like that but multiplied by a thousand. His head landed with a thud as it crashed through the spiky underbrush and bounced off a raised tree root beneath.

Darkness closed in from the periphery of his vision, like the narrowing of the aperture on a camera, the grey sky above receding into the distance, as if he were falling away through the very earth itself. His mind drifted, lazed like on a sunny day on the beach, thinking of nothing in particular, a coolness washing over him that was not unpleasant and made him feel sleepy. The sound of water dripped rhythmically somewhere above him, he listened to the different tones, trying to pick them out like individual instruments in an orchestra. He coughed and the pain in his head and chest jarred him back to reality. Breathing heavily as he started to lever himself up, the cold dampness penetrating his clothing. His jacket – in dire need of re-proofing – now no barrier to the wet, which pushed through the material like the police bursting through a door, chilling him, motivating the muscles in his legs to get to work. He started to swim through the mud. Sliding through the slime of the moss and the muck, his fingernails scraping against wet soil, scratching and snagging on sharp stones and pieces of gravel. It occurred to him, for the first time in his life, that he was really going to need a manicure after this, but, whomever did it, would certainly have their work cut out for them. He laughed out loud at the thought. An image of a brightly lit salon of chrome and glass, of immaculately presented beauticians in red tunics and not a hair out of place, arranging files and clippers and scissors on a white table, like in an operating theatre, as they greeted him with the smile reserved for their best customers. He was guided to a dentist's chair with a white bench in front, Velcro straps wrapped around his forearms.

Are you ready for your manicure, sir? His beautician smiled down at him, leaning a little too close so he could smell her body spray in the daydream.

Why yes, I am, thank you. He returned the smile and raised his hands onto the bench, enjoying the horrified screams of all the staff as they saw two handfuls of mud, nails encrusted black, scratched and chipped, the fingertips bleeding.

The manicurist's worse nightmare.

He laughed again, his face almost rubbing in the dirt, and the image faded as he noticed the coldness of the puddle numbing his balls as still he swam, getting nowhere. Finally, the abused fingers managed to get some purchase, grasping onto a submerged rock, and he pulled hard, sliding a knee up under his belly, struggling to get to all-fours. The sudden movement combined with a blow to the head, and the heady scent of beautician perfume, made him see stars. For a second, he wobbled, his awareness starting to fall away, the lights going out, but he managed to hold on, getting onto one knee, pushing hard up through his leg with a grunt and another cry, which brought him onto his feet, bent double, pushing himself up from the floor. He slowly grew more upright, like he was being inflated. As he reached his full height, his vision misted over again and he swayed like a tree in the breeze, squeezing his eyes tightly shut to make him focus on his balance, his consciousness, to stop the darkness encroaching. The spinning sensation faded with the fog and he slowly opened his eyes, realising how unsteady he was, and now having to cope with vision as well as everything else, he began to pitch forward, like an ancient chimney stack toppling over, staggering to avoid a fall, his body listing, shuffling feet trying desperately to keep up, ready at any moment to fall foul of a prominent tree root and go down like a boxer in the fifth. Uncontrolled he crashed through the undergrowth, wading through dead grasses, ferns and clumps of brambles – *what the hell, add this to the list of blemishes on his perfect skin* – avoiding a couple of slim but solid enough trees that would certainly have delivered the knockout blow. A big trunk suddenly appeared before him and he dropped a shoulder, sidestepping like a winger in full flow, heading for the try line. He staggered and stumbled past tree after tree, like a drunk weaving his way home between lamp posts and parked cars. Just when it seemed his body was running away from him, he managed to get control of both his balance and his breathing. Looking down at the ground and shuffling to a stop, he paused and could feel the *lub-dup* of his heartbeat slowing and his breathing rate beginning to ease. He must've only stopped thirty or forty yards from the barn, but still he daren't turn round to look at the house. What if he was lost? What if he'd stumbled and crashed deeper into the woods as dazed as he was – this place certainly felt quite alien. For the first time in a while, he looked up. In front of his clearing vision, parting like clouds, was a huge silver-grey mass. Bark was a long distant memory, the wood bleached by the sun and polished smooth by the action of the wind and rain. Some six feet in diameter, the trunk of the dead tree sat heavily in a shallow basin. In contrast to the evergreen pine and spruce forest on the far side of the lake, this area was very much mixed deciduous – oak and alder, birch and whitebeam jostling for position, fighting for the warming rays of the sun and formed the almost continuous spidery canopy, with only the beech trees still clinging to their leaves – but nothing encroached around this tree, not even the ubiquitous undergrowth he'd been wading through. With only two branches – large horizontal limbs that could've been beams in a house extending on either side about ten feet off the ground – and the trunk, which had become a rotten basin with only one large splinter, suggesting more height and magnificence in days gone by, reaching up another twenty or thirty feet.

The dead tree.

Gabe now looked back through the trees to the house, sitting by the lake some eighty yards away – about a decent sand wedge as Peter Alliss would say. He could clearly see their bedroom window on the corner – a black rectangle like an eye, with the monochrome sky behind. He had travelled further than he'd thought after his fall, a fall he'd momentarily forgotten about, but now looked down at his clothes, muddy and wet with a darker patch on his trousers like he'd pissed himself. Shivering he turned back to the tree. *The dead tree.* It must be the one Idris had warned him about. But that couldn't be right, this tree was dead long ago, and would surely have rotted into the ground by now, reclaimed by the forest. Been overgrown and overcome.

Unless something had stopped it from doing so.

Where the hell did that idea come from? What could've preserved it?

You know what.

His sub-conscious was wanting to take him down a dark path, somewhere his rational self didn't want to go anywhere near. Idris must have his facts wrong. This tree might've been dead thirty or forty years but not ten times that amount, it just wasn't possible.

Shivering again and now needing to get back to the house to clean up and get warm, Gabe took one more look up at the abstract skeleton, then turned to slowly make his way back to the house.

Ready for his manicure.

CHAPTER 12

IDRIS AND GABE

Hooper turned off the lane onto a gravel track which sloped upwards to a small bungalow surrounded by wooden sheds in various stages of collapse – ancient creosote having nothing in competition with the Welsh weather. The car crackled along the gravel, slowing to a halt in front of railway sleepers fixed together into raised beds of vegetables – winter cabbage growing vigorously in the depths of manure that had been dug in over the years. Carefully pushing the car door open so it wasn't grabbed by the wind, Gabe emerged and stood in the bright sunshine, looking across the produce growing amongst the dead flower stems, beyond the shrubs and fruit trees to Idris Dawson, standing bent over in a bed, pulling out summer bedding that was now well-past its best and throwing it into a wheelbarrow. He seemed to be dressed exactly as he had been in the pub that first night – checked shirt, brown braces and high-waisted tweed trousers. Now the shirt was unbuttoned, almost to the waist, exposing a white string vest and grey hairs, matted with sweat even in the colder autumn temperatures. He also wore a trapper hat pushed back on his forehead, ancient brown sheepskin sticking out around his ears from under the shiny covering.

'Mr Dawson?' Gabe called across to the old man who continued with his work, oblivious to his visitor. As if he had so many. 'I'm–'

'I know who you are, Englishman,' Idris said, standing up with a low groan, putting his hands over his kidneys and arching upwards to stretch his back.

'Sorry. Didn't know if you'd remember me from the pub.' He resisted offering him his hand to shake.

Gabe had spent the rest of the morning cleaning himself up after his adventure in the woods, slowly making his way back to the house, going in by the boot room and depositing his muddy clothing in the utility by the washing machine before Tor saw him. She'd barely looked up from the laptop as he went into the kitchen, a cheery wave was all that interrupted her browsing on Amazon. He dashed up the stairs in his underwear and he did catch her raising an eyebrow at him before looking back down again. The shower had done a good job of getting his fingers clean, save for a thin black line in what was left of each fingernail, but he wouldn't be modelling sovereign rings for *Argos* any time soon. Then he'd cleared his thick head by turning the jet of water ice cold. By the time he'd gone back downstairs and announced that he was going to see Idris, he was feeling thoroughly human again.

'Old and pissed I may be, but senile... not yet.' Idris gave a smile. 'You should know, I don't care for the English.'

'No? Why?'

'You think that Britain and England are the same thing. The whole country is governed by the big English cities – mainly London – and anywhere else must have the same problems, the same things to worry about. Fucking bollocks.' The old man's face lit up with fire and anger as he fired shots across the bows of the old enemy. 'You English think you can stamp your idea of things – your way of doing things – on everyone else. As if it's a good thing. It's as if Wales is an extension of England and not our own country. Tea?' Idris turned and stepped down from the raised bed, striding off toward the front door of the bungalow, loose black work boots, caked in mud, trailing their laces in the soil. Hooper stood there and watched him go, somewhat shocked at the anti-English rant aimed at him, and yet, then being invited in. Shaking his head, he followed the old man.

Chez Idris was a wide squat bungalow sat atop the hill, staring out moodily across the magnificence of the valley, more rolling hills continued behind, giving some shelter from the north and east. Politely, you would call the place 'tired', but rundown or ramshackle would be more accurate. It had probably been painted cream at one time, but was now faded and pale, with paint peeling away from the render. Wooden windows were rotten and double glazed with cobwebs, and the slates on the roof had slipped and slid, now looking like they'd been scattered at random by a drunken roofer. Idris pushed open the door – strangely new in brown uPVC with opaque half glass – and slipped off his boots, replacing them with threadbare corduroy slippers, before hanging his hat on a row of hooks covered in coats for all seasons. Hooper slid off his trainers and left them next to the muddy boots, following Idris into the kitchen.

'This place – never been the same since I lost Ellie,' Idris filled the modern black electric kettle. 'She kept the place up. Well, she told *me* what to do – always had a list of jobs needing done, she had.' A smile crossed his face at the thought, lighting it up, shaving ten years off him, then faded as quickly as it had come, a shadow chasing the sun, barely leaving a memory that it had been there. 'Doesn't seem a lot of point in it now. It's a roof over my head and that's all I need.'

'I'm sorry.' *Because what else do you say?*

'Six years she been gone, now.' Idris bustled around finding mugs that were the least stained by time. 'Seems like yesterday,' he said to himself as Gabe leaned against the worktop. The brown Formica was at least clean – as was the rest of the kitchen as he looked around – just dated and unloved. Idris might also say that about himself, Gabe thought.

'You've invited this Englishman in for tea.' Gabe decided to pick up their conversation from the front garden.

'Yeah. I didn't say I disliked every one of the English, nor do I like every Welshman. Let's just say I'll be reserving judgment on you for the time being.' Idris raised his head from his teamaking, giving Gabe a fierce look.

'I'll watch my step.'

'Here.' Never once having asked how Gabe took his tea, Idris slid a mug along the counter, like a bartender in an old Western movie, the contents of the three-quarter full mug trying to slosh over the sides in an enthusiastic escape attempt. The mug, with a faded print of *Cymru am Byth* stamped on the side next to a cartoon of an overweight rugby player diving for the try line, was chipped on the top. Fortunately, Idris' one-size-fits-all-tea of milk with no sugar, suited Gabe. 'Have a seat, Mr Hooper.' Idris pointed to a leather stool parked next to the worktop. It might've been a breakfast bar, except there was no bar, just a stool next to the back of a kitchen cupboard. Yellow drawers matched the worktops, with light brown cupboards beneath, all once neat and parallel, now hanging on their hinges at jaunty angles.

'Call me Gabe, please,' he said as he perched and sipped the steaming tea. Idris gave him a look that said it would be a long time before he would be doing that.

'What can I do for you, Mr Hooper?' There was a green leather armchair beyond the kitchen units, the small dining table having been moved across to accommodate it. The stitching was frayed and AWOL in parts, allowing the foam stuffing to peep through, too shy to yet make a full appearance. The chair farted almost as impressively as Idris when he flopped down into it.

'Tell me what you know about my house.' Hooper set his mug down and kept eye contact with the older man. 'Tell me what's really happening.'

'That's a lot to ask from a stranger. Coming here, knowing nothing of history, buying a place, then demanding to know everything about it.'

'Who does? When you go house-hunting, you fall in love with the place, the surroundings – you don't immediately hit the local library and start looking for strange things. So, I thought I'd come and see what you knew.'

'What makes you think I'll know anything about your house?' Idris seemed to dismiss him, as if he'd been wasting his time, but then, almost as an afterthought. 'Has something happened?' Idris shrugged into his tea.

'You seemed to know plenty the other night in the pub.' Gabe was beginning to think he was wasting his time with the old man, that he was just smoke and mirrors and his performances in the pub were just that –

showing off as he held court in his domain. Still, he'd made the effort to come up here, so he might as well tell him. 'Something pulled down our windchime – pulling a metal hook completely straight in the process. Then all the pipes started moaning and creaking, but the plumbing is working fine. Then this presence, this thing appears, walking through the house. I think this won't come as any kind of surprise to you..?'

'Thing, you say?' A small shake of the head before another sip of the tea.

'Yes, like… an apparition. Like something was there, *distorting the air*, but with nothing to see.' Hooper threw his hands up in the air, exasperated that that was his best explanation.

'You saw bent air?'

'Look, Idris. *Mr Dawson* if you like. I know you know my house. I know you know more than you are admitting here with your coy answers. I just thought you'd be able to fill me in – I'm not sure what else to do at the moment. If you can't or won't help me, then I thank you for the tea, and I'll be off.' Hooper pushed the stool back, which slid easily on the shiny terracotta tiles. With a slight nod in Idris' direction, he turned and took one step toward the front hallway and the door.

'It's not your house. It's hers.'

∞ ∞ ∞

Gabe sat opposite Idris in the lounge having turned Idris' matching armchair from the one in the kitchen round from facing the television to point in his direction, on the equally matching sofa. The old man had poured them both a measure of Scotch, and he raised his glass an inch in a conspiratorial toast, now that he'd let Gabe metaphorically in the front door. A small log burning stove glowed in the fireplace, it was that sort of autumn day, but Gabe suspected that it was probably lit year-round, regardless of the temperature. Yellow and orange flames licked languidly up and over the logs inside, which glowed red, the movement was continuous, constantly changing, mesmerising.

'Told you she'd come after you.'

'Sorry?'

'Your first night here, in the pub. Told you about the witch and you didn't seem too keen to believe it.' Idris stared down at his whiskey glass, smiling to himself.

'Is that surprising?' Gabe raised an eyebrow. 'Our first night, being told about an old witch haunting our house..?'

'Just being friendly. You had to be told.'

'Well apparently we did, so I guess I should thank you for the heads-up.'

Idris waved this away. 'There's a lot of folks who think we shouldn't be telling people, that it should stay a secret. But she's not shy. She was always gonna come and introduce herself – like the neighbour you don't want.'

'Wait, so more people know about her?'

'Well, yes, o'course. Why wouldn't they? You think you can keep her a secret?'

'I'd never thought I'd have to think about a long dead witch, so who knows what I'm thinking about.'

'Fair enough. There's something you should see.' Idris set his drink down, the remaining amber liquid sloshing around the glass as it landed at an angle on the table. He levered himself awkwardly off the sofa and shuffled across the wooden floor which was scratched and dented with age and wear, to the small window and the captain's chest underneath, it too creaking as he lifted the curved lid. Gabe rose to join him, looking over the old man's shoulder, down at the collection of old photographs, papers and files that seemed to fill the chest. 'Sit. Sit,' Idris urged as he flopped into one of the two dining chairs that were placed adjacent to both chest and window, at first glance, a little strangely, but now seemed perfectly logical as both men perched on them to peer into the secrets inside. 'There's some old photographs of the village,' Idris said to himself as he pulled out two picture frames of sepia prints of a road – little more than a track – with a few squat cottages on either side. 'Don't really know why I've got these – just found 'em in some jumble sale once. They don't really show anything or anyone that means much now.'

'But it helps keep a record of the history of the village.' Gabe studied each picture as it was handed to him, half expecting something to suddenly move or jump out from behind one of the houses.

'I suppose it does.' The old man rummaged deeper, pulling out piles of papers stacked and tied with ribbon, hand-written envelopes that had been carefully slit open and now protected their precious contents, two empty whisky tubes that must've held particular memories in their cardboard, and, finally, three large photo albums that were stacked at the bottom of the chest next to two old shoe boxes, lines of dust having settled between the gaps left by the lifetime of memories piled above. Idris lifted them out, awkwardly, and blew the dust off the top. Gabe reached across to help with bringing the albums out into the open, and an image of tablets being removed from the Ark of the Covenant sprung into his head. He didn't want to think about face-melting, head-exploding Nazis, though. Idris closed the chest and then put the albums down on the lid, opening the top one of the pile to show old notes, newspaper cuttings and articles. The first cuttings were pictures, the earliest were hand written, on thick paper, now, despite the care and protection, faded and tarnished.

'That's Dyserth Church, where they had the trial of Gwen ferch Ellis – the first woman convicted and executed of witchcraft in Wales.'

'When was that?'

'1594.'

'And this?'

'The courthouse in Beaumaris, where Margaret ferch Richard was tried in 1655.'

'Two cases, sixty years apart. Not much witchcraft going on in Wales, then.'

'Oh yes there was. Your gang across the Dyke said Wales was a hotbed of witchcraft and superstitions – fairies and ghosts and the like.'

'And was it?' Gabe was warming to the subject and the seeming knowledge of his tutor.

'You have to understand that there wasn't really any medicine. You might have healers or herbalists that made poultices and balms. Most towns and villages all over had 'cunning folk' as they called them. They were respected too, like early doctors I suppose.'

'And she was one? Our witch. One of the 'cunning folk'?' *Our witch.* As if she was affectionately known now.

'Yes. Here's a note listing some of the things she did. It was written long after she passed, but it clearly says her name and lists some of the healing she did.'

'Is it a report from a magistrate?'

'I've got no idea, I just came across it in the library in Builth, with some other papers.'

'And you just took it, from the library?' He raised an eyebrow.

Idris shrugged. 'I've got a better record here than they have, and they'll probably have all of this one day when I'm gone.' He gave a short laugh, which deteriorated into a cough. 'Still, it shows that she was a healer of some kind. The church didn't like 'em though. Said they were heathens. The pious folk obviously relied on the power of prayer to get them better.'

'Hmm. So, charms and potions for warts, cuts and upset stomachs isn't what I would call witchcraft.'

'It goes beyond that, though. All the cunning folk would get asked about curing all manner of things – anyone with any kind of illness might approach them. You think of the folks with cancers or that've had strokes or something. They either let someone suffer or go to see a witch, to see what they could do.'

'Modern medicine struggles to cure this kind of thing, Idris, so what chance does a medicine woman have?'

'Well, that's where it gets interesting. Some people thought they were curses, as were rashes and impotence. And some healers could cure these things – set aside curses if you want. That's your dark magic, your more sinister stuff, not just your herbs and potions. That's what the church really didn't like.'

'Not their kind of magic then.'

'No. You're right, 'magic' that is the will of God was okay. They could explain miracles because they were from God. Not by your local wise woman.'

'And is that where the pressure came from to put these people on trial?'

'I think so. But, as you say, there weren't many – five people executed in Wales for witchcraft.'

'So, they were tolerated.'

'Yes. The church wanted to move society forward, get away from old-fashioned ways, but without a better medical option than prayer, people still wanted the cunning folk.'

'Why the trials then.'

'Maybe there were people who overstepped the boundaries. Charms were very frowned upon – it's what got Gwen ferch Ellis executed. A charm against a local gentleman did it – persuaded by someone else to put a charm in his house. She denied it, but they had some people come forward and they'd made their mind up.'

'And our witch?'

'Morvith ferch William. Apart from the list of magic she performed, and a list of charges, there isn't much of a record about her, as such. There are some diaries that are said to be hers, but it's how you find them.'

'Why isn't there more of a record?'

'Well, now I'd be guessing. We're not a big place round here – back then even less so – so record keeping prob'ly wasn't very good, or stored very safely even if records were made.'

'Yes, I suppose so. Interesting to think that huge amounts of history is lost because it isn't recorded.'

'But that's not why there isn't a record – I don't think so, anyway.'

'Go on.' Gabe was becoming more intrigued by the story the more he found out – realising later that the old man was drawing him in, making him a believer.

'We know she was one of the cunning folk. And from what I've heard about the contents of her diaries, seemed to keep out of the way. There was no father and her mother lived as a recluse on the hill overlooking the valley.' Gabe looked quizzically at him. 'My daughter got me into going online on an iPad she got me. Who needs to go to libraries?' Idris chuckled. 'We also know that she was asked to go to a child who was dying, and she couldn't save him.'

'That's in the diaries, online?' Gabe thought back to Mal telling him that Idris wasn't on the internet. The old man clearly liked a certain façade to his personality.

'No. It's listed in the charges against her – she's accused of killing the child.'

'But you think it's different?' Gabe found himself leaning closer, drawing the old man out.

'Why would she? She was a healer, and seemed to dabble in some more powerful things but why would she go and kill a child?'

'Isn't that a bit tenuous, for someone you don't know from nearly four hundred years ago?' Idris shrugged. 'So, what happened?'

'She was put to death by the local landowner who lived in Ty Llyn. The child's father. Hung from a huge oak tree with her guts out.'

'The dead tree.' Gabe nodded.

'Very good. It's said that tree died the day she did, and got struck by lightning some years ago.'

'But it can't have been dead for four hundred years, it would've rotted away to nothing a long time ago.'

'It's said the dead tree is the seat of her power.'

'But what power – how? What will she do?' Gabe's eyes widened, looking alarmed.

Idris shrugged his rounded shoulders once more. 'She's defied death and is still around after all this time, I would've said there wasn't a lot she couldn't do.'

'Should I be as worried as I'm starting to feel?'

'I dunno. Don't try and stop her, though.'

Gabe paused and looked at all the old notes in front of him. 'Why isn't her death recorded with the others?'

'Because it was done by a mob not a magistrate. I don't think anything happened to him because he did the authorities a favour.'

'And when was this?'

'November 23rd, 1619.'

'The anniversary of that is just a few days away.'

'That's right, Mr Hooper. It is.'

CHAPTER 13
– THEN –
MEETING IN A MARKET

'Who's that?' The young woman's angular face was looking through the market stalls – lined up in parallel on the main street of the village – at a well-dressed man stepping down from a carriage that had stopped on the main road, his breath visible in the cool air, tousled dark hair an unruly mop on his head.

'I can't believe you don't know who that is, Morvith. He is the Master of Ty Llyn.' Morvith's friend was taller, with a stockier build than her slim, lithe friend. She carried a basket with meat and some material to make herself some skirts, balanced on her hip. Her hat was tied under her chin with a simple ribbon – Morvith's head was bare. They walked from stall to stall, making themselves heard over the bustle and hubbub of the busy street, with people – largely women – coming and going, rushing between the various produce stands to get what they needed before disappearing off.

'Ty Llyn?'

'The big house up on the lake.' Her friend said, as if she must know it. Morvith shrugged, still not taking her eyes off the man. 'He rarely comes into the village. I wonder what he wants.'

'To come to the market, of course.' Morvith shook her head slightly as if it was obvious why anyone was in the village that morning.

'People like him, of his breeding, don't come to the market amongst the likes of us. They have staff that do their shopping for them.'

'I want him,' Morvith said, matter-of-factly.

'Hush your mouth!' Her friend was wide-eyed. 'Do not be saying those things – you are wanton. Besides, he is not for the likes of us.'

'Why, Eiddwen? Is he not a man? Does he not bleed if he is cut? Does he not eat and shit and rut like the rest of us?' A number of women stared at Morvith as she spoke – her voice rising in volume, eyes glittering with life and mischief – shaking their heads as they passed, turning to their companions to gossip, conspiratorially.

'Keep your voice, down, girl,' Eiddwen hissed, grabbing her friend by the arm. 'People can hear.'

'Let them. I care not,' she said, raising her voice still, throwing her arms wide in a challenge to the women walking past who averted their eyes from the strange woman, turning around, daring anyone to respond.

'Their hearing is connected to their tongues, and they will wag, you know. You don't want that.'

'You forget how familiar I am with their wagging. They talk about me, anyway, behind my back, being one of the cunning folk. Let us give them something else to talk about.' Morvith looked at her friend for the first time, the hard lines of her face and piercing gaze softened and she looked nearer to her twenty-three years. 'They say I should be married – that I am old now in years. Perhaps it should be him.'

'You get ideas above your station.' Eiddwen, laughed. 'Cunning folk or not, he is well-bred and not for the likes of us.'

'Perhaps he is not good enough for me,' Morvith said, mischievously.

'He was married, by all accounts.' The two women walked together along the line of barrows that made the portable stalls of the market, reaching the end where a farmer was attempting to corral chickens in a series of wicker cages.

'Was?' Morvith carried little other than some dried lavender and a half dozen eggs.

'She died in childbirth.'

'So, he has a child?'

'A son, I think.'

'Oh.' Morvith pursed her lips as if thinking, frowning, her eyes darting left and right, and then her smile slowly returned. As if something had slotted into place. They rounded the end of the stalls and turned to walk back along the main street, heading towards the Master's carriage, passing by as he turned to reach back in for his hat. Morvith smoothed her white lace dress down over her body so she would look her best, accidentally brushing against his hip as she walked past. 'Oh, forgive me, my Lord,' she said as he turned to look at her, bowing her head respectfully and giving him a little curtsey.

'Nothing to forgive,' the Master replied, looking her up and down. Deference forgotten, she looked him in his deep blue eyes, smiling wickedly this time, before spinning away to catch up with her friend.

'What was that about – silly girl, bumping into him like that,' Eiddwen chided her.

'He didn't seem to mind.'

'You need to watch yourself. You could get yourself into all manner of trouble.'

'Good. I like trouble,' Morvith looked at her friend and laughed out loud.

CHAPTER 14

TAKING ME FOR A GOOD TIME

'What are we having?' Tor asked as Gabe moved around the kitchen, depositing the contents of the fridge and several store cupboards on the worktop.

'Thought I'd make a Thai curry.'

'Nice,' she replied, flicking the switch down on the kettle. 'Cuppa?'

'Nah, I've got a Peroni on,' Gabe replied roughly cutting up an onion, some ginger and garlic before tossing them into the food processor with chilis and lemon grass. The loud whirring sound of the Magimix filled the kitchen and it was 'his' noise. Tor didn't use kit like this when she cooked. By her own admission, her cooking tended to revolve almost exclusively around the toaster, because she had staff that did everything else for her. Gabe smiled as he remembered her saying it. He added a little water to make a paste that he could fry off and turned to the fridge. The one thing they both loved about their kitchen was their 'American' larder fridge – oversized and difficult to fit into any conventional kitchen slot, they had made it work in here by sitting it at the end of the counter next to the dishwasher – open now as he helped Tor unload it as he went along. Gabe had already managed to smack his leg into the open door of it twice in the last two days, his bruised lower shin showing the evidence of the abuse, thankfully bruised at a different level to the one he'd got from colliding with the cellar steps.

'That's the one thing I don't like about this kitchen,' he said. 'Whoever thought putting this dishwasher in this narrow thoroughfare was a good idea, and next to the fridge too. Bloody hell.'

'You can't blame the kitchen designer for the fridge – we put that there. You're right, though, the sh'washer does make it narrow when it's open. Anyway, I'm sure you'll find some other things to dislike, babe, in time, if I know you.'

'Yeah. Start a list, maybe.'

Opening the fridge door wide, Gabe looked for the pack of chicken breasts on the 'raw meat' shelf, pulling it out to come to room temperature while he was pottering around, gripping the plastic tray with his fingers, the nails of which were still black from earlier. He nudged the door shut with his hip and set the polystyrene tray down on the worktop, turning back to make sure the fridge had closed properly, he saw her standing next to it.

The witch.

Wearing the same lace dress of the other day in the woods, the girl was dripping wet, the material clinging to her shoulders, nipples and hips

– red hair hanging in ringlets dripping more water down her body. It was as if she'd just climbed out of the lake.

A pretty, slight girl looking at him with cold black eyes, her skin pale and almost grey as she shivered above puddles of water on the floor. She could've been a young woman who'd burst in seeking some shelter from the rain, this could've been almost normal, just someone needing a little help. But the wound was a give-away. As Gabe watched, blood started to pour from her sternum as a cut opened up, the slash descending from an unseen knife, a crimson stain expanding outwards to form a gruesome inkblot on the front of her dress. The lace parted to reveal a jagged ugly wound, puckered and angry, material and flesh opening like a zipper, from chest to crotch. Small sausages of guts nudged their way out through the wound to say hello, hanging out of her abdomen like the embarrassing piece of food that sits on the corner of someone's mouth for everyone to stare at while the owner is blissfully unaware.

Gabe took all this in in a split second and reeled away from whatever she was. Her head tilted on one side as she studied him, quizzically. Suddenly, her arms jerked forward, and she opened her mouth as she reached for him, jaw separating into a wide gash, the dead skin of her face peeling back like a sharks, revealing row upon row of pointed fangs. There were no lips to speak of. Worms or something even more unspeakable had presumably gobbled up those delicacies long ago. All she had was a gaping maw. The twisted clawed hands tried to grab him, but he pulled away, taking a step to the side to evade her grasp, but catching his ankle violently on the open door of the dishwasher, his body weight already travelling in that direction, but now his foot was jammed. Momentum kept him going – with his foot jammed, his ankle cantilevered against the metal rim of the appliance. Teetering in mid-air for a second, his body hovered over the utensils tray of the dishwasher, full of forks and knives from earlier, all pointing upwards and looking far less innocent than when he'd been eating lunch. Now they had murderous intent. His ability to pause time wasn't in the same league as Trinity, and his body carried on its arc over the open door, increasing the tension in his leg, still pinned at the side of the appliance. Managing to look down, he watched his leg bend, grotesquely, almost at a right angle to his ankle, before, in front of his eyes, it snapped, the door of the dishwasher providing enough of a fulcrum to break the lever. He flew sideways, without the bowing tension of the bone to keep him up right now, his foot still planted on the floor where he'd left it, two bone shafts sticking upright, the leg seemingly only attached by skin and tendon and muscle. Blood exploded out from below his knee, splattering across the front of the fridge, and a bucket load splashing into the dishwasher tray. Gabe went down fast and hard, crashing onto and off the open door, scattering the drawer and utensil tray across the kitchen – skittering across the tiles like a facehugger. Vaguely he remembered seeing a 'making of' documentary from the early 80s about movie special effects, and that they used a knife stabbed into a cabbage to create the sound of any blow to the head. He thought this as the sound of the brassica being assaulted echoed in his ears as his forehead bounced off the floor for the second time that day. Looking down through his daze he could see his trapped ankle completely tear free of the leg.

'Gabe, what the fuck.' Tor was at his side, cradling his head. 'You fell over the dishwasher you numpty, look at you.' This seemed somewhat of an understatement with the witch standing over him and having severed his own foot. Allowing his head to be lifted into Tor's lap, somewhere he heard a sob and realised it must have been coming from him, and he looked down to survey the damage. His leg, ankle and foot were all present and correct and his ankle was untwisting itself from the side of the dishwasher. It hurt like a bastard, and he instinctively knew he must've twisted it, but felt like cheering that his leg was still attached. Looking up at the fridge, the image of the witch, now a skeletal monster, faded in front of his eyes. The floor was dry – no blood anywhere. 'What the fuck happened?' Tor asked with concern in her voice.

'Girl,' he groaned.

'What?' Tor replied, trying to help him off the dishwasher door and onto the floor.

'Girl... by the fridge.' He tried to turn his head in that direction but then winced as pain evidently hit him from somewhere.

'What? There's no one here, just us.'

'But...' He looked dazed and confused, having propped himself up against a cupboard door to look back across the kitchen, only to see nothing.

'You're bleeding.'

'My ankle.'

'I don't think it's your ankle, love, it's your head or somewhere.' Tor pointed at his forehead as blood trickled down, just above the eyebrow.

'I think I bust my ankle.' Tor looked down and saw that his ankle was already swollen, but at least it wasn't at an unnatural angle. The gash on his forehead was deep but was definitely something she could manage herself with their first aid kit – steristrips and a bandage would do, but the ankle was something else. 'Guess I forgot the dishwasher was open.'

'Jesus love, you could've actually broken your leg.' Tor reached for a neatly folded handkerchief on top of the other clean laundry on the worktop, opening it with a deft flick of the wrist and blotted it against the wound on his head. The white cotton quickly becoming saturated, she turned the makeshift dressing, using a clean section to help stem the flow, repeating the process again until the blood slowed but the handkerchief was soaked.

'Or worse.' He laughed, the image of his severed leg popping into his head again for a moment.

'What?' Tor frowned at him.

'Nothing.'

'Look, can you stand up? We might need to get you to the hospital.'

'Nah, I'll be fine.' Turning onto all fours, Gabe managed to lever one leg – the good one – up under him and start to stand. So pleased was he with his efforts, that he placed his other foot to the ground and immediately put weight through it. The pain shot up his leg and drained all the colour from his cheeks, Tor grabbing him as he started to slip back to the floor.

'Easy big fella. I think we need to go to A&E. Christ, you aren't safe to be let out into the community.'

∞ ∞ ∞

'Hi Mr Hooper, I'm Dafydd Linley and I'm the on-call orthopaedic consultant.' The doctor nodded in Gabe's direction as he burst through the light green curtain of this particular cubicle that his navy blue theatre scrubs clashed with. Gabe lay back in the hospital bed in a t-shirt and shorts. Tor had somehow managed to get him standing, and, with him leaning heavily on her so he didn't have to put his mangled foot to the ground, she got him to the car, where he lay across the back seat. It had taken almost three quarters of an hour to drive through the winding lanes to get to Bronglais Hospital in Aberystwyth. They'd waited for just the three hours before the triage nurse came over. Sandra Burnham was written on her name badge.

'So, can you tell me what happened?' She asked. Gabe explained how he'd tripped, minus any references to a strange disembowelled dead woman in his kitchen – he didn't think it had a lot of clinical merit, other than risking him getting shut in a room with a jacket that fastened at the back. 'And what are the main problems for you today?' Sandra asked again.

'You're staring at one of them.' Tor said, unable to hide her exasperation when it was fairly obvious her husband needed some treatment. Within twenty minutes, Gabe had been checked for concussion, been stitched up and had had an x-ray on his ankle. Then Mr Linley arrived with his chiselled good looks, well-spoken Welsh accent, and rugby player physique – *would I look as good in some scrubs, love?* – and the results.

'I think you've been fairly lucky – you've sprained your ankle – one of the ligaments on the outside of the foot has been put under excessive strain for what it can cope with and this has resulted in some 'giving' of that tissue, which is classed as a grade two sprain. This might also have pulled away a small shard of bone from the ankle where that ligament attaches.'

'Might?' Tor asked, eyebrows raised.

'Yes, sorry it sounds a little vague. It's called an avulsion fracture. X-rays are great, but when you are looking for tiny changes in the contour of bone that the x-ray makes transparent, it's hard to distinguish between what is abnormal, and the shape of the bone beneath. It isn't major, and won't change how we manage it – just that if it doesn't settle down how we might expect, we can investigate further. The good news is that it doesn't need surgery to correct, but you will need to wear a boot to walk around in for a month or so. And there'll be no running or disco dancing at weddings for a while either. I'd also like to keep you in overnight for observation as you had a bump on the head.

'Two bumps on the head,' Tor added helpfully.

'Sorry?' the doctor frowned at her.

'No way, Doc, I'm not staying. I'm fine.' Gabe said, already starting to get out of bed.

'Not if you could see yourself in a mirror you're not. If you'd rather go home, that's fine, but take it easy for a couple of days, and if you get increasing headaches, blurredness of vision or nausea, you need to come back.' The doctor held up a clear bag and removed the object it contained. It was made of grey plastic and was reminiscent of a ski boot. 'This is a walking boot. It's got an inner sock which you Velcro around your foot and a hard outer casing to protect it in the same way as a shoe would. The clever part is this.' He held up a small rubber ball with a pipe connection on one end, then plugged it into a black pipe connector on the rear of the boot. 'When the boot's on, if you inflate this, instead of your foot pressing on the sole of the boot, it's surrounded by air. So even if you had a significant ankle break you can still weight bear in one of these things.' Linley handed the boot to Gabe, who hurriedly started to put it on. 'Remember. This boot doesn't have healing properties, so wearing it isn't going to get you better. If you are resting up – take it off.'

'Thank you. I don't need crutches or anything?'

'No, you get the air right – and don't overfill it so it cuts off your circulation – and you'll be able to walk okay. You will be lopsided though as the boot has a fair-sized platform on it.'

Gabe looked down at his foot, now surrounded with the inner sock, made of a neoprene-type material that made it look similar to a wetsuit. As he watched, the material gradually disintegrated into dust on the sheet around his bed. The somewhat swollen ankle – already showing signs of bruising – grew progressively more purple and enlarged. The skin becoming stretched and distended, like an overripe tomato, until it split on the front of his foot, a rip, tearing open from toes to lower shin, dark red, almost black blood oozing out, and running in small rivers round to his heel, soaking the sheet and onto the floor. The skin peeling back, retracting from the split, exposing muscle and tendon below, blood now flowing freely from the open wound. He was now a bad anatomy video, watching tendons shorten as he moved his toes, but then they too tightened, curling the toes upwards, until each one snapped like a guitar string.

Someone needed to work out who was responsible for the increasing pool of blood on the floor, he thought, *and perhaps someone should take another look at him.*

The grotesque tableau at the end of the bed continued and his foot twisted inwards all of a sudden, causing pain in the site of the injury. It kept turning inwards, the big toe curling in to touch his shin. And then he heard it snap. The foot, the ankle, snapping the shin just above the joint, snapping it clean in two and leaving a jagged bleeding wound, the severed foot dropping into the blood on the flour, causing blood splashes to fly off in all directions, leaving Gabe staring at a jagged bony stump.

'Are you okay, Mr Hooper? *Gabe?*' The doctor leaned in at him, a frown creeping across his more familiar, happy countenance. Gabe's foot was encased in its neoprene coat, ready for him to slide the hard plastic boot on. He could wiggle his toes and pump his foot up and down. He stared at it as he replied.

'Yeah, fine. Just all been a bit strange, that's all.' He forced a smile and made eye contact with the medic.

'Okay. Well, if you're feeling okay, you're good to go. Take some over the counter paracetamol and anti-inflammatories to take the swelling down. If it's getting more painful and more swollen, or anything unusual happens, come back and see us.' Doctor Linley gave a final smile, what must be his final sign-off smile, and turned to leave the cubicle.

CHAPTER 15
CHOPPING LOGS

The day dawned cool and crisp, with clear skies. Narrow fingers of mist, like grey candyfloss, hung over more sheltered inlets across the far side of the lake, the mirror-surface undisturbed by any breeze. Gabe had spent a fairly peaceful night, cursing his bladder with every painful step when he had to get up to pee at 3am, but that had been the worst of it. He'd had a belter of a headache in the evening, but even that had piped down with some paracetamol and a couple of 'secret' glasses of scotch, that Tor would've disapproved of. Getting up this morning, he'd been tempted to go without the boot, but Tor's best stern schoolteacher expression told him otherwise. Once he'd slid it on and inflated the air bladders inside he found he could walk without pain, but the Doc had been right, the height of the boot made him limp along. As he hobbled around the kitchen, he imagined himself as Snake Plissken in *Escape from New York*, and hoped he looked as cool limping around – but somehow, he doubted it.

'I think I'll go out to the barn and check out the wood situation – maybe split some,' he said quietly over a bowl of cornflakes.

'You're gonna do what, now?' Tor replied, setting a mug of coffee down in front of him.

'Thanks.'

'How is that 'taking it easy' like the doctor suggested?'

'It feels fine – I'm sure it will be okay if I do it in bursts or batches or something. I'm sure I won't need the boot for long either.' He shrugged.

'Mr Lindley said a month.'

'Yeah, but he said about a month, and if it gets better…'

'Alright. Alright. But don't come running to me if you mess it up again.'

∞ ∞ ∞

Not walking remotely like Kurt Russell, Gabe limped from the house and breathed in deeply, the aroma of the forest on the back of his palette. The log shed stood at right angles to the barn, with large discs of timber thrown inside, waiting to be split. Gabe had noticed several axes and hatchets on the wall in the barn the day before and decided to get some exercise and increase their stores for the log burner in the living room, ready for the winter. There were a range of sizes of axe, one with a handle, the others wooden, and all appearing well-cared for. As he selected the largest one, he wondered why they'd had been left – almost as if the previous owner had departed in such a hurry, they'd forgotten about them. The wooden handle was new, covered in a shiny layer of varnish, but the head wasn't – the metal painted red save for an inch toward the blade which had been left bare, and contained small pockmarks and indentations that showed signs of rust from living in the dampness of the barn. Gabe ran his hand along the blade, believing it to be sharp, but, not knowing much about these things, knew trial and error was his only option.

Going back outside and using one of the discs as a chopping block, he stood his first victim upright, like an executioner – the wood faded to silver and dried bark peeled away as he man-handled it into place. As he swung the axe up and over his head, he wondered how long the timber had been undercover, and guessed it had to have been at least a year and probably longer. For the first time in his life he swung an axe, envisaging the wood splintering and exploding into suitable sized logs with his first blow. The weapon embedded itself in the surface of the wood with a thud, and remained resolutely intact. Levering the axe free, Gabe reviewed his technique – surely there wasn't a lot to swinging an axe, apart from, well, swinging, and aim. Deciding to use more brute strength and rely less on the weight of the axe, he swung again, the head landing heavily into the surface of the wood, sending a wide crack all the way through, the two halves separating as he pulled the blade free. Gabe got into a rhythm of placing timber and swinging the axe. His breath surrounding him in wispy white clouds before disappearing into the trees. It was hard work and his jacket and clothing began to feel hot and heavy. He dispensed with the jacket, but this did little to cool him, so the shirt soon followed – the chill air cooling the sweat on his skin, making him catch his breath – but was forgotten about as soon as he began working again.

'Coffee for the worker,' Tor called as she approached carrying a steaming brew in a mug. 'Jesus Christ!'

'What?' Gabe paused mid-swing and looked over his shoulder at Tor's surprised expression.

'You, you clown. Stripped to the waist in November when it's bloody freezing.' She set the mug down on the roof of the log shed. 'Are you sure you're okay?'

'It's not cold – I'm boiling.' He looked down at his chest where rivulets of sweat raced each other toward his waist, some getting caught in the matting of hair on his chest and belly, some getting a clear run and reaching his trousers first.

'I hope that smack on the head wasn't worse than we thought. I think you're mad.'

'Nah, love. But do you think I could do a Coke ad?' He stood with arms wide, flexing his muscles, cheesy grin in place.

'Oh,' she exclaimed, putting her hand in front of her mouth. 'Just tasted a bit of sick in my mouth at the thought. Gotta go – don't do too much.' She turned and walked back towards the house, lifting her hand in a casual wave. He watched her go with an easy smile, and shook his head at the banter.

The exercise was invigorating. Tor was right about one thing, he thought, it was bloody freezing and he should be shivering, but there was still sweat glistening on his skin. After an hour and a half of exercise, Gabe wondered if it was time to stop – he wasn't used to this level of physical activity and he'd definitely pay for it in the morning. The coffee had gone cold in his mug, although he had managed to drink half of it while it was still warm. The log shed was filled with freshly chopped wood – row, upon row of logs of varying shapes and sizes, neatly stacked up like crazy paving, the air filled with the smell of freshly cut timber. Gabe brushed the debris and sawdust away from his new chopping block, and went back into the barn to hang up the axe.

One wall was covered in hooks and clips for hanging and securing all manner of gardening tools and other outdoor equipment. Gabe had already hung up his basics of a fork, spade and rake, and leant his snow shovel against the wall. But it was the axe that was intriguing. Or, more properly, the axes. The only tools in the shed, it was as if someone had left in such a hurry that they'd left them behind, and yet, despite the pockmarks and rust patches, his axe was still really sharp. He wondered if someone had bought a range of them to chop wood, and yet had left before they could be used. Or had bought them some time before, and they'd remained in their place, watching several of the short-termed owners come and go, desperate for someone to swing them in anger.

Clipping it back in its place on the wall, he took one more look around the room. Some dustsheets off to the side had slipped away – perhaps when he'd found the picture – and revealed the top of a wicker basket. Pulling the sheets back further, through the cloud of newly disturbed dust, revealed a round basket, woven to be strong and sturdy with a roll-top and two stout handles, lined by leather for ease of carrying heavier loads. Gabe picked up his new log basket and carried it outside, filling it with the spoils of his work, and a couple of handfuls of kindling that he'd made by splitting thinner branches, and from splinters from the bigger logs. At the house, he opened the door with his hip, kicking off his one work boot, scattering piles of sawdust that had been smuggled in inside and around his socks, and found himself humming *I'm a lumberjack and I'm alright* as he hobbled across the kitchen.

Tor was sitting on the sofa, her coffee, too, had gone cold on the small table. She was cradling a picture in her hands, tears rolling down her cheeks. Setting the basket down on the hearth, Gabe went across and knelt awkwardly at her feet, sticking the boot out to one side as he rested his hands on her knees. 'Hey, it's okay.' He knew the picture she was looking at.

'I can't help feeling that we've left him behind.' Tor let out a sob, her eyes red and full of tears.

'We're never gonna do that. He'll always be with us – you've said so yourself a hundred times. Where we live doesn't matter – he would've loved it here – and I wish we could've come here when he was around.'

'But what if he can't find us?' Tor looked thoroughly desperate and confused. *Lost.*

'He doesn't need to find us, baby, he's here. He's in our hearts, he's all around us. He *is* us, isn't he?'

'I suppose. I just guess because he's never been here it feels a bit empty without him. It doesn't feel real – he hasn't got a room here.'

'Yeah, okay. But remember how empty the old place used to feel when we could imagine what he'd be doing and where he'd be playing. I could *hear* him in every room there. That's why here is a fresh start. Come on, this was your idea.'

'But without a room, he doesn't seem to belong.' She hugged the picture to her chest.

'He doesn't need one, babe. He's here with us, and that's all he needs.'

'I know,' she said, smiling through her tears. 'I just miss him.' She glanced up across the room toward the window overlooking the lake, Gabe following her gaze, at the small blue urn on the windowsill.

'Me too. Me too.'

CHAPTER 16
– THEN –
TY LLYN

Blu-grey smoke drifted out of the short, squat chimney on the roof of the cottage, rising straight up in the stillness of the air against a backdrop of the trees behind. The fire had been well-stoked that chilly spring morning, before Morvith had gone up into the woods on the east side of the valley, looking for herbs, roots and bark. She had a number of potions and balms to make that morning before going delivering her medicines later on. Slowly walking back down the hill into the shady rear garden of the cottage, she noticed someone climbing up the sloping path to her garden. Putting her basket down by the side door she slowly made her way around to the front to meet them.

'I'm sure this path gets steeper,' Eiddwen called, out of breath from the climb from her small-holding next door. 'Brought you some eggs.'

'Thank you,' said Morvith, pleased with the unexpected booty, taking her panting friend's arm and guiding her up the path, in through her door. The foraging basket temporarily forgotten. 'Tea?'

'Aye. I need a whiff at any rate,' Eiddwen replied, plonking herself down on a wooden chair by the open stove. 'Chilly old morning.' Still wearing grey fingerless gloves that were starting to fall apart, she reached her hands out to warm herself from the flames from several logs that had blackened and blistered, shrinking away as they warmed the cottage. The kitchen was small and dark. The stove recessed into an alcove around which were stacked piles of logs, and herbs hung in bunches up above, drying out. The oak table in the centre of the room was chaotically piled with baskets and bottles, measuring spoons and candles. Several battered and well-thumbed books on herb-craft and the like were in the middle. Books that were banned by the church, no doubt.

The tin tea kettle bubbled into life on the stove top and began to bounce and rattle, Morvith taking it off and pouring the scalding contents into cups containing a collection of herbs tied in a little bundle for the purpose. Leaving it to infuse, she sat down opposite her friend.

'I heard some news,' said Eiddwen, clearly unable to contain herself from the real reason for her visit.

'Oh?' Morvith tilted her head to one side and pretended to be uninterested. This was a game they played, Eiddwen was always excited by local gossip, and Morvith liked to hear her tell her stories, even though she had no interest in the people that they described.

'He's been asking after you.' Eiddwen slapped her thighs as if to emphasise the exciting news.

'Who has?' Morvith's eyes narrowed, instantly wary of anyone new showing an interest.

'The Master.' Eiddwen was a little exasperated that her friend didn't instantly grasp her meaning. 'Of Ty Llyn!' Her eyes searched Morvith's for any recognition, but they were the same dark pits she always saw. 'The man you bumped into on purpose at the market the other week,'

'Oh, yes, I remember. I didn't bump into him on purpose.'

'Oh yes you did. You could not have been more obvious, my girl.' Eiddwen smiled. 'Never one to shy away from what she wants.'

'And why should I?' Morvith lifted the herbs from the tea and handed a cup to Eiddwen. 'What's he been asking?'

'Some of the women in the village said he'd been asking for the best of the cunning folk.'

'Who did they say?' Morvith's eyebrows raised. The cunning folk were only ever desired, talked about or even popular when someone wanted something. They were otherwise shunned. This was the doing of the church. Generations before they would have been revered, put on a pedestal because of their ability to heal and advise. But the church had put a stop to that, poisoning the minds of the people against them for heresy and ungodly practices. They still used them – probably just as much – when the power of prayer failed, but their name was blighted by the clergy and their God. With several women practising herb craft, there was always some competition between them as to whom was most highly regarded.

'Eiryth Williams, of course,' Eiddwen said with a dismissive wave of her hand and quietly took a sip of her tea. 'Your face, Morvith! You look a picture.' She grinned broadly. 'Of course, they all said you.'

'Eiryth knows her herbs,' Morvith said defensively, as if she could've understood if the women had named her.

'Didn't you say that Eiryth was a pretending witch that wouldn't know her own arse if she could smell it?'

'That doesn't sound like me.' Morvith shook her head, face impassive as her friend stared at her, then could hold her pose no more and burst out laughing. 'Yes, I think I would go round to each one of those women's houses and put a curse on them all if they'd truly said her.'

An uncomfortable silence descended over them as Eiddwen thought about Morvith's power – her ability to make a curse – that she knew she had made charms, both of which were banned and punishable by death.

'So, they said me. Is his son sick?'

'Yes, I think that's what they said something about…' Eiddwen's face fell, colour draining from it. 'Oh no. Did you make him sick?' Her eyes wide with realisation. 'Did you make his son sick so you could get closer to his father?'

'I might have.' Morvith smiled. 'Why do you think I needed to bump into him?'

'Oh Morvith, that is a wicked, wicked thing to do.' Eiddwen looked shocked.

'The boy will be well again, and he will have women fussing all over him and bringing him nice food and treats. He will have the time of his life.'

'But… it is immoral.'

'It will be well, and his father will be grateful. You will see.'

Eiddwen remained pale, her shock still palpable – whilst she knew of Morvith's power but didn't know of the extent to which she would use it, particularly for her own ends.

'Now what?' Morvith said to jerk her friend back into the room.

'They didn't really say. I imagine the Master will visit you..?'

'I'll be waiting.'

∞ ∞ ∞

The front garden was the only part of her land to get direct sunlight and Morvith was busy digging the earth – readying it for planting the herbs that would be the basis of her craft during the summer, and then to dry for the next winter. She sang to herself as the spade sliced through the soil, screeching against the stones beneath the surface, but the birds that were chirruping in the trees around Eiddwen's smallholding next door, stayed away from her. Morvith was sweating from digging and shifting soil, mixing it with manure that she'd brought by the bucket-load from Eiddwen's, and digging it back in with her tiny plants. Breathing heavily, a sheen of moisture across her chest, she paused to take a rest, only then hearing the sound on the lane below, like cartwheels rolling over the compacted dirt. She looked up. A fine carriage appeared out of the trees as if by magic, pulled to a stop by the gate at the bottom of her lane, and the driver carefully climbed down onto the thin metal rungs of the steps, down from the seat at the front. He was thickset, dressed in a dark suit and hat, and could've easily splintered the rotten wooden gate with his large bare hands, but they were surprisingly careful, respectful even, she noted, as he swung the gate in despite it almost hanging off its hinges. She continued with her planting and waited for the man to make his way up the steep slope, noticing the top of his head appear over the brow of the hill, the rest of him slowly appearing. She looked up as he approached.

'Good morning,' he said, stopping, doffing his hat and interlacing his hands in front of his waist. 'Are you Miss Morvith?'

'I am.'

'I am from Ty Llyn – the master has sent me.'

'I had heard you might be coming.'

'Ah. Well, my master would like to see you.' The man wrung his hands, clearly uncomfortable with this amount of conversation.

'Shall I get my coat?'

'If you would, please, miss.' He looked relieved that he wouldn't need to speak any more. Morvith got up from her kneeling position in the patch of soil, brushing first the dirt away from her dress, and a whisp of hair from her face, leaving a smudge on her cheek. She carried her basket and her remaining small plants and disappeared inside. Deciding not to rush, she put the kettle on the stove and stripped out of her dress so she could wash the sweat off her body. The already warm kettle didn't take long to boil and she poured it into a bowl on the kitchen table. Stripped to the waist now, she washed with wanton abandon, knowing the Master's man was out there. She changed into a simple white lace dress that she liked to wear to make a statement – usually where men were concerned – then packed her bag of herbs and potions.

The carriage driver eyed her when she finally emerged from the cottage. She wondered if he was having lewd thoughts about her – she knew that men did, and she knew how to make them react to her – but she wasn't going to do that to the driver. Following him down the path she looked back down the valley and across to the lake, before stepping into the carriage, taking the proffered hand of the thickset man, stepping up the wooden steps into the carriage.

∞ ∞ ∞

'Thank you for coming.' The Master greeted her and offered his hand to assist her down the steps once more.

'I don't think I had any choice.' She paused, eyeing him with her head tilted to one side. 'Lord,' she added, with more than a hint of sarcasm.

'Yes. My apologies, but there is some urgency. My son–'

'Is sick?' she interrupted.

'Yes,' he smiled, grimly. 'He has a fever and is very weak. He wastes away in his sweat, and gets more frail. Others have come and brewed him this and that, clergy have prayed, but all to no avail.' They stood facing each other, him a good head taller. 'But I heard tell that you had other… abilities. That you might be able to help.'

'I see. It sounds like he has been resistant to other things, but I can try all the herb craft I know.' She smiled thinly at him. 'Let me see him.' Barging past the Master she headed for the house, the pleasantries over, and the sooner the better, she thought.

The housekeeper turned in the doorway and led the way inside Ty Llyn as she saw Morvith approaching, in through the narrow front hallway to the steep stairs, dimly lit by candles and a fire in the huge hearth at the far end of the house. At the top of the stairs was a long hallway with several dark rooms leading off it. The housekeeper stopped at the last door on the right before the large room at the end – the Master's bedroom, no doubt, Morvith smiled to herself. The housekeeper stepped aside and Morvith brushed past to step into the boy's room, a small window harshly illuminating half the room and giving a view of the lake, throwing light onto the shivering child laying on a small cot, covered by a thin, soiled sheet. The boy was tiny on the bed, and she mused that he must've appeared like he was shrinking – his illness making him waste away. Skin was stretched over the skeleton of an eight-year-old, breath coming in short, sharp gasps, beads of sweat on his forehead. A maid sat by his bedside and mopped his brow, squeezing out the water into a bowl.

'Leave us,' the housekeeper said from the door. The maid rose, nodded and disappeared into the hall. Morvith perched on the side of the boy's bed, feeling the damp sheets, the chill in the boy's flesh, shivering. She looked up at the Master, who had followed her into the room and was now bending forward, peering over her shoulder. 'These sheets need to be changed every day, to make him feel fresh, and he needs to be kept warm.' The Master nodded and turned to look up at the housekeeper, his eyes like thunder, wondering why his son's sheets were not changed every day.

Leaning forward, she placed her palm on his forehead, wiping away beads of sweat before re-applying her hand.

'He's definitely warm,' she said.

'What does that mean?' The Master asked.

'It means he has a fever and we need to try and bring it down. It will settle his body – stop this shivering.'

'Can you do that?' he asked, his voice hopeful, leaning in to peer over her shoulder.

'Yes. I can. I have some lavender oil with which to bathe him and I will pack soothing herbs on his forehead.'

'The other women,' the Master interjected. 'They tried these things.' He waved his hand in the direction of her bag. She looked at him, defiant, above her station.

'But they weren't me, Lord,' she said with confidence.

'This medicine is powerful in the right hands – small variations can change their effect. Let us see how this does.' Morvith rose and turned, her bag of herbs on the table behind her, spinning quickly around and striking the Master's nose with her shoulder. Recoiling, he cupped his hands to his face, blood already seeping from between his fingers.

'Oh, my Lord, my apologies, please forgive my clumsiness,' she said, and reached for a cloth from her bag. 'Allow me to help.' The master stepped backwards, but she pursued him and eventually he lowered his hands, allowing her access to his bloody face. The pristine white cloth soon turned crimson as she mopped the blood up from his nose and around his mouth. 'Grip this between your finger and thumb over your nose,' she commanded. He nodded and his hands replaced hers on the cloth. 'Sit, please, Master.' She guided him to her chair, and he waved away her further apologies. After a few minutes she pulled the cloth away to see if the bleeding had stopped, but it soon started appearing at the base of his nose again. She re-applied the cloth, using a clean part this time, applying his hand once more. After checking several times, Morvith was happy that she had stemmed the flow and she took the now blood-soaked rag away, tossing it carelessly into her basket. Taking a clean cloth, she rinsed it in the bowl they had been using to bathe the boy and carefully cleaned the remaining blood from the Master's face, now dried in streaks on the bridge of his nose and across his cheeks. He sat, impassive, as she wiped his face.

As the Master sat quietly nursing his swollen nose, Morvith opened her bag and brought out an array of fresh herbs and roots that she had foraged that day, and dried ones she'd had in storage. She pounded them together and mixed with roots and fresh water fetched by the housekeeper. She applied poultices to the boy's forehead and abdomen, made a paste that she fed him from a wooden spoon, and asked the housekeeper to bathe him in his bed. 'We will do this every day, and see how he responds.' She looked at the Master, who nodded.

All was quiet and still in the room save for the rasping sound of the boy's breathing and the fluttering of his chest. Alone with him in the room, Morvith sat by the bed, her hands working quickly and skilfully, fashioning something. Working with willow twigs and thin strips of leather, she bent the twigs and tied them with the cord, forming a shape. Looking carefully at her design, she adjusted and re-tied, bent and replaced some of the wood that wasn't as she wanted. Satisfied she took a piece of material from her basket and draped it over the willow frame, tying it again in place, tucking the material in here and there until she raised it up and smiled at the fruit of her labour. Getting up from her chair she went to the door and slowly opened it, poking her head into the hallway to check it was empty. With the coast clear, she turned to walk into the master bedroom, noticing the three small windows on the lake side, the sun beaming in through them. Quickly she went to the Masters' bed, reaching under the mattress on what was clearly his side of the bed – a journal and candleholder sat on a narrow table on this side, where the table on the opposite side was empty – using a small knife she made a slit under the mattress and tucked something inside, pushing it along so it wouldn't fall out of the cut she'd made. Checking over her shoulder, she put the mattress back down again, smoothed the bedclothes and left for the waiting carriage.

CHAPTER 17
-\/-
NORMAL DAY

Gabe collapsed into bed, the boot discarded untidily on the floor, his body aching, not just from the falls of yesterday, but from the physical exertion of today. He tried to remember the last time he had exercised or physically worked as hard as that, but he couldn't. The cool sheets caressed him, and the duvet settled over his body with a soothing pressure that he envisaged was easing away his tension, like a masseur.

'You okay, my little coke-ad man?' Tor asked him, closing her book and setting it on the bedside cabinet.

'I thought you felt sick?' he chided her.

'Just joshing with yer,' she smiled, gently punching him on the arm.

'I'm alright,' he replied. 'Be glad to get into the land of nod, though.'

'A normal day.'

'Sorry?' Gabe's eyes had closed and was willing himself to sleep, but he was interested in Tor's comment.

'It's just that every day has had some kind of weirdness since we got here, and today has been, well, normal.' Tor flicked the rocker switch on the cable leading to the lamp and the room fell into darkness.

'It's not all been weird,' Gabe said a little defensively, as if he had to stick up for the house and their early experience of being here.

'No, but today is the first normal day we've had. No ghosts or girls in white dresses, no funny noises, no dodgy pipes, or crazy old men that think they can spook the new people. No mangling ourselves. These first few days have been a crazy couple of months.'

'Well, when you put it like that…' Gabe mumbled now, his consciousness already starting to drift.

'Goodnight you. Good effort today.' Tor rolled over to face her husband and rested her hand on his hip as she always did, listening to his breathing getting deeper almost immediately as he fell away from planet Earth.

∞ ∞ ∞

Gabe stirred. Something wasn't quite right, but the fog of his consciousness wouldn't let him process anything. He murmured, but then wondered if he'd actually murmured out loud or just thought he'd done it. Maybe that was what had woken him up, like a loud snore. And then he definitely did murmur, a low moan. He couldn't help himself, something made him groan out loud. Quickly, he did a systems check on his body, to see if he could work out the cause in the darkness. By the time he reached his waist, and his wits were more about him, he realised what was happening. Another wave of pleasure hit him as the stroking fingers slid along his manhood, which was itself beginning to wake up.

'You're not very sleepy,' he muttered as she began to caress him with more purpose, more directly, knowing exactly how to get a rise out of him, and doing just that. He arched his back as she held him firmly, both he and his little friend now fully awake. *And less of the little.* He couldn't remember the last time they'd been intimate. He'd been desperate to, oddly not because of the sex *per se*, but so they could reconnect, to become husband and wife again, to start to come together – no pun intended – again. He'd longed for her – felt lonely in their bed, sleeping side by side, sometimes never feeling more distant and yet just inches away.

Then she was swinging herself up on top of him, her nightshirt not impeding her as she straddled his hips, reaching down to slide him inside her, causing him to make another moan, louder this time, and joined by her somewhere above.

Nightshirt?

Settling down onto him, she put her hands flat on his chest, leaning forward on them for leverage. Her hips started to rock back and forth, pushing down onto his pelvis as he rose to meet her. His hands sliding down her body, to hold the curve of her bottom through the slight roughness of the lace.

Lace?

Their rhythm increased, her driving them forward, becoming frenzied in her very obvious desire. All he could do was keep up, holding onto her hips, and wonder how she was wearing lace when Tor slept in a nightshirt. Or nothing. Gabe opened his eyes, and through the watery moonlight seeping in around the curtains he realised that it wasn't Tor sat astride him, riding him for all she was worth, but the girl in the white dress. The witch, Morvith, here, on top of him in their bed. For a few seconds he continued, his primal urges overriding anything else – his morality, or revulsion. Surprise and shock were now too late as he had reached the point of no return, nothing could stop it and he groaned one last time, crying out.

And she was gone.

She hadn't climbed off him or rolled away, but disappeared in that instant of climax, as if in a puff of smoke. Gabe's whole body had tensed in the moment, every single muscle, it seemed, had contracted and now he subsided back onto the bed, suddenly realising what he had done and turning immediately to look over at Tor, dreading what his wife had seen and heard and felt in all that had just happened in their marital bed. Tor was sleeping soundly, her face relaxed in the moonlight – the little frown lines she sometimes had when she was dreaming were absent and she looked serene, her breathing so slow as to be almost imperceptible. Gabe flopped back onto his pillow, his breathing rate still high but returning to normal, sweat across his brow and chest. She was here. She *was* here. Fucking him. Fucking him, *why*? To make a point? Because she could? Because she wanted to control him? Because she was horny?

The thought of a four-hundred-year-old dead witch with the horn was a very strange one bouncing around his head. But not the strangest. He felt a cold wetness in his shorts and felt ashamed, like having a teenage wet dream but a thousand times worse with this being disturbing and supernatural. Throwing the duvet back, he carefully swung his legs out of the bed so he didn't get the cold, wet patch against his skin – he didn't want to be feeling his stuff on him. Sliding his shorts down so they puddled onto the floor, he gathered them up and dumped them in the linen basket in the corner of the room, quietly sliding a new pair out of the chest of drawers, before limping off to the bathroom to clean up.

CHAPTER 18
– THEN –
CHARMED

Morvith climbed down from the carriage and smoothed the white lace dress down over her hips. The Master greeted her at the door in a familiar tweed suit and she could see his eyes rove over her body.

'How is Morgan?' she asked.

'The same, I am afraid.' He nodded, pursing his lips.

'Oh. I am sorry. Let me see him, please.' She pushed past the master, pausing only to hang her small navy jacket on the coat stand, before heading to the stairs and up to her patient. The small figure did look unchanged from her last visit two days ago. His chest still rose and fell rapidly, skin pale and clammy. Immediately she produced several pouches of herbs from her basket along with a pestle and mortar, and began to grind sprinklings of numerous herbs and roots together. Adding some hot water, she'd made a 'tea' and bent over the boy to support the back of his head and bring the cup to his dried and cracked lips to allow him to drink. He coughed and spluttered at the taste.

'It isn't the nicest, drink. Sorry, Morgan,' she said, lowering his head back to the pillow and wiping his mouth when he'd finished the tea. 'Sleep now,' she said standing up, turning away from the bed and seeing the master leaning against the doorframe. 'We need to see how the medicine works – it will need some time.'

'Nothing to be done then.'

'No. I suggest we retire. Perhaps we should spend some time together.' Her eyes glittered as she looked at him, and, taking his hand, led him to the bedroom, the master meekly following. Stopping by the bed, she turned to face him, and they stood awkwardly, facing each other for a moment, but Morvith closed the gap between them, her hands pressing against the master's chest, feeling his warmth, his heartbeat. She pushed him backwards, the bed preventing him stepping back to save himself, and he sat down firmly onto the mattress, looking up at her standing over him. Taking his hand, she brought it up to her breast and pressed it against her. Needing no further invitation, the master's hand squeezed her and she moaned at his touch. She bent to kiss him, not concerned about appearing forward or wanton in front of him, her lips found his and they crushed together, tongues quickly finding each other.

Straightening up, she pushed his chest again smiling triumphantly as he fell backwards against the bedclothes. Reaching down to grasp handfuls of the lace material, she hitched it up, slowly unveiling her hips to his gaze, then climbed on top of him.

CHAPTER 19

YANNICK

Mist hung low over the lake that morning, like a diaphanous sheet, suspended just above the water. There had been a frost that night, and the frozen dew floated around him like tiny snowflakes. Grasses and dead perennials, petrified in white, stuck up like icy fingers, defiant in one last stand before their inevitable collapse during the depths of winter. Frozen spiders webs laced between the balustrades of the deck. Gabe sipped his coffee and enjoyed seeing his breath plume into its own little clouds to disappear into the sky as he stood on the boards, his toes hanging over the edge of the last one. He'd opened the curtains that morning and seen the lake hidden from view – a cotton wool matting covering the whole surface.

As he walked unevenly down the stairs, the boot clanking on each step, he realised that the cloud was above him – it was floating at the height of the first floor ceiling across the whole lake. *How the hell does that happen.* The chill was palpable when he threw the doors open.

'Hey, bonehead, I'm stood here in a vest top, jammy bottoms, and nothing else,' Tor said, with a frown, as she put coffee bags in mugs, waiting for the kettle to boil.

'Why do you think I opened it,' he grinned mischievously, which faded quickly when a memory of last night popped into his head.

Now, still stood at the edge of the decking – the edge of the world, covered in mist and frost and gossamer, and he himself would be blanketed by frozen dew if he stayed still for long enough – he stared out into the picture framed above and below by the mist and water, and the trees either side.

'Watcha thinking?' Tor said as she walked across, hands wrapped around her mug as if it were the only way of keeping warm. She'd pulled on a blue fleece and was wearing moccasins as she joined him.

'Thinking about writing again,' he replied, still looking across the water.

'But you haven't–'

'I know.' He turned to look at her, a small smile playing on his lips.

'You've found the words again – you always said you can't force it, that they had to find you.' She held his hand, interlacing her fingers with his.

'I think they're there. I'm gonna set the computer up in the spare room. See how we go.'

'Nice. That's really good, babe.' She gave a nod, as if that rubber stamped the whole procedure, and thus, it would be so.

'Well, there's no point in not writing if–'

'Is this sentence going to end in some kind of 'new start' type speech?'

'It might be,' Gabe pretended to whistle innocently.

'I see…' She wore her best disapproving look, that did its best to hide the faintest of smiles.

They stood in silence for a while, each lost in their own thoughts. Gabe wondered what was so strange about the morning, yes it was colder and the thin wisps of cotton wool mist they'd had before were eclipsed by this heavy blanket, but as he stood there the realisation slowly came to him.

Silence.

Not matter how quiet it was out here, it was never silent. There were always some wildfowl messing around in the water, the breeze coming up the valley and off the lake made some kind of sound in the trees, and, off in the forest, some creature or another would move or stir or scatter something else. That's forgetting the bastard squirrels.

Now, there was silence.

Was that something? Did it mean something that there was nothing? Something or nothing. Was he reading too much into everything given what was happening or had he got every reason to question everything at any time?

'It's like we are on a ship – Franklin or someone – up in the arctic, trying to find the Northwest Passage, and all we have to see is water and sky and nothing. That's our world,' he said.

'Yeah. I can see that. But all I've got in my world is a frying pan, some eggs and a load of washing. And my undercarriage is bastard freezing. See you in a bit, Shackleton.' Tor turned and walked back across the decking, Gabe enjoying watching her hips sway – a little more than usual, so all for his benefit, he thought. He smiled and headed in himself, ready to make some proper coffee.

∞ ∞ ∞

'Did you hear that?' Gabe asked, pausing with coffee cup midway to his mouth, the world's deadliest dishwasher open and half unloaded.

'Hear what,' Tor replied as she walked by, a pile of 'darks' in her arms ready to go in the washer.

'It sounded like a cry – weird sounding. I'll go check.' He turned and headed for the doors, half slid open as usual to let some air in.

'Hope it's not a fox,' Tor said over her shoulder as she walked into the hall.

'Cheeky.' Gabe stepped out onto the deck, and saw the creature.

On the beach just below the deck, something walked slowly along. It was so badly hunched over, its head seemed to almost grow out of its chest, long spindly arms thrust deep into the pockets of a dark woollen overcoat, only the wrists visible in the gap at the bottom of the sleeves. A huge mane of thin hair appeared out of the upturned collar of the jacket and flowed out and down like a yellow scarf to the waist. Sticking out from within the depths of the mane, a long, pointed nose, crooked and hooked, pointed downwards and all it lacked were large warts to make the figure a modern-day witch that was passing by. Gabe smiled to himself – another mirage, another illusion from her to frighten them this morning. Then it sneezed again, and wheezed immediately afterwards like a keening cry – the noise Gabe had heard inside – and somehow, this time, he knew it was real.

'Can I help you?' He called to what must be a man, he thought, but in the loosest possible sense. The figure turned his whole body toward the house, the heavy overcoat moving stiffly as one, a face vaguely appearing from within the mane of hair, thin and pale.

'Just walking,' the figure said – yes definitely a man – his higher pitched voice like shale on a beach.

'Oh okay. Are you alright?'

'Yes. Why?'

'It's just the sound you made… your chest?' Gabe was acutely aware he was in his pyjamas and wondered about what Tor had said before about frightening the neighbours.

'Sorry. My asthma is bad and this change in the weather is never good for it.' The figure turned his whole body back in the direction of the shore he had been walking along.

'You look cold. Can I offer you some tea or coffee?' Gabe walked halfway down the steps on the decking, one arm pointing towards the house in open invite, the boot making him look even more ridiculous.

The man stopped shuffling along. After a short pause he turned to look at the house, the upper half of his body seeming to ratchet itself more upright so he could make eye contact. 'Thank you. I wouldn't want to impose…' Where is his accent? Gabe wondered.

'You wouldn't. Please.' Gabe stepped aside to let the man awkwardly climb the steps, holding on to both handrails. 'It's nice to meet people, our neighbours and such – you are local I'm guessing?'

'Yes. Up there.' He turned his body with a flick to indicate behind him, meaning somewhere on the far shore. 'I like to walk the perimeter of the lake from time to time – when my health allows.'

Gabe escorted the strange man in through the sliding doors, which he closed as their guest looked frozen. Tor was just coming back into the kitchen from putting the washing on, and stopped in her tracks, staring at their visitor.

'This is my wife, Tor,' Gabe pointed in her direction. 'And I'm Gabe. Gabe Hooper. Please do have a seat – may I take your coat.'

'Thank you,' the man replied, shrugging the heavy jacket from his thin shoulders and balancing his skin and bone on one of the bar stools by the kitchen counter. The coat now hung on a chair back, the mane no longer bunched around his neck like a scarf, but his dark-blond hair simply hung down, beyond the waist of his trousers. 'I'm Yannick. Yannick Pederesen.'

'Good to meet a neighbour, Yannick.'

'Tea, coffee?' Tor asked, flicking the switch down on the kettle which blinked red as it told the heating element to raise hell.

'Coffee. Black. Thank you.' Sitting in a woollen shirt on the stool, Yannick's upper body was almost completely 'C' shaped, his upper back bent forward at almost ninety-degrees to his slower spine, giving the impression of his head coming out of his chest. 'Please forgive my appearance.' He managed to finish his request before coughing and wheezing again, in his own inimitable style, then reaching into his jacket on the counter in front to get his inhaler. Two good strong pulls clearly did the trick – as far as the wheezing was concerned, anyway. 'I have a couple of medical conditions. The bones in my spine are soft so I started to get hunched working at a desk, then I developed a rheumatological condition which resulted in them fusing. So, I got a hunch and I stayed like that.'

'Your appearance is just fine, Yannick,' Tor said, kindly, setting a mug of steaming black coffee in front of him.

'Well, thank you for saying that. I am a bit of a shock to some, but… that's where we are. Thank you for the coffee.' Yannick reached his long spidery fingers for the cup and wrapped them around the handle, almost too many times, Gabe thought, as if he had twice as many joints in his fingers than anyone else. Raising the tall black mug in both hands, he sipped at the contents – wincing at the temperature. 'Settling in?' he asked, setting the mug back down on the counter and uncurling his fingers.

'Yeah. Yes, we are – aren't we, love?' Gabe looked at Tor for affirmation.

'Yep, just getting everything where it needs to be.' She smiled at Yannick and then pulled a face at Gabe wondering why they were pretending it was eutopia.

'But we've had a few strange goings on since we arrived.' Gabe shrugged with an *as you do* expression.

'Uh huh.' Yannick nodded sagely and sipped his coffee, as if he knew exactly what the strange goings on would be, without any further discussion.

'What do you know about the witch?' Gabe blurted out, and Tor immediately gave him *the look before rolling her eyes.*

What? He mimed back.

'Been talking to Idris Dawson, have you?' Yannick smiled down his long thin nose and nodded as he raised his mug again.

'We met him on our first night,' Tor replied.

'Oh, he would've loved that.'

'You two don't get along?' Gabe asked.

'I just think he talks too much – probably the Strongbow. Shouldn't be telling people about *her* before their engine is even cold.'

'Why not?' Tor sat at the breakfast bar opposite their guest, becoming more interested in the direction of the conversation.

'Well, it's just odd isn't it. Welcome to the village, oh, by the way… She's not exactly major news if you don't live on the lake. I know you do, but he tells everyone. It's like she's his trophy wife.'

'Hardly like his wife.'

'Oh, you might be surprised,' Yannick answered cryptically, and Tor and Gabe exchanged a glance.

'You're not from around here, obviously,' Tor said, lifting the silence left by Yannick's strange comment.

'No. Retired down here. Well, semi-retired.'

'Why here?'

'Gabe.' Tor admonished him for being nosy.

'No, carry on. It's nice to have people to tell your tales to. I've done a lot of work around here over the years, and, well, look at it – you can't get more spectacular surroundings.' Yannick pursed his lips then shrugged.

'What kind of work?'

'Environmental analysis. Monitoring, really. Not as much of a call for that any more. All automated.'

'I suppose that's a blessing with your illness..?'

'Yes, the day to day of sitting in front of an old keyboard in damp bunkers monitoring screens of water flow does take its toll, and here I am.' He smiled, wistfully.

'You said that you were semi-retired?' Gabe asked – throwing a glance at Tor who threw one to the ceiling in a *what are you like* kind of way.

'Yes, I still keep my hand in a little. Keeps the old grey matter whirring.' His soft Swedish accent rolled the 'r's to add another syllable. 'Just a little consultancy. It's fine having automated stuff, but someone needs to check it's still working!'

'But don't companies have their own guys for that?' Gabe shrugged.

'Yes, but out here, with only a small resource – and her. Nobody wants to come out. Makes sense to them to sub-contract it out to me. And I'm not complaining.' He nodded and smiled.

'Her. Does it always come back to that?' Gabe had genuine concern in his eyes.

'You can't ignore her, and she has a certain reputation. People hear things and whilst they might not know the story much at all, it's enough to put them off.' His smile broadened. 'Anyway. I've taken enough of your time. Thank you for the coffee, Tor. And do swing by my place on the far side of the lake if you have the chance. I like having visitors, even though my road doesn't.' He stood and retrieved his jacket, buttoning it up to the chest, the mane bunching up once more.

'Yes, we will. It was nice to meet you, Yannick.' Gabe stood at the same time as their guest and resisted the temptation to take his arm as he was leaving. Yannick shuffled along and took the steps down to the beach quite awkwardly, teetering as he reached the shingle slope, before turning to make his way back in the direction from which he had come, slowly disappearing up the shoreline.

CHAPTER 20
-\/-
BATH

'I'm going to take a bath,' Tor called from the bathroom, throwing the bath mat onto the floor.

'Ooh, now there's a risk – can I watch?' Gabe replied, walking out of the bedroom in his lounge trousers and t-shirt.

'What does *that* mean?' Tor said, her voice edged in sarcasm as she started to run the hot water.

'Well,' said Gabe, leaning against the bathroom doorframe, 'it means that pipes–'

'Can we stop going on about the fucking pipes?' Tor threw her arms in the air in mock indignation, but Gabe, smiling, continued his mansplaining.

'Pipes that haven't been used for a thousand years–'

'Or whatever.'

'Or whatever,' he nodded. 'Aren't, necessarily, going to produce the most crystal-clear water.'

'Hence you are here for the floorshow.' She smiled sweetly at him.

'Hence I am here,' he said, hefting an adjustable wrench, 'to be as much assistance as possible with any problems you have with your plumbing, my lovely lady wife.'

'How kind. And you've brought your big tool.' She smiled, turning the hot water onto full. 'Husband.'

They both looked at the water pouring out of the old-style mixer tap mounted on the wall and churning around the tub before finally disappearing down the plughole in a turbulent vortex.

'Looks pretty clear to me,' he said.

'Not quite so smug now,' she said, stripping off her jeans.

'Just keep an eye on the temperature – don't know how good the hot water store is. And even though it looks clear, by the time it fills up it might be a bit discoloured, but don't worry about it.'

'Okay – thanks.' Gabe turned and left, heading down the stairs. At the bottom he opened the cellar door and pulled the light cord, as usual, every step creaking and groaning like an old man getting out of a chair, combined with the plasticky noise of the boot landing on each step. Cobwebs hung from the rafters above and festooned the walls – he'd thought that the workshop was the domain of the spider, but perhaps that's where they went on holiday – although quite what they fed on down here was anyone's guess. The boiler was roaring away on the far wall, filling Tor's bath. He checked the pressure gauges and they all looked fine. Things were promising for her to have a nice long soak.

Back upstairs, the steamy bathroom was empty and he could hear Tor moving around in their bedroom along the hall. Deciding to have one last check on the water temperature, Gabe went into the bathroom and froze. Steam rose up from the taps, initially a good sign, the scalding liquid emerging from the faucet, water evaporating, billowing into its own cloud system below the ceiling, dropping down to make the glass of the corner shower cubicle opaque, and drifting across the room to the far side, coating the mirror as the steam cooled, sank and disappeared. It was like a geography project on the formation of weather systems. The cloud did little to obscure Gabe's view of the bath, however, which was why he was so startled. The water, now up to about three-quarters full, was deep red. Not red-coloured water, not rusty water, not see-through as if she'd used a bath-bomb, but opaque – like wine.

Or blood.

The water was more viscous than it should have been, sticking to the porcelain, sliding down like people trying to climb a slippery wall, clinging to the surface until Sir Isaac Newton intervened. Gabe stared at the ripples and waves on the crimson surface, wondering if this was the extent of the weirdness or if something else might happen. As if in response, as he watched, something began to happen on the surface, a dome slowly forming in the middle of the water – or whatever it was – rising upwards like a red sheet draped over a child's head at Halloween, the blood running off and splashing back down into the bath, splattering the walls. *It was definitely blood, it couldn't be anything else.* And it was definitely a head that was rising out of it as the liquid dripped away from two eyes, blinking in the light and staring right at him with anger and malevolence. Dark hair was matted to her head as she rose, shoulders and breasts lifting out of the water, face twisted into a sneer. Blood ran from her face and head, running over her shoulders in a hundred tiny rivulets, down her arms and to the tips of her small breasts, dripping off her nipples.

'Gabe?' Tor called from the bedroom.

'Two minutes,' he answered in the direction of the door, hoping he didn't sound as shaken as he felt, struggling to stop himself screaming aloud and running from the room. Turning back to the bath, the water was clear and steam slowly rose up from the surface, filling the room like a sauna. The noise of water pouring in once again dominated the room. Looking back to the door then to the bath again, seeing nothing of the apparition or hallucination of before, he made a decision. He shut off the tap and reached in to grab the chain, pulling the plug, allowing the water to start to gurgle and spin out down the plughole.

Tor looked up as he walked into their room, dressed snugly in a white bathrobe, her hair held up in a clip. 'What?' she asked as he stood there looking at her.

'Bad news about the bath, babe, it had run cold.' He shrugged apologetically.

'Cold? But it was boiling a couple of minutes ago. It is a combi, right?'

'Yeah. Don't know if it's a pressure thing or something.'

'I thought the pressure only mattered for the central heating?' She said, exasperated, sitting down in front of the mirror and crossing her legs, angrily pulling the hair clip out.

'Yes, but if the mains pressure coming in is too much for the burner, it won't heat the water quickly enough.' *Damn his wife knew too much about the mechanics of a house to get fobbed off with a lame story of 'pressure.'*

'So, what does that mean?'

'I'll test it again tomorrow. Maybe it just needs to get used again, or maybe it needs a new burner and a service – there's bound to be a plumber round here that'll do that.'

'Okay. Bugger. Was looking forward to that.'

'Shower instead?' At least the shower cubicle should be harmless enough.

'Not really the same though is it?'

'Yeah, sorry. Glass of wine to cheer you up?'

'Why not.'

∞ ∞ ∞

Gabe poured the wine and they shared a couple of glasses catching up with shows on Netflix. He half wondered why they watched some of the stuff they did – some very formulaic, predictable stuff, but then, you knew where you were with them. It was comforting, even if not innovative. Starting to fall asleep on the sofa, Tor gave Gabe a nudge and suggested they go to bed. In a familiar routine they tidied the cushions and returned remotes to their usual baskets – until tomorrow – then filled glasses with water when they had got the cold tap running very cold. Upstairs, Gabe sat on the side of the bed, satisfyingly tearing back the Velcro straps of the outer shell of the walking boot, folding them back on themselves, tidily, ready for the morning, before slowly easing the outer shell off. The relief was immense, the pressure removed and his foot felt lighter than air. He unwrapped the neoprene 'sock' and tucked it in the boot, thinking that in only a few days that sock was going to get pretty funky. Now that dressing his lower half was much easier without the bulky footwear, he idly changed into shorts and a t-shirt before carefully walking back down the hallway to the bathroom to clean his teeth, foot turned out to one side so he wasn't rocking backwards and forwards on it. His leg felt lighter – naked in a way – having got used to the restrictive, cumbersome device. Rinsing his face in the sink, he prodded and pushed at his skin – he was in good nick really – although recent bags under his eyes made him look like the lovechild of Barry Norman. Massaging moisturising cream into his face, he spent time on his cheeks, desperate to avoid the jowls that his dad had developed, willing the smooth muscles to maintain their tone. *Better cut down on the drink as well then, darling, eh?* His wife had admonished him when he'd spoken of his cosmetic fears a few months back. Skin saved for another evening, the dentist placated and bladder voided, as if he himself were Niagara Falls, Gabe finished his evening ablutions and limped back down the hallway to the bedroom – the ankle not painful at all, but he still wanted to make sure he was careful – to not make things worse. Tor had already slipped on an old *Flintstones* hoody over her pyjamas, and her and Fred were off to carry out their own nightly rituals. Gabe tossed back the duvet and swung his legs onto the cool crisp sheets – one of his favourite things before covering his legs – waiting for the weight of the duvet to cause pain in the ankle, but nothing came. He shuffled up the bed and arranged his pillows just right – one flat, one upright, before reaching to take Stephen King off the nightstand. He'd just opened the book – wondering how many pages he'd get to read before his head started nodding or he'd wake himself up with a snore that would get Tor telling him to turn his light off – when Tor screamed. A scream to create nightmares and chill the blood, it cut through him, piercing his heart, which was suddenly now gripped by fear. Bolting out of bed, he put his injured foot down quickly with a wince, but this just served to make him more alert, and, injury be-damned, he was by her side in the bathroom within seconds. Tor was sobbing and frozen in place, arms crossed across her chest, almost facing him – eyes transfixed on the medicine cabinet above the sink on the right of the door. Gabe stepped in behind her and placed his hand on her shoulder, making her jump and scream again.

'Hey, it's okay,' he said, a comforting tone to his voice, his lips pressing gently against her hair, inhaling the mango smell of her conditioner.

'Is it?' she turned to him – anger in her voice, her face red. 'Is it really? I wonder if it can be.' She pushed past him, shoving him backwards, storming off to the bedroom. Perplexed, and turned around by her shove, Gabe scanned the rest of the bathroom, to see what had upset her. His eyes fell on the bath – the first culprit after earlier – but it was clean and almost dry with just a trickle of water dribbling down the plughole, and not a trace of red anywhere to be seen. There was nothing in the corners of the room either. He turned from wiping his hand along the side of the bath, looking at the sink, then letting his eyes travel up, seeing the glass of the cabinet for the first time, and realised now why Tor had screamed. Across the glass, written, or more accurately, *scrawled,* in what looked like lipstick, or could conceivably have been blood was one word:

DIE

'Is this supposed to be funny?' she asked, standing in the doorway again, her eyes full of tears and anger, shoulders shaking in her white vest.

'What, you think I did this?' he replied, annoyed himself that this was even a question.

'Well, who else could've?' she pointed in the direction of the cabinet for emphasis.

'I'm not sure, love, maybe the person who's just been spending time in the bathroom,' he snapped.

'And so now I did this?' she asked, holding her hands to her chest, inadvertently looking all femme fatale.

'Well, I wasn't in here and you were.' Gabe pointed at the glass. 'Who else?'

'Jesus, I can't believe you think I'm faking this. You were just in here – I heard you pissing like a horse.'

'I'm not saying you are, but I can't believe you are suggesting that I've done it.' Gabe turned on his heel and went back to the bedroom, angry and his heart pounding, up for a second round of the fight, but realising how sore his ankle had become walking back and forth without looking after it. If she was gonna accuse him like that she could have it back with both barrels. He held Stephen King in his hands once again and re-read the same sentence half a dozen times as he thought of his altercation with Tor, waiting for her to come to bed. Despite his distraction, he made a real play of being engrossed in the novel as Tor walked into the bedroom, eyeballing her over the top of the tome, noticing how she didn't look in his direction. She switched off the main light and went round to climb into her side of the bed, throwing her hoody on a chair. The duvet rustled as she flicked it back and slid in, keeping her back to him as she pulled the covers over her, and reached up to switch off her lamp, snuggling in under the down.

His heart was still beating fast from their argument and in readiness to continue where they left off in bed. But she'd shut it down and now he was laying there with no release – like she'd stopped sex halfway through and rolled over to go to sleep. But he didn't know any argument-porn websites he could look up to satisfy his craving for one. His mind bounced from one subject to the next – the *Monty Python* sketch where someone wants an argument and all they get is contradiction, the scene in his book, where the plot had been left on a knife-edge at the end of a chapter, switching to a totally different set of characters with none of the peril he'd just been reading – something he found infuriating about King, but knew it would build to something similarly compelling before switching back in the next chapter.

He contemplated his choices. Continuing the argument wasn't one of them – even when post-row angry, Gabe reconciled that sniping at each other some more was not going to help at all. Or he could just leave things as they are – go to sleep on a row, accept the frostiness of the morning, and hope that she was more amenable to a measured discussion about what really happened. But, perhaps the best option was that he should just put the book down, turn the light off and cuddle into her – spooning together from behind. She'd go tense for a moment and resist, then would allow him to wrap his arms around her but saying nothing. He'd hold her close, nuzzle her neck and shoulder, and then, after a few minutes he'd–

FUCK HER.

What? Where the hell did that idea come from? He wasn't thinking that at all. He was planning that after spooning nicely and both calming down, he would just–

Shove her on her front and fuck her hard from behind!

Jesus. What is going on in your head? In his mind he was going to tell her that he loved her, that he wouldn't do something stupid like that in the bathroom, that it must be the witch, she was getting into their heads, driving a wedge between them. He thought of all those things, banishing the other thoughts from his mind, shoving them into a corner – putting them into a box and closing the lid, and enjoying the thought of holding his wi–

The bathroom door slammed. Not the sound of someone pulling the door closed with a bit too much force or the breeze from an open window blowing it shut, but a frame-shaking slam that reverberated along the hallway, bursting through the bedroom door as if to say *surprise!*

They both jerked upright in bed, Tor reached for the bedside light and flicked it on, looking at Gabe, their argument forgotten, but the adrenaline pumping no less fiercely round their veins. He looked at the doorway, then back at his wife, before getting out of bed.

'Gabe,' she hissed in a stage whisper. He glanced back at her and she shook her head, her eyes wide – *don't go out there.* He gave a little nod and held the palm of his hand toward her, to say it would be okay. She shook her head again, but he turned and tried to tiptoe into the hallway, but his ankle wouldn't tolerate it and he simply limped toward the bathroom. Jumping out of bed, more because she didn't want him to leave her alone than to support him, Tor grabbed the nearest thing she could find to use as a weapon and raced to join him in the dark hallway, as he approached the now closed bathroom door.

'What are you gonna do?' she whispered, her hand on his shoulder.

'Go in,' he said as he reached out to the old brass doorknob.

'Gabe!' she whispered again, quite why she didn't know, as if something with the power to slam doors or write ghostly letters on a mirror might not have the greatest hearing.

The knob rattled, a screw was missing from the mounting plate on the door itself so the handle slid back and forth when turned. Tor's eyes widened at the noise, her expression telling him in no uncertain terms that he was making a racket. Looking back at her, he noticed for the first time that she was carrying a shoe. He shrugged and pushed the door open.

The bathroom was empty and as it should be. Nothing was out of place. He didn't know what he expected – maybe a person or presence in the room, maybe for it to be wrecked with the sink ripped off the wall and water spewing out of the pipes, and Gremlins running around everywhere. But it was calm and serene. Relaxing, and exhaling slowly, Gabe turned to sit on the edge of the bath as Tor followed him in.

'Nothing,' he said, unnecessarily.

'Did we really hear that? That was some door slam. We couldn't both imagine it.'

'Look,' she said pointing at the medicine cabinet. The writing had gone – like a supernatural clean-up crew had come in and cleaned the mirror of any sign of what had been written there. Less *Mr White*, but *Mr White* dress. And that really did make them question what they had seen and how real it had been. After one final look around, they left the room, being careful to pull the door tightly this time, and retired to bed.

CHAPTER 21
-\/-
BUNKER

The morning routine had been a tense affair. After seemingly calling a truce on accusations of who wrote the words on the mirror, they seemed to largely avoid each other. One making another coffee while the other showered. Followed by separate breakfasts. Gabe started to work on unpacking some more boxes upstairs, and finally Tor went to speak to him. She walked into the spare room to find Gabe sat cross-legged on the floor, the boot awkwardly pushing against his leg, staring wistfully at a picture of the three of them.

'Remember that? he said, cradling the picture frame.

'Yeah, course,' she softened, sitting on the side of the bed just behind him, and ruffled his hair. 'It was a great day at the seaside.'

'It was bloody freezing.'

'Yep, so windy. We had down jackets on and it was May or something.'

'Wasn't it his birthday?'

'No, but he'd got new wellies for his birthday, I think, and that's them in the picture.'

'Didn't we go to that little café on the corner afterwards?'

'Yes, had chips. Don't you remember we ordered cones of chips and coffees to go and they took so long bringing the coffees we'd finished and were ready to leave. We were a bit unimpressed and the waitress woman kicked off and had a right go, as if it was our fault they were a bit crap.'

'That's right, she was a right case she was.'

'I wouldn't argue with her.'

'You bloody didn't, it was muggins, here.' Gabe jabbed at his chest.

'That'll learn ya.' She smiled.

'It's amazing how those clips of your memory fade.'

'Getting older love.'

'Yeah,' he smiled sadly. 'I want there to be something after… this. A place where we go. An afterlife.'

'Just so we can see him again.' She nodded.

'Yeah. Even just once more if I was passing through.'

'Going up or down?'

He snorted, a tear staining his cheek. 'Jury's still out on that one.' He turned to face her. 'But don't you see, if this, *thing*, is real then it proves that something beyond us exists.' His eyes searched hers, as if Tor agreed with him, it would make it so.

'If what is happening to us and our house is being done or caused by an evil spirit, it proves the existence of an afterlife? Is that what you're saying?' She looked at him, eyebrows raised. 'And if it does, then our little boy might be caught up amongst it all?'

'That's not what I'm saying.'

'I hope not, because my normal, highly rational husband has just explained that our new definition of normal is talking rationally about evil spirits or whatever the hell we seem to be saying this thing is?' Tor snapped.

∞ ∞ ∞

Gabe thought it best to get out of the house for a while, to give the two of them some space. He'd not really explored the perimeter of the lake by road and decided to go for a drive. The road was becoming more familiar on this side now – the twists and turns, dips and humps were almost like old friends. Gabe went past the turning for the pub, and then the turning up the lane to Idris' cottage. He was almost at the top corner of the lake, just before the road turned right over the bridge and then into the village, when, through the trees, he saw a car parked in a small clearing. Idris' car. Nosiness, rather than a great desire to speak to Idris, got the better of him and he braked firmly, looking for a turning, almost missing the track which was little more than a gap between the trees, bordered with bracken and lined with pine straw like the rest of the forest floor in this corner. As he slowly negotiated his way down the slope, the lake opened out before him as he approached the edge of the trees. Idris, having heard the car engine, stood watching him approach.

Gabe pulled up alongside the old man and killed the engine, which revved once in protest before dying. Immediately it felt silent, but this was permeated by the trickling sound of water by the shore. He pushed his door open and got out, leaning against the side of the car. 'I saw your car, and thought I'd say hello.'

Idris pursed his lips, nodding. 'Hmmm. I come down here quite a bit,' he said nodding out at the water.

'It's a lovely spot.'

'Aye. Used to walk down, but bloody old legs won't do that anymore. Knees are knackered.' He shrugged.

'At least you can get down in the car.'

'Would be proper fucked without that, and no mistake.' The old man turned and looked out across the water, the breeze in his face, causing him to narrow his eyes to little more than slits, his crow's feet growing to size tens. He stood like that for a while, Gabe watching both him and the water, wondering if Idris had dismissed his presence and he should go. 'They had the army here, you know?' He said finally, as if he'd been weighing up in his mind whether to divulge that particular nugget.

'Oh?' Gabe raised an eyebrow.

'In the early seventies, I reckon. A fella bought Ty Llyn. Ambitious he was. Was gonna make it into a resort or something – build cabins in the hills around the place – fishing and all that. Then Morvith made herself known.'

'And that was the end of that.'

'Oh yessir. But he was an old army type and he must've spoke to someone about what went on, the next minute there's uniform crawling all over.'

'To do what?'

'In all honesty, I don't know. They were asking a lot of questions – did a big search all around the lake, up on the other side, into the next valley.'

'Looking for her.'

'Right. But they didn't find anything. Kicked around the leaves a bit and pushed over a few trees.'

'What do you think the old army guy said to them?'

'Well, I don't think it was, 'hey boys come down here and see if you can find a witch, will you?' I don't know, in truth, but something got them interested.'

'But then they left? After making a lot of noise?'

'Aye, they left alright. But then the scientists arrived. Had some sort of lab and a 'containment' thing.'

'A what?'

'A cage or something to hold her in if they caught her.'

'Bloody hell – so many questions. Aside from *Ghostbusters*, I've never heard of a branch of science looking into ghosts and witches and spooks.'

'I don't know who they are. Anyway, they were looking into energy or something. Never really talked to them and it was a long time ago.'

'Did they stay around for long.' Gabe was warming to the subject now, the writer in him making mental notes, fascinated that this had happened in his back yard.

'Seemed to be a few weeks, but then they kept coming back every so often for a while – like every few months. It was as if they were checking on things.'

'How do you know?'

'Saw 'em. Saw 'em in town. Helen at the B&B had them staying there… word gets around.'

Yeah, I just bet it does in a place like this. They probably hadn't even unpacked before everyone knew. 'But how do you know what they were up to?'

'Like I say, I saw 'em. They were down here – parked where we are – easy to find, and where they were in their little lab thing.' He shrugged and curled his mouth through his stubble.

'They had a lab?'

'They had a hut – like a shed – a zinc thing they plonked here and their clear cage that they were going to put her in if they caught her. But they never did.'

'What was in the lab?'

'I dunno. Instruments, computers, telephones – who knows.'

Unlikely to be computers in the seventies they would fill a whole room.

'I haven't seen anything like that.'

'No, it's gone. I think it kept getting blown around by the wind, so they moved into there.' Idris raised his arm to point in the direction of the sound of running water. Following his arm Gabe could see a squat concrete structure, set into the bank, half covered in pine needles, brambles and rotten trees. The concrete had weathered and was covered in moss and lichens. It was about fifteen feet wide and the term 'bunker' could've been invented purely for it.

'You know, even though I'm standing right next to it, I wouldn't have noticed the thing if you hadn't pointed it out. Did they build it?'

'No,' Idris snorted. 'It's a pumping station. Regulates the level of water in the lake. This bank is higher than the village, so, they need to keep an eye on the flow through it, into the stream that goes through the village. I spose it was convenient for them to use rather than their rickety tin shed.'

'How long did they spend doing experiments or whatever they were doing?'

'Well,' said Idris, interlocking his fingers across his chest and giving a thin-lipped smile. 'That, I don't remember. A year, maybe more, but not coming back very often towards the end.'

'And that was it? Gone and never to be seen again?'

'Er, yes.' Idris looked a little unsure, as if he didn't remember – or didn't want to. Gabe frowned at the reaction.

'I don't get it,' Gabe responded.

'You English always struggle to get things.' If Idris was younger, he would probably say LOL after that comment. But in this universe, he wouldn't know what that meant.

'You are probably right. But humour me.' Gabe wandered up to the side of the bunker, and noted a set of stone steps at the side, going down into the gloom and a side door – probably metal, by the looks of it, with grey paint peeling away. Soil and brambles had invaded, so it would be a struggle to get in there now.

'Alright. What don't you get?'

'You say the scientists came after the army left. So someone, somewhere, wanted something investigated. They wanted it enough to set up some sort of mobile lab, and send something to catch her in if they managed it. No matter how implausible, all that thought process, the kit, the cage, someone believing in the witch enough to want to study her, to then just disappear empty handed. I don't get it.'

'Maybe they thought there wasn't any merit in it. In her. Maybe they thought that there was no way of catching her – it wouldn't be just a matter of putting some cheese in the cage, would it?'

'No, it wouldn't, but equally, they couldn't have just thought they would rock up, capture her and drive off with her on a horse and cart, paraded through the village. Particularly if they weren't there very much. I just don't think they gave it very much time.'

'Maybe they ran out of money.' Idris said. 'It all boils down to money, one way or another.'

'That's true – makes more sense. Money and motivation to try and secure more money.'

∞ ∞ ∞

That evening, Gabe found himself standing in the upstairs hallway in front of the painting, a glass of whisky in hand. He sipped and admired the work – he was no art critic or anything but this was exquisite. The brush or knife strokes creating texture and movement. The image of the lake, the moonlight shining down from above illuminating the ripples on the water. He studied every corner of the image, the trees around the banks, the hill on the far side, heavily wooded and leading to the cottages in the valley below and the plumes of smoke from their coal fires being taken by the breeze. The picture was so striking, so real that he could almost feel the breeze off the water causing the ripples, the breath of it against his face, ruffling his hair. The movement of the water made the moonlight shimmer on the ripples. And then he realised that it didn't give the impression of shimmering, no brilliance of artist or brush, but there was actually movement on the water. The picture was moving. He held his hand up in front of the frame and he could feel the breeze, cool against his palm. It was no longer a picture but a window, hung on an internal wall facing in the wrong direction for the lake, but a window all the same.

He became aware of a sound, growing from nothing, slowly rising in volume and intensity. It was the sound of a cry, a high-pitched shriek – a scream from across the water, travelling from the far side of the lake. Yet it was also like it was coming from back in time – an ancient scream getting louder now it was free, freed from its confinement in the shed covered in sheets, dust and dead spiders. It was moving now, gaining altitude so it was above the lake, and flying closer and closer and closer, the shrill volume increasing as it approached until it hurt his ears, the image distorting, the lake fading and being replaced by an ancient woman, flesh made grey and blue in the moonlight, whose black sunken eyes were holes into an abyss, whose every wrinkle was evil and whose gaze followed him as he moved. Slowly she opened her mouth, her jaw dropping like she'd had a stroke, and her whole head tilted back like the flip-top of a pedal bin, revealing a twisted chasm, a maw of ragged grey tissue pulsating in the breeze, dominating the frame of the picture, and the shriek became something else. It became a roar – the noise of a huge waterfall or the combined cry of a pride of lions – it struck him in the chest and blew him backwards. The blast increased and pinned him to the opposite wall, it felt to Gabe as if he were standing immediately behind a jet engine at full throttle, being knocked off his feet. Suddenly, hundreds of hands shot out from the gaping mouth, tentacles from the depths, reaching out from the picture itself, across the hallway to grab his shoulders and arms and abdomen, holding him in place, and then gradually, slowly, pulling him forwards, drawing him in. Feeling the pressure of each of the tiny fingers digging into his flesh, he was dragged toward the gaping chasm. It was no longer a picture, but the frame was a hole opening out into the domain of the witch, her body horrendously twisted and exposed, and despite leaning backwards and pushing hard with his legs he was inching inexorably closer. Leverage from the floor wasn't enough, so he lifted one foot up onto the wall, then quickly brought up the other one so he was straddling the picture frame, bracing to prevent being pulled in, the height of the boot making it difficult to balance and use equal resistance through each leg. He was parallel to the floor being pulled into a picture by a ghost. The arms were bending him double, like a weightlifter collapsing under the weight of the bar, pulling with no mercy, but slowly, incrementally, he fought back. Bit by bit he managed to straighten his knees, the burning pain in his thighs keeping him focused no matter how insane this was. Finally, his knees locked, giving him the leverage to start to extend his hips and low back, ratcheting himself from being in a ninety-degree bent position to being gradually straighter and straighter. More and more tentacle arms shot out from the monstrous mouth and wrapped themselves around the back of his neck, unwilling to relinquish their prize, but he'd gained momentum, and despite the mounting pressure around his spine, he straightened. And then, he was locked out like an arrow, his legs quivering with effort, his body completely horizontal, so he could feel the opposite wall brushing against his head.

'Gabe?' He heard Tor calling his name from what sounded like a long distance away. 'Gabe!' She was shouting now, more insistent, and there was a noise, which might have been feet on the stairs. The thousands of arms holding him disappeared back into the mouth in front of him which closed, and the face of the witch gave a last sneer before the spell was broken and he was in mid-air, three feet off the ground. He landed hard amidst the broken crystal of his whisky glass, groaning as he rolled from his back to his side. Tor reached the top of the stairs and ran toward him. 'Gabe, what the hell is going on? I heard a racket – did you fall?'

'Yeah, I must've tripped or something.' He sat up, rubbing his head. 'I'm getting good at that.'

'But there were some weird noises, it didn't sound like just that.' Concern was etched on her face.

No, it was the picture, it came alive, like a window into the lake, and then there was this monstrous hag that tried to pull me into it. Simple really.

'Yeah, I stumbled against that bloody picture, got the boot caught on the carpet, almost knocked it off the wall and juggled that and my glass, and then ended up on the floor.'

'Are you okay? Should you be moving?'

'Yeah, I'm fine, just a bit bruised. That picture's going though.'

'There's nothing like blaming an inanimate object.'

'Very rational, I know.'

'You go downstairs and chill out, I'll get the hoover and dustpan and sort out your mess.'

Not being in a fit state to argue, Gabe went downstairs. He filled another glass with scotch and threw half of it to the back of his throat to calm his nerves. Sipping at the remainder, he looked up through the patio doors and out across the lake, finding himself being drawn toward the picture image like the one he'd just been looking at. He stared across the water, watching the ripples glowing in the moonlight as they were pushed along by the breeze, sipping his drink as if hypnotised. *It was the same view as in the picture, but from upstairs in their bedroom.* Then he saw a figure down by the shore, a woman or rather a girl, in a white dress looking back up at the house, the skirts of the dress rippling in the breeze, and the hem trailing in the water. Hearing a noise behind him he looked back up the stairs – Tor had probably dropped the hose of the hoover – before turning back to the window. She was right by the glass, less than a foot away, making him jump, staring in at him, her young features angular and blemishless, but with cold, black eyes. For the second time in half an hour, Gabe found himself about to drop his glass – and this one would've been harder to explain away.

Tor came down the stairs, causing him to turn away and break the spell. 'Bloody glass took forever to get out the pile in that carpet – don't go barefoot upstairs until I get chance to go over it again tomorrow.'

'Okay. Thanks.'

'You obviously got interrupted, making the drinks,' she nodded at his glass.

'Can't rush these things, was just planning yours and on the way over to make it. Cucumber or lime, Hendricks or Whitley Neill?' Gabe walked across the kitchen and opened the drinks cupboard.

'What do you think? And forget all that salad shit.'

'Hendricks it is then.' He poured the gin over ice in a large glass, added slices of dried blood orange before topping it up with Fever Tree tonic. For someone who hated gin, Tor always said he made the best G & T she'd ever had. They chinked glasses.

'Think we'll be happy here,' Tor asked as she looked out across the lake. Standing next to her, Gabe thought about all he'd seen tonight, wondering how to process such a thing. It was like Idris had said; she was there, she was showing herself. But surely they could co-exist, to find a way to get along together.

'Well, I think it'll be eventful.'

CHAPTER 22
-\/-
MIKEY

Breezing into the room with a wide smile, the tall surgeon nodded to Tor and Gabe sat on either side of Mikey's bed. Dave Singleton was big and thickset, like a second row, and dressed characteristically in Metallica t-shirt and plain trousers. Combat shorts weren't too unusual in the summer.

'How you doing, champ?' He asked Mikey, fist-bumping him. Mikey's face lit up with a smile, dry lips curling up toward the canulae delivering oxygen to him through his nose.

'Good, fanks, Doc!' he said, his voice slightly hoarse and quiet.

'Oh yeah? Good to hear. Not quite sure why the heck you are in hospital then.' He smiled down at the boy, dressed in a red t-shirt with an 'FF' across the middle.

'Because I have cancer, silly.' The boy giggled and Tor thought her heart might break. Mikey's shock of black hair, that looked like it had been dumped on his head over a series of months by nesting birds was long gone, his pale skin slack, and face hollow. He was a small five-year-old at the best of times, but looked even smaller in this hospital bed.

'Oh yeah. Course. What sort of a doctor am I?'

'Not a very good one.' Mikey giggled again.

'Mikey,' Tor said, trying to sound like she was admonishing him, but failed, particularly when Singleton laughed.

'You're not a bad judge, my friend,' he said. 'They treating you okay in here?' Singleton was stood over the bed now, but such was his rapport with his patients that they felt comforted rather than intimidated.

'Yes.'

'Okay.' He nodded. 'Getting enough to eat?'

Mikey nodded. 'Mhm.'

'And is the food okay?'

'No. It's horrible.' Mikey shrugged. 'But the nurses sneak me some pizza when they order it.' Mikey looked between his parents who were already exchanging a glance. 'I don't think I'm sposed to tell anyone though.'

'Secret's safe with me, buddy. Hey, catch you later, okay?' Singleton raised his hand at Mikey like a gun, index finger pointing, thumb raised. Mikey quickly raised his, and before Singleton could move, the boy's hand jerked and recoiled like he'd got off the first round. Mikey brought his finger to his mouth and blew the gun-smoke away.

'You got me, again, kid.'

'Twelve-three.'

'Is it? *Really?* Trust you to be counting. I need to practice.'

'Yep. You *are* rubbish.' The boy was beaming, but was already looking tired, as if the effort of this short interaction was too much for him.

'Mikey, I need to borrow Mum and Dad for a minute, okay?'

'Okay, doc. Bye.'

Singleton looked at Mikey's parents and inclined his head toward the door. Across the corridor was a relative's room, and they sat in the comfortable chairs arranged around a low table.

'Mikey really loves you, you know. Thank you for his t-shirt, by-the-way,' Tor said when they were sat.

'The kid's got impeccable taste in rock music, it's the least I could do to teach him some bad habits. Thank you for saying that though, it does mean a lot. We try and be as informal as we can with these kids – they are in a strange place with things happening to them that aren't nice, so they need friendly faces and as much fun as we can muster around them.'

'And pizza,' Gabe said.

'The night shift nurses are rather partial, and Mikey's a superstar.' Singleton smiled thinly, but it faded on his face like a memory, and his expression hardened. 'Which makes this all the harder. There's no easy way to say this, but I've had his scan back and the bloods. The tumour has grown… and it's spread.'

'But the chemo…'

'I know, I know. We threw everything at him – more really than we should at a boy of his age, but I wanted to give him every chance. But… it's got hold of him too well and won't let go.'

Elsewhere in the ward were the sound of footsteps and voices, the clanking of machines and the suction closing of lift doors. There was silence in the room, which grew deafening, the air suddenly hard to breath.

'So, what now?' asked Gabe in a voice that Singleton could barely hear.

'We have a really good palliative care programme. We'll get him home, make him as comfortable as we can, with all the equipment you need. Our community nurses will be on hand and on call.'

'Palliative? You mean that's it? We give up?' Tor's voice increased in volume as she looked at the man who was supposed to save her son.'

'There's nothing–' Singleton's voice cracked and he looked down at his lap to compose himself. Looking back up again, with tears in his eyes, a thin-lipped smile and a nod. 'I'm so sorry.'

∞ ∞ ∞

Mikey's funeral was two months later. As well as his family, everyone in their street and the whole school, it seemed that most of the Paediatric unit turned out that day. Dave Singleton gave a eulogy. He'd written some things about Mikey, some of the little things he'd said and done when they'd been together on the ward, some of the things that had driven him, had made him scared, had made him laugh. Dave had finished with a short poem he'd thought of when Mikey was close to the end and he'd visited him at home.

> If only you lived for just one day
> If only life was just a game to play
> If only there was more to say
> Live, laugh, love, today

If only angels had music to play
If only Lego put itself away
If only there was another day
In our hearts, you will, forever stay

The poem broke the whole church. Where people had been holding onto their grief, it flowed out in a huge wave, swamping every aisle and every pew. It was a collective outpouring for Mikey that swept everyone up and brought them together as one, particularly his family.

Mikey was cremated later that day in a quiet service for family only. They put his ashes in an ornate blue urn that he would've thought funky, and kept him close to them on the mantlepiece, every so often wondering aloud whether they should scatter his ashes somewhere, like the park where he flew his kite or the beach where he could splash around in his wellies for forever. But they could never face it. Then they started talking about moving one day, moving away from all the places where he'd left an indelible mark, wherever you turned and saw him, saw the things he'd done, saw where he'd *lived*. To move because it was too heart-breaking to stay, because it was draining the life out of them, because it was *destroying* them as people and as a couple. And those discussions became more frequent, acquired an urgency, becoming an overwhelming demand, until they found Ty Llyn.

CHAPTER 23

A NEW DRESS

'This is like watching Matilda,' Gabe said as he handed another cardboard pouch to Tor, the familiar swoosh logo on the front.

'Thank you! Been waiting for this!' Tor grabbed the package and dashed up the stairs, bare feet rattling on each one. Gabe returned to the stove, where his Asian broth was at the very gentlest of simmers, and he threw in some finely sliced carrots and ginger, before shredding the chicken breasts he'd steamed earlier. Working through his processes, he steamed rice and boiled noodles, toasted cashew nuts and prepared some other garnishes. He finished setting the table and was pouring prosecco into glasses, the reassuring fizz bubbling up the sides, when he heard Tor starting to come down the stairs, clomping down in her clog sandals.

Looking up, for a second, he thought she was wearing her wedding dress, but then realised it was made of white lace – uncannily similar to the one worn by the girl – the witch – on their walk. Gabe stared open-mouthed as she descended the stairs to the kitchen, but Tor was beaming, twirling around for his benefit when she reached the bottom and walked towards him.

'What do you think?' she asked playfully, unable to quash her smile.

'A white lace dress?' he asked, a surprised smile on his face. 'You look incredible. It really suits you.'

'Thank you, kind sir. Yes, I was really rather taken with it – and isn't it lovely?' She twirled round again for him and he enjoyed seeing the tight material clinging to her curves, accentuating and flattering. He could've watched her twirling all day.

'So, are you trying it on just to show me or are you dressing for dinner?' He waved a wooden spoon in her direction.

'It's nice to dress up once in a while… don't you think?' she pouted and he smiled again.

'If only I'd known, babe, this broth is probably the least practical thing to eat whilst wearing a white dress.' He shrugged as he stirred the brown liquid.

'I'll take my chances, chef,' she said as she put napkins by the side of the place mats and set their glasses on the table.

Gabe served the broth over the rice and noodles and piled high the garnishes of cashew nuts, sliced herbs and crispy onions, carefully carrying the hot white bowls to the table one at a time. Taking off his striped apron he gallantly rushed round to Tor's side of the table to help slide her chair in as she sat, before taking his place, and raising a glass. 'Cheers, darling, you do look beautiful.' They chinked their glasses together. 'Not quite sure where you'll get to wear it round here – it's a little formal for the pub.' He smiled and took a sip, letting the bubbles explode and evaporate on his tongue.

'You think?' Tor said, tasting the broth for the first time, taking a small sample of soup, garnish and rice all together. 'This is really good. Lively!' she said, her eyes growing wide for a moment to emphasise the spice level.

'Too much?' Gabe asked, a frown momentarily corrugating his forehead.

'Don't be daft – bring it on. What does Torode say – that his lips will be burning?'

'Yeah,' laughed Gabe. 'And he reckons to like his spicy food.'

They ate and chatted, like a couple out for dinner, only he hadn't got the memo about dressing smart in his cargo trousers and t-shirt. Gabe got up to refill their glasses, and took ice cream out of the freezer at the same time to make it easier to scoop.

'I do like wearing this for you,' Tor said as she finished the last of her dessert.

'Good. I'll look forward to you wearing it again,' he smiled, savouring the last mouthfuls of Hagen-Daz' finest. Tor got up from her seat, drained her glass then walked around to stand next to him. She pushed her hip between him and the table and sat down on his lap, draping her arms around his shoulders.

'Thank you, husband, that was very lovely.' Her eyes glittered and she kissed him on the cheek.

Gabe put his hands on her hips and looked up at her. 'You are lovely, and never more so than now.'

'Aww, that's a lovely thing to say.' She bent to kiss him, her lips gently meeting his. She cupped his face in her hands, fingers feeling the first signs of five o'clock shadow starting to poke through. She kissed him again, harder this time, their lips crushed together, then parting and her tongue slipped through to meet his.

'Let's clear everything away,' he said, kissing her chastely and easing her off his knee to stand up.

'Washing up is such a passion-killer,' she pouted as Gabe bustled past her, clearing their plates from the table and setting them down by the sink. He turned around, bumping into Tor as she came up behind him. 'Let's not clear up any more,' she said, her hands at his waist. Reaching down and grabbing the material of his t-shirt in two handfuls, she dragged it up, ripping the shirt over his head and tossed it onto the floor. Their lips met again and she ran her hands over his chest as he found her breasts through the dress, an urgency gripping him. She unbuttoned his trousers, reaching into his shorts, freeing his arousal, rubbing him. Tor turned and cleared a section of the kitchen worktop, using her arm to sweep heat proof mats into the drawer beneath. Gabe raised an eyebrow as he watched his wife bend over the newly cleared worktop.

'Fuck me,' she said, turning to look straight at him.

'What has got into you?' he asked.

'Not you, at any rate. Now come on, I want you.' She reached back and gathered the material of her dress, drawing it roughly up her legs, over the curve of her bottom, revealing her nakedness underneath. She looked at him again, he had stayed rooted to the spot since she'd first bent over the counter. 'Want me to post an invite,' she mocked him, and it jerked him back into the here and now. Moving round behind her, already half undressed, his arousal pressing against hers. 'Come on,' she insisted and pushed back to meet him as he thrust forward and entered her from behind, grasping her hips. They rutted like animals, urgent and fierce, grinding hard against each other, with no love or caring or tenderness, just pure animal lust. Gabe looked down and it occurred to him that the other night he'd dreamt he was having sex with the girl in the white dress, and now he was – he just hoped she wouldn't turn into the witch. The boundaries between fantasy and reality, between normal Tor, and a Tor that was much more sexually aggressive or demanding, between his wife and someone else who seemed to be developing an increasing fascination with the witch, seemed to blur, and he found himself driving into a stranger.

The witch.

As if he was having an affair, that this was his mistress, his fantasy figure – someone from his 'allowed' list. And then they were crying out together, like two lost souls, swimming in a fish bowl, magically coming together, in every sense.

CHAPTER 24

THE ENCHANTED FOREST

'What're your plans for today?'

'Well, there's a mountain of laundry to put away and we seem to have generated ironing when neither of us is working or needing anything presented respectably, so I don't quite know how that worked out.'

'Not exactly domestic bliss.'

'No but I might go for a walk around the lake, too.'

'Really? On your own? Do you wanna maybe wait 'til I get back and we'll go together?' Gabe frowned at his wife's suggestion, the furrows on his brow deep enough to sow potatoes.

'No, it'll be fine – I won't go far – besides, I can't be afraid of where we live, otherwise there's no point living here.'

'True enough. Okay. So, I've gotta go to the supermarket get fuel and go and see Idris, to find out what he knows. He seems to me like someone who lets you know a snippet of what you need to know each time you see him and nothing else.' He shrugged, his expression saying *what can you do?*

'Do you trust him?' Tor leant forward over her steaming coffee cup.

'I trust that he seems to know more about local legends around here than anyone else. Beyond that – I don't know. *Can* you trust someone you hardly know?' Gabe got up and kissed Tor on the forehead, going over to the plate containing the car keys before slipping on an old trainer – permanently undone for ease of putting on, to accompany the ever-present boot. 'See you later.'

∞ ∞ ∞

Tor watched the car disappear up the driveway from the open door and around the corner at the end, the tall pines blocking her view like sentries on duty. She waited until she could no longer hear the engine, imagining Gabe waiting at the main road to turn onto the carriageway then accelerating away. She couldn't really hear the engine noise fading in the distance could she..? She smiled to herself. *Alone at last.* Then disappeared into the house.

Naked.

She was in good shape. She didn't exercise or particularly look at diet, but her body was trim and she wasn't carrying much in the way of extra weight, other than the slight curve in her tummy since she'd had

Mikey, but she regarded that as a mum's badge of honour. Of course, after last night, she could be using the shag your way to fitness concept that they'd just invented. Lots of calories burned that way for the first time in ages – their new start paying dividends already. She wasn't sure why she was particularly horny, but she'd definitely felt like that in recent days. In a way she wished that Gabe was here right now, to scratch that particular itch once more, but then, he would be wondering why she was getting the white dress out of the wardrobe and pulling it over her naked body again. The lace scratching at her nipples, arousing her further. The feeling of freedom underneath being something she'd never experienced.

I think I'm wearing no knickers.

She remembered a TV show from years ago, where a character said just that. What the hell was that show? Was it a parody of someone Scandinavian? She couldn't remember. Anyway. She'd been asked not to wear anything under the dress. The same way as she'd been told to buy the dress in the first place, a few days ago. And now she was putting it on for the first time. Sure, she'd worn it for Gabe, and they'd had a good time with her in it. But this was different. This was for her. And for Mikey.

Tor smoothed the dress into place over her body and tidied her hair. She had no idea what Morvith expected her appearance to be, so she didn't fuss over it too much. Downstairs, Tor put on a simple pair of pumps – not quite in keeping with the dress, but not as bad as a pair of walking boots or Wellingtons. She pulled the door firmly closed behind her and crunched across the gravel of the driveway and into the trees. As she stepped passed the threshold of the treeline, it felt like she was bursting through a membrane that sealed behind her. The air was still – smelling of damp forest floor and clean wet pine. There was an air of movement around her – life – like voles and worms, slugs and pheasants were going about their business this morning, and just idly keeping an eye on her to check she wasn't some psycho-human out to catch them. Passing the barn she saw a puddle, and some deep boot prints next to a pile of mud and surmised this was where Gabe had fallen and hit his head. As far as she was aware, he'd returned to the house after the incident and not gone wandering into the woods to find unusual looking trees.

The mud around the barn was replaced by leaf mold and pine needles, and she bounced from step to step on the springy carpet, feeling like Neil Armstrong. Despite trying to plan a route through the woods, tree trunks seemed to appear in front of her, as if they'd moved sideways, barring her way, meaning she must change direction, or divert around impenetrable clumps of ferns and brambles. Soon, her planned, fairly linear route was gone and having zigzagged her way deeper into the woods, she was totally disorientated. Turning left and right, then looking behind her, to see if she recognised something, anything familiar – a landmark she'd noticed on the way through, perhaps, but she'd gone on such a convoluted route that she could've got here from anywhere. The house was nowhere to be seen either, adding to her confusion – she couldn't have gone so far that she'd left it behind – out of sight – it had to be there and just obstructed by the forest. Tor started to panic, out here in this flimsy dress and the temperature was dropping.

Was it? Was it getting colder?

Goosepimples were raised on her arms and she folded them, rubbing her hands up and down them to create some warmth. Part of her wondered if it was just the cold or a combination of that and fear itself – she was lost in woods she didn't know. In reality, if she'd stopped to think, she knew the lake was off to her right and the road up to the left. So, she could turn either way and be able to orientate herself and find her way back to the house. But that rational, sensible self, had been banished to the back of the queue in her mind, with far more populist scaremongering, clamouring for attention in front of it. Tramping through the underbrush, sharp upright sticks – the remnants of long dead plant stems which had succumbed to the winter chills – scratched at her legs, while brambles and gorse pulled at her. Just as her fear was getting out of control, beyond something she could keep a lid on by locking it in a corner of her brain with breathing exercises for company, she saw an outline in the gloom up ahead. Little more than a stick-figure silhouette at this range, every step closer brought new layers of detail – the white dress, dripping wet hair falling around her face, bare feet covered in mud. A young woman in her twenties – pretty, an easy smile on her lips, head bowed slightly but eyes set in dark hollows watching Tor. A young woman in her twenties – but with ancient eyes and a sly expression. Her lips curled into a smile as Tor approached, as if she was happy to see her similarly dressed friend.

Approval.

Tor reached an open, shallow basin that dropped gradually down about fifteen feet into a flat clearing in which stood one tree, denuded of all bark, the silver-grey trunk and one large limb a still-life image of what once must've been a magnificent tree. Mirroring each other, on opposite sides of the basin, the women walked down into the dip, sound seemingly muted. The atmosphere was electric as if they were in the middle of a storm – Tor could feel the static in the air and imagined her hair was starting to stand up, the air itself cracked and popped with tiny flashes, large forks of lightning repeatedly streaking across the sky overhead. As they followed the slope down, the grey skies started to fade, to lighten, and the surrounding trees lost focus – grew thinner and disappeared. Everywhere around and above felt like it was closing in, that they were enclosed in a magical bubble made by the basin and the sky. Somehow, it was a lot warmer in here too – Tor's goosepimples had disappeared and she was quite comfortable now in her dress. The wind speed increased, whipping around the basin, the bubble, further blurring the trees beyond from view, blowing Tor's hair around and tugging at her dress, like the clumsy hands of a drunken lover. The witch stood unmoved on the far slope, then suddenly she was off to the right of the tree, closer, yet standing motionless, then she disappeared again and materialised beyond the tree. Time and again, but faster and faster the witch seemed to jump from one location to another. Suddenly, she was by Tor's side, wet hair blowing in the wind, staring at her. Now, in close-up, the witch tilted her head as she maintained eye contact, the wind whistling around them, swirling and moaning. Tor returned the witch's gaze, transfixed, eyes searching each other for understanding, for meaning, for some way of communicating. She had a confident smile that was unnerving, and broke her gaze with Tor to look around her at the bubble she'd created, as if to say, this is my power, this is what I can do.

The wind was almost visible, whipping dried dead leaves up around her in a whirlwind, a gust passing her with a whisper, some words hissing by on the breeze then fading as they echoed off into the basin. They came back around again, like your family on a carousel and this time she could hear distinct words flying around her head, hovering just out of reach of her ears, before, finally, allowing her to hear. Tor gradually realising that the wind was the witch's voice.

I can reach him.

The words on the wind swirled around the canopy of trees above, twisting and dancing around her, echoing across the clearing, bombarding her from different directions. But they were unmistakeable. Reach who? Who did she mean?

'Who?' she built up the courage to ask a four-hundred-year-old dead witch.

I can reach him.

I can reach him.

I can reach him.

The words echoed around the basin, bouncing around her head, to the left, to the right, in front and behind, creating a Doppler effect as if the witch was in either ear at any one time.

'Who?!' She screamed defiantly, as if that would stop the wind and bring her back into control.

The boy.

I can reach him.

And there he was. Or rather, there was a boy in front of her, small and frail, his head covered by a light grey hoody, hiding his features. Red wellies and blue tracksuit bottoms making the figure look just like Mikey.

Mikey.

Did she really mean him?

'My son?' she asked, her voice cracking, sounding desperate, staring at the figure in front of her.

I can reach him. He is here.

'My son is dead.' Her voice caught on the last word, no matter how long it had been.

He is here. I see him.

'Here, where? Where is he?' Tor reached forward to the figure, the material of the hoody was very real, the cloth soft and slightly damp.

'Can you help him?'

Yes. The wind whispered the word, little more than a hiss that echoed around her.

'Will you?' Her voice climbed an octave as she bent to the small boy in front of her. Even if Mikey was *there* with her, wherever the witch was, whatever 'there' meant, she had still reached inside Tor's head for an image of him, of him wearing an outfit that she remembered, from a particular day. The witch had thumbed through her memories like going through a photo album, picking one out that she liked, and dangling it in front of her now.

Need.

'I'm sorry? Did you say 'need'? You need something?' She was squatting in front of the figure now, the witch, dripping wet and ageing before her eyes was just behind. The young girl had gone, wrinkles developed and deepened, spine rounded, breasts sagged – her eyes intensified as they sunk into her face, and the hairline dropped backwards, gradually turning grey and thin.

Need. The eyes of the witch grew wider, her mouth curling into a smile.

'What do you need? Something from me?'

Must die.

'Who? Who must die?' Tor was confused – desperate to understand – delighted to be thinking about Mikey – not just as a picture in a frame and a load of painful memories. Not going near the idea that Mikey was dead, not thinking about what the witch might really be telling her of where he was and just what was meant by how she could 'help' him.

The witch's skin started to fade, becoming grey, and her dark eyes rolled back in her head to leave bloodshot white discs. Her head lolled to one side and somewhere, halfway up her spine, there was a kink in the opposite direction.

Must die! The wind whispered in her ears like a lover – caressing her delicate flesh before slipping inside. The witch was a hag now, and sneered down as Tor gently lifted the hood off the tiny figure.

'Who must die? Please tell me,' she implored the monster, glancing up to make eye contact with orbs that had turned as black as coal, waiting for a response. In front of her the hood dropped back but there was nothing, just empty air, the clothes comprising the figure falling away into a crumpled heap on the floor before bursting into flames. Wondering if this was all a wicked game, Tor looked up again, wanting a response, which came directly from the slack gash of an almost lipless mouth, yet seemed to surround her at the same time, slithering into every pore, hissing and poking at her soul.

Hus-band.

CHAPTER 25
—\/—
SUPERMARKET

There was a law of physics that Stephen Hawking had missed, that Galileo overlooked and that Heisenberg wasn't certain about. It was that no matter how carefully you selected your shopping trolley, there was always going to be one wheel that behaved completely differently to the others. A quarter variance constant, or something. Gabe pondered on this as the right front wheel of his particular trolley juddered wildly as he pushed it along, as if he were Lewis Hamilton about to get a flat. He could've changed it for another, but that isn't what men did. They endured and put up with, or maybe they were just too lazy to go and change it, or even too stubborn to admit there was a problem (with their selection).

He breezed through the fresh fruit and veg isle of the supermarket, ticking off a list, swerving around other shoppers with a smile and a nod, that was more often met with a stare and a scowl. Stares that didn't seem to go away when he did. They followed him. Now that he'd noticed, he saw people from across the central produce isle staring at him over the clementines and courgettes. And not just staring, but nudging each other, leaning in and whispering, exchanging secrets or stories that no one else should hear – all without breaking their stare. As if to look away was to break some sort of spell or maybe to let him escape. It seemed like he'd walked into *Dawn of the Dead.* He promised himself, if he saw *Bub* with some headphones, he was going to leave.

'Hey. It's Gabe isn't it?' A vaguely familiar man appeared in front of him such that their trolleys collided.

'Ye-es,' replied Gabe, extricating his cart from that of the other man, lips curling into a half smile to stall for time as his short-term memory sifted through reams of paperwork like they were the police in the 70s. Finally, a breakthrough in the case and the identity got passed from the short-term unit to his frontal lobes. 'Mal! Hi. Nice to see you again.' They shook hands, both gripping with a firm, three-quarters of the way to causing a fracture, bloke-type grip. Gabe regarded the landlord from the pub in a different light now he'd recognised him – it was amazing how different people looked out of context. 'It's my first time in here, and I kind of get the impression that everyone's staring at me.' Gabe decided not to mention *Dawn of the Dead* at this stage.

'Don't be paranoid,' Mal laughed. 'You're just the new guy.' An older couple tried to make their way down the aisle that Gabe and Mal were blocking, so they shifted to the far side, squeezing past and nearly knocked over a pile of cornflakes boxes – collecting a pack of Oats So

Simple on their way, but again, staring at Gabe as if he were a freshly landed alien.

'How long does that last?' Gabe gave Mal a quizzical glance. 'The new bloke thing?'

'I've been here fifteen years, and I'm glad that now, you, are the new guy!'

'Oh.'

'Alright boys.' A tall, thickset man appeared in front of them, his booze-filled trolley crashing into both Gabe and Mal's. 'Sorry – bad driving,' he said with a grin. 'I'm Bobby Seymour.'

'Hi, nice to meet you,' replied Gabe.

'Likewise.'

'Bobby runs the local cricket club,' Mal interjected.

'Do you play?' He asked hopefully, eyebrows raised.

'No, not at all.' Gabe almost laughed at the idea of him in whites.

'No problem, we always need scorers,' Seymour said, happily, as if that was now set in stone – Gabe's involvement with the cricket club a foregone conclusion.

Gabe looked down at his new friend's trolley, packed to the gunwales with bottled beers and trays of canned lager. 'Got a lot of cricket going on in November, have you?'

Seymour snorted. 'Big Champion's League game in the club tonight. Liverpool are playing. Come down if you fancy it.'

'Thanks. I might.'

'There's always something going on with us – have a look on Twitter.' And with that, Bobby pulled his trolley free from the others and headed off for the fresh meat isle, and still managed to give Gabe a quizzical sideways glance that unnerved him somewhat.

'Good bloke, Bobby.'

'He seems nice,' Gabe replied in the absence of anything meaningful to say.

'So how are you settling in?' Mal asked brightly.

'Oh, it's okay – lots to do. And things are a bit… strange.'

'Strange? How? Don't tell me that Idris was right.' Mal looked slightly concerned and disappointed in equal measure.

'I'm afraid he was.'

'He will be pleased with himself when he finds out. Best not to tell him, I reckon.'

'My lips are sealed.' Gabe replied.

'So, have you…. seen things?' Mal's eyes were wide, he was almost leering and Gabe wondered if everyone else in the store knew who he was – not just the new bloke, but the new bloke at Ty Llyn – and that they would all like to know what was going on. Perhaps they should put this conversation over the tannoy? But as Mal said, that was surely just paranoia.

'Yes. Ghost stuff – apparitions, noises, weird things.' Gabe shrugged, being deliberately vague.

'Oh. Nothing specific then?'

'It does feel like the place is haunted.' Gabe watched for a reaction as he divulged this revelation and wondered about him asking about specifics – as if he expected certain things to be happening.

'Really?' Mal reacted as Gabe thought he would, with interest and excitement. *What was going on around here? he thought.* 'Have you seen her?'

It was like Mal was getting excited by all this witch-porn and it was time to stop feeding him. 'No, not really, she doesn't appear to us – just things moving… odd.'

'Oh.' Mal's non-poker face couldn't hide his disappointment as it avalanched downwards.

'We're just hoping she gets used to us and stops the Halloween stuff. We don't mean her any harm, so, in time, let's hope she gets it and lets us carry on.' Gabe shrugged.

'She has tended to keep hounding people. That's what I heard about previous owners.' There was a twinkle in his eye that said, *look out buddy*.

'Well, we don't want to fight her. Show her we aren't a threat, and hope she'll leave us be.'

'Good luck with that,' Mal said, without meaning a word of it.

'Yes, thanks a lot. I'll see you at your place, soon.' Gabe gave him his biggest smile and moved away, the wonky wheel wobbling away on the front of his trolley.

CHAPTER 26

-\/-

A CLOSE SHAVE

Gabe reached into the boot of the car and grabbed the bags of shopping in one go, three in each hand. He tramped across the drive and up the steps of the decking, idly noticing muddy footprints leading up to the door. He had yet to become an expert in levering open the front door with elbow or hip whilst his hands were full – it would come with time, it was, a minor problem in universal terms, but one he knew he would solve. Finally clattering through the door, protesting as he barely freed its catch before shoving through, he set down the bags. Tor walked toward him from the kitchen wearing her white bathrobe and towelling her long brown hair.

'Get all we need?' she asked absently, vigorously rubbing her head with the towel before tucking her hair behind her ears.

'No, I decided to leave half of what we needed in the shop and buy some random shit, not on the list, instead.'

'Normal for Gabe-shopping then?' Tor responded to the sarcasm.

'And we are Mistress-Two-Showers now are we – and it's not even mid-day?'

'Yeah, that was a bad idea this morning. Got pretty muddy and sweaty on my walk.'

Gabe's eyes settled on her boots, which were clean and parked in their space next to where he'd put on his trainers this morning. They hadn't moved.

'Uh-huh. Where'd you go?' He slipped off his jacket and hung it on the coat rack above.

'Out past the barn and that way. Saw the skid mark you left the other day when you fell.' She smiled at him, before turning to walk back to the kitchen. 'Cuppa?' she asked, looking back over her shoulder.

Gabe watched her go, leaving damp bare footprints in the clay tiles. The same size footprints that were on the deck. 'That'd be lovely, thanks.' *What the hell?* 'You saw the dead tree then.'

'No. Didn't notice anything like that, but there were a few trees that had fallen and were a bit rotten – no good for the fire.'

'You can't have gone far – you can't miss that tree.'

'Yeah, I walked for ages. You'll have to point it out the next time we go that way.' He could hear his wife humming as she busied herself taking the lid off their cafetiere with its metallic pop, joined by the sound of the kettle bursting into life like the rumble of a jet engine. The sound grew louder in his ears, as if all his focus was on Tor making coffee, the only sound that mattered, the only thin–

'What?' Tor was staring at him.

'Sorry?'

'You were miles away – is everything okay?' she asked, concern wrinkling her forehead.

'Yeah, sorry, just thinking. You didn't get as far as the corner did you?'

'The corner,' she beamed at him. 'The corner of what?'

'The corner of the lake. That's where the inlet is and the cave where Idris said was the witch's lair – remember?'

'Yeah… maybe. No, I don't think I went that far – didn't see anything resembling that if I did.'

∞ ∞ ∞

'When's food?' Tor padded through the kitchen in the t-shirt and joggers she'd changed into after her shower that morning. She'd spent the afternoon attacking some of the overgrown bushes on the woods side of the house with secateurs, loppers and a bow saw. Large sections of cotoneaster, lonicera and broom had been dispatched and by the end of the afternoon, more light was coming in through the windows on the far side of the house. Now, long glass in hand, she sipped at a warming zinfandel.

'Whenever you are you making it?' Gabe looked back her, confusion on his face, *I thought you were cooking?*

'No need. I have staff that do it for me.'

'Do you now. Wow. What great staff,' he replied, stirring the pot containing pork shoulder, tomatoes, olives and garlic making a Mediterranean stew of sorts.

'Smells great. When?'

'Gosh, sooo demanding,' he said rolling his eyes. 'Maybe needs twenty minutes. I'm gonna go shave.'

'Oh yeah?' she smiled. 'Wanna impress someone?'

'You never know, my love. You never know.'

Steam rose like a mushroom cloud from the bathroom sink as Gabe arranged his shaving paraphernalia on the side of the enamel. Never liking foams in cans or gels, he preferred the old-fashioned approach of a shaving brush and some cream in a tin. He enjoyed the ritual, splashing his face with the slightly-too-hot-water from the basin, massaging it into his skin to open up the pores. Working up a lather with the brush, he quickly made himself look like Captain Birdseye, then wiped the fog from the mirror. Slowly and carefully, he pulled the razor across his skin, sliding effortlessly on its gel layer, slicing all the tiny thick hairs to leave his skin smooth and dry behind it. He always imagined it was like a piece of farm machinery – a combine harvester leaving a field of wheat in front, a clean-cut strip behind. The first batch of foam and whiskers were swilled off in the sink water – tiny dark bristles floating on the foamy surface. He placed the razor next to the clean strip he'd just made and pulled it along, a sharp pain denoting a cut – unusual with these razors with their three fine blades, unless they were getting beyond their useful life. Blood immediately welled out of the wound and started to run down his face, but he continued with the stroke, oblivious. The blades, no longer floating on their gel layer, were digging in, extending the cut, slicing the side of his cheek open. He finished at his jawline and looked at the flap of skin that had opened up, hanging down, the initially shallow cut deepening, having sliced through muscle, leaving tendons and glands visible beneath, like *The Terminator* ripping off his skin glove to reveal the robotic tendons sliding backwards and forwards beneath. Thick blood oozed down his cheek, collecting on his jaw before dripping down, turning the sink water a deep crimson, with drips and rivulets running over the sides and down onto the floor. Curious, he started on the other side of his face, watching the reaction of the witch in the mirror, her face grey and dead as she stood behind him, skin sallow and slack, lips purple, but her eyes alive and shining, positively encouraging him to carry on. This time there was no gliding and sliding of the razor, but, fascinated, he dug the blade in, feeling it cut down through the skin immediately, the shaving stroke lifted a flap of tissue away as he dragged the blade down. Another stroke and another, and he'd pulled away the bottom half of his face to hang in grotesque ribbons from his lower jaw. He looked at the witch who was smiling as best she could from her dead face, enjoying the triumph of making the man do this. Her face faded, the skin changing from dead blue-grey, growing lighter, becoming more flesh-toned, the eye colour changing and the cheeks blurred slightly as the bones moved beneath, and Tor was stood behind him, looking at his reflection in the mirror.

'Oh shit, Gabe, you've cut yourself,' she exclaimed, opening the medicine cabinet and pulling down some cotton wool pads she used to remove eye make-up.

'No shit,' he replied, looking at his face again. The small cut on the lower part of his cheek was oozing blood which she quickly blotted, applying some pressure to stem the flow. The rest of his face was smooth and, apart from a couple of thin streaks and a blob on the earlobe, was free of shaving foam. He felt disconnected, watching in the mirror as Tor worked on him, replacing the soaked pad with another as the bleeding slowed. He was inside the mirror, and the world outside was false, although it looked exactly as it should. His eyes flicked between Tor and her reflection, but she looked the same. Then she crossed the glass again, reaching for a plaster to finish the job, her face turned to the mirror, their eyes met and it was the witch. Only for a second, just the tiniest moment, he saw her again – the grey skin, the black eyes – before the reflection, and the witch, disappeared.

'You okay?' Tor had pealed the backing strips off the plaster, and held a sticky end between thumb and forefinger, ready to close the wound. But she'd stopped and was staring at him. 'Gabe? You look like you've seen a ghost.'

Shaken back to reality – the sight of him shaving the skin of his face off with the witch behind seemingly less shocking than the final glimpse he'd just had of his wife *becoming* her. 'Sorry. Miles away. Thanks for being my nurse,' he said with a weak smile as she applied the plaster.

'You are most welcome, sir. Just don't expect me to put on the uniform.'

'Now there's a thought,' he said, thinking of no such thing.

'I'll bet.' She kissed him on the cheek and walked out of the bathroom, with the thought of Tor dressed as someone else still firmly on his mind.

CHAPTER 27

ARGUMENT

'You're back then.' Gabe had heard the door catch clunk open and then shut. Have a good walk?' A few seconds later, Tor walked round the corner into the kitchen, smiling at him, skipping along, her bare feet leaving a trail of muddy footprints. She lifted down a glass whilst running the cold tap, the white dress, now a little grubby, riding up as she reached up. 'Don't want a cuppa to warm up?' he asked.

'No thanks,' she said, raising the glass of water to him in a 'cheers' motion. 'This is fine.'

'Okay.' He'd wondered how to play this, wondered how he should broach the subject. He'd been simmering since she had been away. Not because she'd gone for a walk when there were things to be done, not because she hadn't asked him, but because she had been with her, and it seemed quite weird to him that Tor's only friend now was a long dead witch. He'd played over this scenario in his mind, thought about a number of ways to discuss it. And they all went to hell.

'Did you see her?' He tried to ask lightly, but he knew there was an edge to his voice, and 'her' didn't sound like 'her', but '*her*.'

Tor stopped as she was turning away with her drink. 'Yes. I did.' She turned back to him. 'Is that okay?'

'Yeah, course.' No, it wasn't. 'Just that you've done that a few times now – it's like you're friends or something.' He tried to smile, but it was weak and, if he was honest, barely curled the corners of his mouth up.

'Don't you think it's fascinating?' She asked him, wide eyed, as if he'd just asked the strangest question ever.

'What – her?'

'Yes. Her story – what she is.'

'Don't you find it scary? Her story – what she is.' Gabe pulled a *really* face. 'She's done all these things to us in our house, threatened us, has power we can't imagine and so is highly dangerous, and you call her fascinating. She is, but she's a whole lot more than that.'

'She doesn't scare me when we're together – quite the opposite.' Tor stood defiantly facing her husband, jaw sticking out as if she was daring him to challenge her.

'Oh,' Gabe responded, recognising Tor on the edge of an argument.

'I think I'm getting attuned to her.'

'What?'

'To Morvith.'

'We're calling her by her name now?' Gabe asked, alarmed.

'Why not?'

'Because she died a long time ago and if this… whatever it is has got something to do with her, then she's a nasty piece of work. I think of her as the witch.'

'Don't you think she was wronged? That she was unfairly treated?'

'Maybe. Yes, you might be right – if Idris' account is true, of course. But she was also someone with power and hold over the villagers. They believed what she said, and that always has the potential for abuse. Maybe she did do some of the things they said. Or maybe she let people think she did and it came back to bite her.'

'I don't think so,' Tor said, with finality.

'But you can't know that.'

'I do,' she said wistfully looking out to the lake.

'Anyway, what do you mean by getting attuned to her?'

'I think I can feel her, like when she's around.' She smiled at him, as if this was a good thing.

'You think you can detect the presence of the spirit of a witch that might be haunting our house?' Gabe's eyebrows raised another notch.

'I think I can feel a tortured soul, of someone who was wronged so badly such a long time ago that she can't rest.'

'Jesus.'

'What?' She snapped at him.

'You wouldn't entertain the idea of ghosts, an afterlife or religion a few weeks ago, and now we need to see if Amazon sell Ouija boards?'

'No, we don't – don't talk like that. Maybe I'm just feeling more at one with the house and I can sympathise with her story – that's all.' She looked at him out of the corner of her eye.

'Well, that sounds a bit better, and I can see that as more likely.' Gabe missed the slight smile that curled on her lips before she turned away, unzipping the dirty dress and stepping out of it.

'I like being with her because she's different. She tells me things, things that give me hope.' Tor's eyes brimmed with tears.

'Hope? Hope – for *Mikey*? It can't be hope for here or for us, because she's not a part of us and we've only just got here. She's giving you hope for someone who can't have any.'

'You have to have hope, because sometimes, that's all that there is.' Tor cried at him, tears rolling down her cheeks.

'Tor, I love you, but this seems like it's going down a very dark road.' Gabe was exasperated.

'You say you love me – but it's not enough,' Tor said, crying hard now as she stood at the kitchen counter, hands braced wide apart, head dropped.

'Not enough? What does *that* mean?' Gabe replied, shaking his head on the opposite side of the unit.

'It means that it doesn't mean anything anymore.'

'It always used to.'

'Yeah, it did. But now it doesn't. Now it's just words. And I couldn't care less. I need something more.' She raised her head, meeting his gaze.

'You need something more than me loving you.' It wasn't really a question.

'Yes. I need something more than you saying it anyway.' Her eyes were sad and she looked tired, as if she were carrying a great burden.

'I'm not just saying it.' Gabe was exasperated, *what more can I do?*

'Really?' Her eyes flashed with anger. 'Not going through the motions?'

'No.'

'Not just saying 'I love you', because you feel like you should?' A smile flickered at the corner of her lips, mocking him.

'No – never. I say it because I mean it, not because–'

'Not because you are going through the motions?'

'No. Stop saying that.'

'Come on Gabe. We are just drifting. We sit across the table at dinner with nothing to say. We haven't done since Mikey…'

'I thought we were doing better. I thought we got through this because we loved each other. It's the kind of thing that would break a lot of couples, but it didn't us. I thought we would be okay.'

'You might not really love me, but I know she does.'

'Who?'

'Morvith.'

'The witch?'

'Must you call her that?'

'But isn't she?'

'She fought for her life against overwhelming odds. She used all she had to help someone – that says something to me.' The tiredness in Tor's eyes had been replaced by a fire, a defiance – almost as if she were angry at him.

'Is that what she's told you? Your new friend? But what if she's lying to draw you in. She doesn't get a lot of company.'

'I believe her – she tried to help.'

'Didn't work though, did it?' Gabe was prepared to be harsh and cruel in the face of Tor's rose-tinted glasses.

'She loves me.'

'And why does she do that? This ghost, or spirit or whatever you want to call her, what does she get out of it?'

'We're friends. We like spending time together. And she wants to help us…'

'She hasn't seemed like the helping kind so far.'

'Mikey.' She brought the conversation back around.

'Babe. Mikey. Is. Dead.' The word caught in his throat and he barely managed to croak it out. 'We couldn't save him, and we said goodbye to him. There isn't a day goes by when I wish we could've done something – and God knows you tried everything you could, but he was just too sick. And now he's gone. He's long gone. And we have to accept that. We can't help him now.'

'But she can.'

'But he's *dead*.' Gabe repeated. Colder, his voice hardening as if to try and put a stop to such talk.

'But dead is just a state of matter, what if we could talk to him, find out if he's okay?' she implored him, pleading.

'But he's not okay. That's what being dead is, it's very much *not* being okay.' He shook his head and leant his hands onto the kitchen worktop.

'His body isn't, but he might be,' she said quietly, her hands cuffing in frustration at the tears dripping off her chin.

'Are we talking afterlife now? We've gone from atheism to considering the afterlife in quite a short period. And it's this witch putting ideas into your head.'

'So what? Wouldn't you just like to hear him, hear his voice again? Wouldn't that be amazing? What if we could speak to him every so often? It would just be like he was living away from home.'

'And she's offering you this?'

'She said she can reach him – who knows what might happen after that. We've gone from not believing in anything paranormal to having a dead witch as a neighbour. Nothing is off the table.'

'I think she's just drawing you in, subverting you to her way of thinking.'

'But why, though?'

'To have a companion, a friend. She's been on her own a long time.'

'And you see, that's the point,' Tor slammed her hands down on the worktop. 'She's dead and she found some way around it, and we believe that, so why not Mikey?'

'Do we believe that?'

'What you don't believe her? Which bit.'

'All of it – I don't know. What if none of this is true. What if she's just some mad girl – a long lost daughter of Idris who's run off and they concoct this story to cover it.'

'Oh Jesus. That's almost as unbelievable as the witch. And get the whole village to believe it?' She snorted in derision of the idea. 'And what about all the strange goings on – the pipes, the wind chime – you said these things yourself.'

The bath, the picture, Gabe thought. 'You can explain a lot of this stuff easily.'

'And her passing through me? Can you fucking explain that? Did I just have wind or something?' Gabe stared at her, knowing she was right, knowing that they were way past the point of believing in all of these happenings. But sometimes you have to draw a line in the sand to say; this is as far as I go.

They had crossed that too.

CHAPTER 28

-\/-

WORD GETS AROUND

The sun dropped to just below the line of the hills to the southwest, bathing the valley in fire, blinding Gabe as he drove along – the windscreen visor doing little. He emerged from the trees to reveal the village in front of him. Crossing the bridge over the overflow stream from the lake, he turned onto the main street. The shadows were lengthening by the second and he could see the steeple of the church set in the trees away to his left. Halfway along the road he took a small turning, hidden between two shops, denoted by a small brown sign with 'Eglwys' pointing to the church. The lane immediately narrowed and meandered around stone garden walls, making driving at anything more than a snail's pace a rally experience. The lane continued on up this side of the valley, disappearing into the trees, heading for who-knew-where. On the left it opened out into a car park in front of a high stone wall surrounding the church yard. Gabe slowed the car to a halt and gaped at what he saw. The sunset lit up the whole of the grey stone of the church in brilliant and vivid orange so that it glowed – a bright and almost alien light shining down. He parked the car and limped to the wrought iron gate, recently re-painted in black gloss, but with a predictable creak that showed the care and attention hadn't extended as far as oiling the hinges. Walking up the winding path through the graveyard, he vaguely noticed inscriptions on the headstones nearest to him – the Welsh meaning nothing to him. Approaching the side entrance, he lifted the latch, pushing the large wooden door open and walked across the small narthex, with its table for collections and leaflets promoting religious events and places of interest, before stepping up into the rows and rows of pews in the nave. Pausing, he breathed in the smell of damp and stale carpet that he would always associate with churches. He looked up to the high vaulted ceiling above and at the alcoves of stained glass. Further inspection revealed paint peeling away from the walls and new beams sitting alongside old in the ceiling – repairing what needed to be and nothing more. Despite his lack of faith, there was always something about a church – he could see how it would cast its spell over someone – the height, the space, the splendour of the woodwork, the glass, the organ. They made you feel small and insignificant – presumably so in the face of God.

'Reverend Pickering?' he called out to the vicar who was tidying several books near the alter. His voice echoed down the empty building, getting funnelled as it narrowed toward the far end. She looked up, black cassock neatly trimmed in purple and fastened up to her neck, leading to the kindly face of a woman in her mid-sixties, with simply parted grey, shoulder length hair.

'Hello,' she replied with an easy smile, striding towards him. 'You're lucky you caught me. We've just had a wedding rehearsal – you might've seen the couple as you came in..?' Gabe shrugged and gave a shake of the head. 'Were you looking for some quiet reflection, my son, or was it me you wanted to see?' She smiled again now, stopping next to him, hands clasped in front of her, a frown crossing briefly across her face as she looked down and noticed the boot on his leg.

'I was hoping to speak to you, Vicar, if I may?'

'Why, yes. Yes of course. Do go on…'

'I'm Gabe Hooper, and I've just moved–'

'Into Ty Llyn. I know who you are, Mr Hooper. Welcome to the village.' The same easy smile again.

'Thank you.'

'How are you settling in? And Mrs Hooper..?'

'Tor. Yes, well that was why I wanted to speak to you, really.'

'Oh, I see. I wouldn't be very good at unpacking boxes, Mr Hooper, I'm afraid. I've never really moved around much.'

'No, we are fine for that.' He nodded at her humour. 'I wanted to talk to you about the witch.'

'Ah.'

'You've heard of her then?'

'I know who she is, yes.'

Gabe blew out through his cheeks in relief. 'I did wonder if you might think I was mad, asking you that.'

'No, not at all, but I can understand your reticence. These are not easy questions to ask of strangers. But my boss happens to be an all-powerful entity that created the universe in six days, and who guides souls leaving people's bodies to come and live with Him for all eternity. So, it isn't beyond me to consider the idea of powerful beings and spirits and so on.'

'Wasn't she one of the cunning folk?'

'Idris has taught you well.' She smiled.

'I think he likes to tell his stories.'

'He does that.'

'So, was she?'

'As far as I've heard and understand, she was.' The Reverend nodded, raising her arm to show him toward the door of the church so they could walk and talk.

'And is that why she was outlawed? Is that why she was shunned?'

'You have to understand that, at that time, Christianity, whilst not a new religion, was still not widely practised – not like it is today.' Gabe was tempted to argue about the decline of religion in modern society, but decided that was a debate for a different day. 'A lot of people, particularly in rural villages like here, retained pagan beliefs, and so, whilst attending church, would go and visit the cunning folk for medicines or what have you.'

'Why did the church dislike them so much – after all, they were not offering a viable alternative for treatment of illness, for example.'

'I'm afraid the clergy of the time believed that anything that could not be healed by the power of prayer, either couldn't be cured or wasn't worthy of it. There was a terrible snobbery around religion – and, of course, that can still be seen today.'

Gabe's interest was piqued but, again, it wasn't something he wanted to get distracted by. 'So, Christian on the weekend, pagan in the week?'

'Something like that, yes.'

'Do you believe in ghosts? In hauntings?'

'I believe that there are restless spirits that are yet to meet God, yes.'

'And this is what Morvith the witch is?'

'I suppose so, Mr Hooper.'

'Have you ever tried to deal with her… professionally?' Gabe pushed the heavily glossed door open and stepped outside, turning to continue the conversation as the vicar followed, running her hand over the black leather cover of a large bible on a table by the door.

'Like an exorcism, you mean?' Her smile grew broader.

'Yes. If that's what that means.'

'No. I have visited your predecessors – more than once – and joined in prayer, and asked for her to move on and for God's help in guiding her.'

'Didn't work though, did it?'

'If you are here asking me these things, Mr Hooper, I'm guessing it didn't.'

'So, if centuries ago, religion couldn't help you, you turned to the cunning folk. What do you do nowadays when religion fails?'

'I'm aware of your history, Mr Hooper, and you have my sympathy and my prayers.'

'Word gets around.'

'It does, yes. But Google is more efficient.' The vicar turned to pull the door closed behind her, pausing, as if making a decision. 'She came here once – not long after I started,' she said quietly.

'Oh?'

'We'd been having a choir practice in the lead-up to Christmas concerts, so I'd wanted to do it in the church for familiarity, rather than in the village hall where we'd started.' Gabe nodded. 'Everyone left at the end, but I have a… thing, I suppose. These days you might call it OCD. But, before I leave, I like to visit every place in the church and touch each bible. To express my thanks for God, and to feel close to Him – the two of us together in this building.' Reverend Pickering jangled some keys and slotted an old skeleton key into the lock, turning the mechanism with a clunk.

'I can understand that,' Gabe nodded again.

'So, it might have been about fifteen minutes after everyone had gone that I was leaving, and I locked the door, turned to walk down the path, like now, and saw this shape, this figure over to the right – over there.' She pointed around the side of the church, just next to one of the stone walls. 'A graveyard has a lot of upright structures, Mr Hooper – gravestones, tombs, pots, pillars and statues. But even after just a short period of time, one gets to know what should be there and what shouldn't.'

'Like the skyline in a city.' Gabe nodded, as they strolled down the path.

'Exactly, yes. She was just an outline, really, but my eye was drawn to her.'

'And it couldn't have been one of the choir, walking over in that direction?'

'That was the first thing that came to mind, but everyone was long gone. It could've been a dishevelled young woman in need of sanctuary – I've thought that on a number of occasions since, but, for some reason, I just knew. I'd heard all the stories–'

'Word gets around.'

'Yes! I just knew who she was straight away.'

'What was she doing?'

'Standing there, head bowed a little, but still watching me. There was one thing, though.' They stopped at the gate, the stone arch above with a painted wooden sign proclaiming the times of the weekly services.

'What.'

'Her head was tilted to one side. Like she was looking at me quizzically.'

'I thought you said her head was bowed?' But Gabe knew this was definitely Morvith.

'It was. It was like she was looking up through her eyelids – but it was definitely on an angle – regarding me with one eye, maybe.'

'I see. And what did your predecessor tell you?'

'My predecessor was here for fifty years and died at the pulpit, so I don't know what he thought.'

'What do you think she wanted?'

'You know, Mr Hooper, this is something that has pre-occupied me since it happened. When I'm alone at night, I'll see her face and it'll make me think again, and I'll relive that short moment when she looked at me in the shadows. There were so few details I could see or make out, so I'm purely guessing, but I'm happy with what I thought on the day and what I've concluded since.'

'Which is?' Gabe got the impression that the Reverend was partly nervous of divulging her thoughts, but also partly enjoying the build-up – like an awards ceremony, when they have a huge pause after saying, *And the winner is…*

'I think she wanted to check me out. Give me the once over you might say. To see if I was any competition.'

'Competition?'

'Well, a new broom might want to come in and drive out any ideas of witchcraft or evil spirits and so on, and I suspect that's what she wanted to see with me. To see if I was a threat to her.'

'What did you do?'

'I nodded to her, and went home.'

CHAPTER 29
-\/-
FIRE

There was something about the fresh air of the hills and the lake. Maybe it was because there was no pollution, maybe it was because they were so busy with the house, or even the nervous energy of Morvith being 'around'. Regardless, Gabe was finding himself falling asleep in front of the TV on a regular basis. This particular evening, Tor had gone to bed early – exhausted herself, no doubt, from her latest walk in the woods. It had been too early for Gabe and he'd been doing a scrolling lottery on Netflix to find something to watch, or fall asleep in front of. Now, sitting up, the glow of the TV illuminated the room like he woken up in *Poltergeist.* It showed the menu screen where whatever he'd chosen to watch – and he couldn't even remember what it was – had obviously finished. Pressing the red power button on the remote the screen collapsed in on itself to a white dot which disappeared. Levering himself upright he limped into the kitchen, looking down at the boot and thinking there was no way he was going to tolerate it for the full month. Setting his empty glass down on the counter, he looked through the sliding doors, out across the lake, the faint moonlight diffused by high cloud to give a glow to the late evening landscape. Frowning he approached the doors and slid them open, walking out onto the decking, sounding like some one-legged pirate from days of yore, approaching the balustrade, he squinted across the water to the trees at the far end of the lake. It was like one of those clever camera effects where there is one patch of bright colour on an otherwise monochrome image. An orange glow – a discreet ball of light – was visible through the trees. It must've been a fire, he could sense movement, getting bigger and smaller as if the flames were sometimes growing higher before dying back down. For the first time in his life, Gabe wished he had a pair of binoculars. He was too far away to spot anything else. Was he just being nosy, becoming a busy-body? Or was it worth having some real concern about a fire in some woods that really shouldn't be there. He wasn't sure at all why he did it, but knowing Tor was asleep he grabbed his keys and slid on a jacket and his old trainers, quietly locking the door behind him on the way out. Why is it whenever you try and be quiet, everything around you knows and turns its own amplifier up to eleven. The decking creaked, the car door closing could probably be heard in the next valley, and the engine turning over wouldn't have been out of place at Silverstone. He was relieved to be slowly driving away up the lane to the deserted main road. He'd had half a bottle of wine and a decent-sized measure of scotch, but at 11pm round here, he didn't think anyone would mind. There was now some comfort in the familiar winding and twisting, climbing and dropping of the road. He cruised past the place where the trunk had dropped on their first night, heading for the village after the turning for the pub. The road dropped into the base of the valley beyond the lake, and turned sharply right over the stone bridge over the stream, which rushed noisily over the rocks beneath and raced down through the village, away to Church Lane, and the main street where it ran by the hotel, where they'd stayed when they came to view Ty Llyn, and the one restaurant next door. Over the bridge the road turned sharply left heading down toward the streetlights and houses, all silent and still at this time of night.

At the apex of the curve, a narrow track led off into the darkness to the right, a sign – handwritten on a piece of plywood nailed to a tree – pointed along it with an arrow, indicating 'Willard's Farm'. Beneath this was a small sign from the water company quietly announcing that the 'Monitoring Station' was along the same lane. Despite having never noticed it when coming to the village before, Gabe knew the track must run along the bottom of the lake and so must be the closest road access to where he saw the fire, and instinctively wrenched the wheel to the right to take the turn, tyres squealing as they were asked to grip and make such a sharp turn, the rear wheels fighting hard not to slide on the loose shale at the start of the track. The lane was just that. A rutted farm road, with patches of tarmac which suggested a far more pleasurable driving experience once-upon-a-time, interspersed with hardcore where the top surface had been washed away, and some areas where muddy wheel ruts had to be negotiated. Even at twenty miles-an-hour he bounced around the passenger cabin and had to slow to even more of a crawl to prevent being battered senseless in his own car. Without streetlights, the road was pitch black, only illuminated by his headlights, now set at full beam. The road climbed gradually and snaked from left to right, bordered by low hedges separating it from the surrounding fields, their gates firmly closed to prevent the livestock getting out. Up ahead to the right was an open gate – the only one he'd seen – and he decided to take it. It might've been about level with where he'd seen the fire, it might not, but being open made it different to all the others, and worth investigating. The field was laid to grass and was growing to about a foot in length. From the gate, and along a narrow strip hugging the hedge, however, it was flattened down, all the way across the field. Gabe was clearly not the first to drive along here of late – maybe even tonight. There had to have been a number of vehicles – it wasn't one strip flattened but a general area. He bounced through another open gate at the far side and onto another track, which wound around a small copse then into another grass field, again with its gate invitingly open, sloping upwards to be bordered at the top by saplings and younger trees competing with bracken and ferns for light and space at the edge of the woods. He stopped the car and watched for movement up ahead in the beam of headlights. After a few minutes, having seen nothing at all, he killed the engine before grabbing the large torch from the passenger seat and climbing out into the chill air. Spotting a gap in the foliage that had been well-trampled, Gabe strolled under the overhead canopy formed from the increasingly dense planting of trees. The ground was flattened and muddy, the torchlight shining on a number of distinguishable boot prints that forensics would have a field day with. The forest was very different at night. By day it was like a giant pergola – a dense roof allowing light in at the sides like watching a widescreen movie on an old TV – darkness above and below. Strange and scary things had happened, but it wasn't, by definition, a scary place. Now, in the pitch black, the trees were indistinguishable from the gaps between, he would turn and immediately in front of him would be a huge trunk he hadn't noticed was there. It seemed like they were moving to block his way. Every noise was strange and foreboding – was that really the cry of a fox this time or was it the girl in the dress – the witch – back once again? He aimed his beam of light diagonally toward the ground and it illuminated a clearing about twenty yards in diameter, bordered by stately trunks, like faceless sentinels casting their shadow, creating hiding places, keeping their secrets.

She could be here. Right here. Hiding in the shadows. Waiting to pounce.

Although, from all he'd heard about Morvith, she didn't seem like a hiding in the shadows kind of gal.

He heard a noise up ahead. Freezing, his eyes searched the limit of the light, moving back and forth like an eagle-eyed Action Man, trying to peer further into the gloom – wishing he'd eaten more carrots as a child – that would've helped, or that's what his Gran had said. But eating all that cabbage hadn't put hairs on his chest either. Although only seconds past, he struggled to remember the noise he'd heard, maybe fear had driven it from his memory. *If he'd heard it at all*, he wondered. It had been a shriek and he found himself wondering what noises badgers make, and whether that could be the culprit. The rest of the forest had gone silent, awaiting the outcome or perhaps needing orders from *her*. As if she were waiting behind a tree to step out into the spotlight and sing a showtune.

Stepping forward again, into the clearing, the sentries remained at the edge, as guards watching over the glade. The remnants of the fire smouldered in the middle, wisps of smoke rising straight up in the still evening, a glow from the embers beneath slowly fading. The fire had been tall and well-fed, producing the flames he had seen from the house all the way across the lake. Now, without shadow, Gabe could sweep the torch around, seeing indentations in the grass and bracken at the perimeter of the clearing. Near to the dying fire, the torch illuminated a large box, made of clear plastic or glass, seemingly dumped there, leaning at an angle, green with algae on one side, and with ivy growing over the top. Slightly taller than it was wide or deep, it was about his height and had tiny airholes drilled high up, all the way around. On one side was what looked like a crack in the wall, but closer investigation revealed a thin line running the length and width of the plastic – a door. But machined with such small tolerance that there was almost no gap between it and the rest of the box. Hinges were made of the same material, as was the clasp. What was a clear plastic box doing out here in the middle of the woods? Was it something to do with the witch?

The containment facility. Idris had said the scientists had brought one with them to somehow capture her, and presumably had left it behind when they'd gone.

Turning away from the strange box, he found himself almost putting a foot in one of the impressions, oval shaped, the foliage compressed. It looked like a person had been lying or sitting on the ground, making the hollow. Counting them, there were twelve places where people had been. A dozen people, in this clearing, sitting or lying around a raging fire and this box acting like an altar maybe, near the lake where the witch might be.

What on earth had been going on here?

Another noise – a soft cry – came from beyond the treeline. Gabe looked up but was immediately less concerned than he had been ten minutes before. The evening couldn't get stranger than it had already. He took another sweep around, looking into every depression and kicking around the ashes of the fire, but seeing nothing else of note. Through the trees he could see the moon reflecting off the water, having shoo-ed away the cloud. The almost yellow disc reproduced perfectly in the mirrored surface. He became aware of the sound of running water – a stream draining into the lake perhaps, there must be a lot of those running off the hills round about, or maybe another overflow going in the opposite direction. The noise refocused him, brought him back to the here and now. The witch could be anywhere, and had every one of those twelve people left? Whomever the hell they were. What if someone was still around and waiting for him?

With a last pass of the torch around the clearing, Gabe slowly backed away, repeatedly looking over his shoulder to check behind him. He reversed up to a tree so he could clear the next section he had to walk and make sure it was safe, before finding another tree. It was like he was taking part in FBI training, bursting into each room with his gun drawn and clearing each corner before he could move on to the next.

Repeating this until he finally emerged from the trees and climbed into the welcome familiarity of the car, he immediately threw it into reverse and turned it around so he could bounce and jolt his way out of the field again. Continually checking his mirrors, although not sure what he was expecting to see, Gabe found his way back to the track and through to the first field, turning left onto the lane and back to the main road. As he headed for home, he didn't see the car following behind with no lights on, slowly making its way to the same bend in the road junction, turning onto the main road and heading back to wherever was home.

CHAPTER 30
-\/-
BRAKES

As Gabe joined the main road the heavens opened, the cloud must've come in over the hills as he drove back through the lanes – lucky he wasn't still out in it. He flicked the wipers on through normal speed to fast, the downpour and lack of streetlights meaning visibility was almost non-existent.

The road bent round to the left and climbed, widening into the fast, winding road that ran all the way back home.

Home. Is that really what it felt like? Not much more than a week of living somewhere and now it was their *home*. Would anywhere feel like home again without Mikey, without his laughter, his mop of unruly curly hair and his never-ending questions about life and science and poo and naval hair. There was a lot going through his mind as he drove, carefully and deliberately along the winding main road. Concentration on the tarmac ahead allowed his mind to drift and he mused on the clearing he had found and the fire across the lake.

Who were the people gathering in the clearing and lighting fires? Was it just local kids messing around, getting away from their parents? He hadn't thought about it at the time. Maybe it was. Maybe they'd come down there because they knew about the story of the witch and wanted to get as close to the lake as possible and tell scary stories. Maybe they'd got hold of some alcohol from somewhere and passed it around the fire and the couples would snuggle in and cop a feel as the stories rolled out. But there were twelve indentations – that's either twelve kids sitting apart or twelve couples, and there probably aren't that many kids round here of a similar age. And there was no rubbish. No empty cans and bottles or cigarette butts that he'd seen. There's no way that local kids would come down here to party and then clean up after themselves. No. It wasn't kids.

So, who was it? Some kind of cult? Druids or something. He thought about this for a moment as the road rose and fell around a right hander, and realised he knew nothing about druids.

The road up ahead straightened out and there were two humps about a quarter of a mile further on. The rain had stopped, the clouds clearing to allow some moonlight through and it shone on the wet road, making it glisten. In the middle of this was a dark patch, at the apex of the hill – Gabe thought it likely to be a patch of repaired road that wasn't holding the water – more porous maybe, or running off more easily. From this distance it looked like a shape. No, not so much a shape, like an amorphous mass, but a figure, standing in the middle of the road. Gabe peered into the night, his full beam headlights not quite reaching that far yet, still thinking what he was looking at was a mirage, smoke and mirrors, when it was a patch on the road. Until it moved.

Less than a hundred yards away the dark shadowy figure that was probably tarmac at the top of the small hill turned and faced him.

Eighty yards. He swore he could see arms raise up from the side of the person.

Sixty. The headlights were still not reaching far enough and Gabe started to get a bad feeling in the pit of his stomach. Lifting his foot off the accelerator he moved it steadily across to the brake and applied some gentle pressure.

Fifty yards. The woman was clearly illuminated in the lights now. She was dressed in the remains of a dark purple shift that contained several large dirty holes through which her grey dead skin could be seen.

Forty. Gabe applied the brakes with more vigour, wanting to slow down before he got to the witch, who raised her hands and seemed to throw them at him, as if throwing a spell – chanting a Latin name from a Harry Potter book, maybe. Later Gabe wouldn't be able to decide whether the car slid because he stood on the brakes too hard on the wet road or because of the spell. He didn't think he'd pressed on the middle pedal with too much pressure, but equally, the idea of the spirit of a witch casting spells to make him lose control of the car seemed infinitely more ridiculous, so he wanted to hang on to the idea of driver error. With a squeal of tyres, the back end started to slide out into the middle of the road and he turned the wheel into the skid, feeling like Lightning McQueen when Doc first takes him to the old race track. Steering into it did seem crazy, did seem like he was going to spin out of control or flip the car, and then there was the witch ahead of him – was he going to hit her, and what the hell would that mean if he did?

Thirty. Fighting with the wheel, the car sliding at a forty-five-degree angle along the tarmac, the witch staring straight at him, her face rotting and with one eyeball hanging down onto her cheek. He could see her sneer.

Twenty. The cars inexorable slide was going to take it right over the witch and Gabe was only a second or two from doing so. Ten. The skid was set in stone now and the passenger door collided with the unsuspecting spirit. Except there was no impact – nothing. He saw a purple colour flash before the window, then it was gone.

Zero. The wheels finally gripped the tarmac, screeching to a halt, the car lurching forward on the suspension, brakes steaming, a ticking noise coming from the now silent engine. Getting out of the car, which was angled across the middle of the road, Gabe looked around, the moonlight beaming in through the trees, the shine on the wet road. There was an empty spot where the witch had been standing. He half expected to see a smoking pair of shoes where he'd hit her, and she'd disappeared like the Wicked Witch of the West, but there was nothing but patched tarmac. Realising that the car, parked across the middle of the road, was a blatant hazard, he got back in and re-started the engine. Slowly pulling away and joining the right side of the road, he smiled to himself and shook his head.

What the hell just happened?

Shaking his head again his eyes were drawn across to the lake, to take in the moonlight, the shimmering of the glow on the water. The girl in the white dress was sat in the passenger seat, her soaking wet hair hanging down in ringlets around her face, dripping onto the material. She smiled at him, her eyes sparkling and alive. Gabe stared open-mouthed at her sitting next to him, never taking his eyes off her – wanting to reach out and prod her to see if she was real, if she had tangible form. She laughed then. Not a snide or sneering laugh, but one of joy and happiness, as if she always enjoyed car trips with Gabe and how he made her smile. He was transfixed by her, drinking her in, mesmerised. The steering wheel started to pull to his left, drifting off with the camber, falling off the road, and he quickly looked ahead seeing only trees before him in the headlights. Wrenching the wheel to the right, he tried the brakes, but had no traction, leaving him no option but to change down and put his foot to the floor. Complaining tyres scrabbled and screeched, stones skittering out from under them in all directions, being thrown up against the bodywork, sounding like hammer blows on the doors. The car continuing to drift off the road, creeping inch by inch toward disaster, but finally got some purchase as the road bled into the verge and dropped away into the brush of the forest. The front wheels clambered back up to the road but the back end of the car slid around in a cloud of dust and gravel. Wrestling one hand over the other he spun the wheel to counter the skid. Trees raced by at touching distance and it seemed only a matter of time before the rear wing clipped one of them, but finally all four wheels got some purchase and slid back onto the road, the car snaking wildly as he unwound the oversteer he'd used. Gabe realised they were just at the dip and left-hand bend where the branch had fallen into the road on their first night. He looked at the passenger seat and the girl in the dress had gone. She'd been replaced by the hag – the white dress was now filthy, grey and rotting, her hair was wild and wiry, sticking up and out in clumps. She looked at him with one eye, the other was steadily rolling down her face, past the ragged hole of a nose that her skull was visible through and down to the nearly toothless maw that moaned a sigh of death and decay to him. When she was the girl in the white dress, there had been a faint musty smell of lake water and wet clothing – like a wet dog – but now the hag stank of rotting flesh, decay and filth – so strong that he nearly gagged. The car dropped on the dip, and bounced at the bottom, veering across to the other side of the road before Gabe wrestled it to the left, screeching to a halt at the edge of the road. Turning to look at his passenger–

She was gone.

He reached, tentatively, across to the seat and found it dry – not wet and stained like it should be from his passenger – but as normal as he would expect from a normal day – without the psychopathic witch. Gabe eased back into his seat, allowing his breathing to return to as close a semblance of normal as he could remember.

Then headed home.

CHAPTER 31

ASHES

Tor had to stop herself from skipping past the barn, heading deeper into the woods, the white dress swirling around her, the movement and flow of air across her naked body beneath making her feel one with her surroundings. She wasn't sure about the bare feet, now becoming muddy and crusted with leaves and twigs like always – she thought she looked like a Hobbit would – but at least the mud layer made it less painful to walk without every stone and thorn sticking into her. And her feet had started to go numb from the cold so that was better. Why had she gone out there naked underneath? She wasn't sure – Morvith always expected her to be that way – how wearing underwear would make you less connected to a forest she couldn't explain, but as the breeze whistled around her, it did feel the proper way to be.. As one.

The witch appeared in front of her, her own dress as immaculately clean as usual, her feet not encrusted with the debris of the forest but clean and pristine. She smiled, her pale skin edging towards grey.

Did you bring it? Said the voice in Tor's head.

Yes, she thought, taking the small rucksack off her back, opening the flap and reaching inside to remove a small cloth bag and handing it over as she approached Morvith. Taking the bag, the witch turned and walked away, and Tor could see over her shoulder the Dead Tree in the distance.

Stopping near the gnarled and twisted root system of the tree, the witch squatted down, setting the bag on the ground next to her. She moved dead leaves and pine cones, scraping away leaf mold and moss until she had bared a dartboard-sized area of earth. Untying the bag and awkwardly loosening the string at the top with clumsy fingers, she poured the contents onto the soil, a pile of grey ash, whilst looking up at Tor with a smile. Walking crablike forward in her squat position, she hoisted her dress up to her hips, pale bare thighs spread, eyes never leaving Tor's, and Tor heard the unmistakeable sound of her pissing on the little pile of ash and bare soil. Standing again, her dress falling into place around her, she reached her hand out towards Tor who approached and they clasped their hands, forming a circle of two stood above the patch of soil.

Piss, said the voice in her head, the witch backing up her command with a nod. Leaning forward they balanced their foreheads together, looking down, the witch smelling of decaying leaves, soil and lake mud – the kind of smell that fills your nostrils on a forest walk on a Sunday afternoon. It was a natural smell, and not at all unpleasant, but in the background, there was something else. Something faint. Something unpleasant. As if you find the decaying corpse of an animal on your walk and the smell lingers in your nostrils no matter how hard you try to inhale the clean pine air. Their hands locked on each other's forearms and Tor tried to relax her bladder – feeling like this was totally normal to try and wet herself like this in front of another woman – and a random thought entered her head that thank goodness she hadn't worn any underwear. The first trickle of urine started to run down her leg – hot and stinging against her cold flesh, her face red with embarrassment. It ran down her thigh, threatening to run out of steam by her knee, to dry on her skin. Then another sensation – that of excitement. Here she was with a real live witch. *Live?* Doing something illicit, something bizarre, something that would probably get her locked up in the funny farm for a decent stretch, something that could best be described as practising witchcraft.

Witchcraft. And as the thought entered her head, and the smile grew on her face, the sense of excitement at the forbidden act took over and she let go, voiding her bladder, her urine cascading down the insides of her thighs in rivulets, racing down her legs to be the first to reach the ground. The hot fluid feeling like it was burning her cold skin as it continued to flow. Looking down between them she saw liquid appear on the witch's lower legs, rushing down to her ankles and feet, flowing onto the ground and into the small hollow she had just made, soaking the soil, making it black as it flowed, being met by her own fluid, flowing over each other, filling the hollow. Their eyes met and the witch's looked vibrant, alive, bright and glistening, her face lit up by her smile. The urine washed against the small pile of ash, eroding away at it, lapping at its edges, the sides slowly sliding into the liquid, making the pile unstable until it gradually collapsed into the steaming fluid, which frothed and roiled as if powered by an unseen current. The slurry started to bubble and boil and Morvith squatted again, streaks of urine drying on her legs, and covered over the puddle with leaves and an old birds nest. Then, taking Tor's hand, she took some steps back, and Tor had a random thought that they hadn't washed their hands, but then again, did they need to? The witch was chanting – a series of incantations under her breath, repeating, over and over, increasing in volume, the words, or whatever they were, easy to follow and repeat and she nodded at Tor when she started to join in. The women held hands, standing arms distance apart, swaying back and forth as if in some dance, chanting, the words echoing around the basin, bouncing back at them as if there were dozens more people in there repeating their words to them. The witch stared at the little pile of leaves and the tired old nest as she was shouting the words now, screaming them at the top of her voice, croaking as her throat could barely cope with the volume she was trying to reach. Then she stopped, frozen in place, eyes fixed on the pile, smile slowly developing on her face, her free hand pointing, beckoning as if encouraging something to happen. Tor didn't know what she was looking for, didn't know whether she was expecting to see something, didn't know how long this would take. And then, suddenly a shoot appeared from the pile of leaves – like the first fresh green shoot of spring. It appeared through a crack in the soil and sprang upwards, pointing to the canopy high above.

And it looked like a finger.

CHAPTER 32

-\/-

WATCHER IN THE WOODS

The track wound its way up the hillside, ruts and holes badly filled with hardcore making the car bounce, ensuring Gabe was creeping along like a soldier in stealth mode. Gabe had already passed the gate he'd gone through the previous night when he'd been looking for the fire. Or at least he thought it was the right gate – it all looked so different in the daylight and someone had shut it since then. So, someone had been out between the time he left and now to shut the gate? Or had the farmer passed by and noticed it open? He was certain he was starting to overthink things.

The track wound and levelled out, getting closer to the treeline, before merging with a better maintained lane – it was still a narrow country road, with no room for more than one car, but felt like the M4 in comparison to what he had been driving along. It climbed out of the valley on the west side of the lake, the high hedge on the right disappearing so he could see the water glinting on the lake below, as he threw the wheel sharply round to the left to continue his traverse up the hill. Several times the road switched-back on itself as it gained altitude, like one of those roads in Europe that the *Top Gear* boys go and test supercars on. Holes and cracks in the road surface were abundant, and the car juddered and was thrown up and down – *I like having visitors, but my road doesn't,* Yannick had said. Finally, it levelled out, although the hillside still extended above him, the lane widening into a parking area in front of a white-painted cottage, seemingly balanced precariously on a shelf cut into the hillside. The cottage looked drab in the shade it occupied for half the day, dampness surrounding it, rotting the few plastic plant pots that had faded or broken with time, still containing soil and the skeletal remains of long dead bushes or flowers. The paintwork had faded – dirty pebble dash showing through as the emulsion had eroded away. Yet the windows – crisp uPVC – looked new, as did the matching door. And whilst he was no builder, Gabe also thought the lead flashings and tiled roof were new as well. Someone took care of this place but didn't look after it. Barely had he wrapped firmly on the door with his knuckles before the door opened.

'Mr Hooper.'

'Gabe. Hello Yannick.'

'Don't get many visitors up here, so I am very pleased you came,' said the man who looked even more hunched over than he had on their first meeting a few days before. 'Please, come in.' Yannick turned and headed back into the dark cottage, leaving Gabe to show himself in. The front porch opened out into a spacious lounge diner, with an oval table that could easily sit eight people. Easily, that is, if you moved the computer keyboard, two laptops and half dozen screens all bolted to it in different ways. The screens showed graphs or scrolling numbers on specialist software or apps, the laptops were open to the more familiar Outlook emails and Facebook. A few dining chairs were scattered around, but a large padded chair with arms and a neck support sat in front of the workstation.

'Coffee, Gabe?' Yannick offered over his shoulder as he disappeared into the kitchen at the back.

'Yes, please. Thank you.' Gabe walked around the table after failing to work out what the graphs and numbers meant. He stood at the patio doors, offering a magnificent view of the lake, which emerged out of the shadow of the hill, tracing the far waterline up toward Ty Llyn, but the house itself was obscured by the tall trees growing on this bank. He could make out the slash in the treeline that was the main road – like a canyon in the desert, and a much smaller gap that demarcated the lane down to the house, but then the canopy blocked the rest of the view.

'You won't see your place – not from here. Not in daylight anyway,' Yannick called amid sounds of mugs being placed on worktops, water running into the kettle and a fridge door opening.

'No, I've spotted where it is, but a rather selfish tree has grown too tall for me to see over.'

'Trees, eh? You can make out the lights through them at night, though.'

'It's a fair walk down to ours that you did. What with the slope and all. Particularly if you…'

'Are as frail as me?' Yannick carried two steaming cups of coffee through to the dining table, his stooped form meaning he looked like he was about to put them down at any stage.

'That isn't what I was going to say.' Gabe pulled an apologetic face to show Yannick shouldn't be offended.

'You were. In some form or another.' His accent was thicker now. 'But that's okay. I appreciate the concern.' He finally did set the mugs down and pushed one, on its wooden coaster, across to Gabe. 'It's important to keep fit. Bones are piezoelectric, you know. They produce an electrical charge in response to stress – in this case, load. And that charge helps encourage bone cells to produce more bone. So, to keep my bones strong, I need impact loading like walking.' Yannick smiled, the science lesson over. 'But it is a fair walk down to your house, you are right.' He paused for a second, then changed the subject. 'I know I said you were welcome to visit – and you are, or course – but I suspect this isn't a social call, or your needing to borrow a cup of sugar..?' That smile again, before he folded himself even more in half and sat in his operators chair, which caught him with the whine of a leaky gas strut. 'Sit. Sit,' he insisted, indicating the dining chair next to him. 'No biscuits, I'm afraid. I'm not British enough to have some on standby on the off-chance I might have visitors.'

Gabe smiled and sat, taking up the coffee mug. 'You're right, it's not a social call. Sorry. I wanted to ask you about what you said when you visited us – the monitoring work that you did – the consultancy work, to keep an eye on things...'

'Yes.'

'It's my house isn't it? It's this whole lake? That's what you are monitoring.'

'Yes.' He nodded, waving his hand in the direction of the monitor screens.

'I've been thinking about that night at the house – we'd only just moved in a couple of days before. I was out on the decking – I'd seen something moving on the far bank but couldn't really make it out. I was concentrating so hard, but then I heard a twig snap beyond the car and on the edge of the woods. I wasn't imagining it, and I'm sure it wouldn't have been an animal, not as early in the night as that. It was you wasn't it?'

'Yes.'

'Crouching down and hiding.'

'Yes. Really played havoc with my knees and back, staying as still as that.'

'The witch.'

'Yes.'

'Is that all you've got?'

'What do you want, Gabe? Yes, it was me when you first got here. I wasn't spying on you, though. I think your removal lorry must've knocked over one of our motion sensors on the edge of the woods and I'd gone out to fix it. At one point you were standing about four feet from me and I had my handkerchief over my mouth to stop my breathing sounding wheezy.

'Motion sensors? Jesus.' Gabe shook his head, incredulous.

'You have to remember, I was here a long time before you were, doing this work. I'm sorry you've walked into this little government experiment, but that's where we are.'

'It was you, wasn't it?'

'Who, now?' As frail and bent as Yannick was, his eyes still had life and fire – were playful, as they were now.

'All those years ago, you were one of the scientists coming to monitor the witch that Idris told us about.'

'You don't want to take a lot of notice of Idris Dawson.'

'So you said. I'm right though, aren't I?'

'Yes. Yes, you are. I was... I am a government scientist. At the time I was involved in all kinds of secret projects but based in London. The army came in here to investigate the witch, but found nothing. Then, some enterprising middle manager decided that if there was a grain of truth in this, we needed to watch her, see what she did, how powerful she was.'

'In case she needed to be 'neutralised' or whatever the army would say?'

'Something like that. But then it became something more. If she had power, could it be used?'

'Like a weapon? Like a witch-inator or something?' Gabe was aghast at the thought.

'That was one of the things that was discussed – there were other scenarios as well. Anyway, it made sense to them to study her.'

'So, they built a bunker. Right next to where the stream runs over the small weir at the southern end of the lake?'

'Yes, you've been there. With Idris, no doubt. They sank a concrete room, ostensibly to monitor water flow and so on, but with a series of basic sensors – seismographs, temperature, movement – all hardwired in, running cables from all round the lake, with monitoring systems that were probably the forerunners of computers. Very basic. But we'd spend long hours in that bunker looking at those readouts.'

'He said it was already there and was better than a zinc shed. Spending all day in that thing - could drive anyone mad.'

'Yes, you have to have a special kind of patience and concentration. But we'd take it in turns to run a sweep to check the sensors, so some days you spent all day in there, some out and about.'

'I don't understand how they believed all this stuff, to go to the lengths that they did. Anyone says 'paranormal' these days and they get called crazy.'

'No, they don't. They get called crazy by their friends, or even the Press if they shout loudly enough. But there will be a government department somewhere who will make a note of it. And they'll start to keep an eye on them. They can't afford not to.'

'You're saying we have an X-Files department? I hope Scully is as fit as she was in the TV show.' Gabe shook his head.

'I'm saying there are some departments that keep an open mind. Imagine if we'd closed our minds out to splitting the atom, if Watson and Crick had been labelled as nutcases with their DNA work, if we'd said it was impossible to leave our atmosphere or land someone on the moon. Right now, they talk about a base on Mars in fifty years, and it's not Asimov anymore.'

'This is different.'

'How is it?' Yannick leaned forward in his chair, eyes wide, his posture making him look like he would pitch forward and land on the floor. 'Studies in Russia in the eighties proved that telepathy was possible.'

'Bullshit.'

'I've seen the results. Seen the data. Talked to the guys who ran the experiments.'

'If that was the case, why don't we know about it.'

'Because those guys aren't around anymore. I never saw them again after seeing their work. It'll have been moved 'in house' with the KGB. God knows what they've done since.'

'That was a long time ago, surely it would've got out?'

'We are only just finding out about the extent of athlete doping by the Russians, gender suppression, hormone treatments – all of those were done throughout the seventies and eighties. To win gold medals. To make them look better than the hated Americans. Why would we hear about something that had several levels more secrecy?' Yannick shrugged with his hands; his shoulders unable to. 'My guess is they can't control it.'

'*Stranger Things* more of a documentary then,' Gabe said with a shake of his head. The room was silent apart from the bubbling of the large fish tank on the wall, Gabe watched as Nemo wriggled in and out of an anemone and a larger fish with a blue throat drifted past on the current generated from the powerhead pumps at either end. 'They are still no further on with the witch, though?'

'What do you mean?'

'Well. You're still watching her – or computers are. They haven't come in and contained her, or dropped a bomb on the place.'

'I think they are biding their time.'

'To do what?'

'Above my pay grade I'm afraid. I'm just a watcher in the woods.'

'Just you? Are you the only one left? You said there were two of you before.' Gabe looked at him quizzically.

Yannick snorted and broke into a wide smile. 'There were two of us, yes. And did Idris tell you who the other one was?'

'No.' Yannick smiled again and nodded by starting the movement at his hips – everywhere north of that being fused stiff.

'Like I said. You don't want to believe a lot that that crazy old man tells you.'

'Why?'

'Because it was him.'

'Him what?' Confusion crossed Gabe's face.

'He was the other scientist.'

'What? It can't be he doesn't–'

'Look like a scientist?'

'Oh okay, but he said he'd always lived here.'

'And he has. He was doing some desk job somewhere local – Carmarthen, I think. They needed someone on the ground quickly. I was coming up from London – a geek who understood all the monitoring and sensors that we used back then. He was good with reports and a Welsh speaker, which is what they wanted.' Gabe just stared back at him as he tried to process all the things Idris had said since they'd met, and superimpose this new twist on it.

'But he's not working with you now.'

'No, thank God. We stopped using the bunker fifteen years ago, computers had far outstripped any technology in there – even with updated systems, your iPhone is probably more powerful than anything we had then. Idris left – retired – but they persuaded me to stay on. This place was needing a lot of work, so they took over that, and installed all my workstation here and remote monitoring systems.'

'If they can be monitored remotely, why do they need you?'

'Because then a removal lorry will knock one of the sensors over and need to be put upright again. There are two hundred and forty of them in these woods and your house.'

'In my house?'

'Don't worry, there's no webcam in your bathroom. But we can see infrared, audio, that sort of thing.'

'You can monitor our conversations?' Gabe looked aghast.

'Not inside – we'd need all kinds of clearances for that and we haven't got the evidence to justify it.'

'Well, that's more… reassuring,' Gabe replied, looking nothing of the sort. 'Idris said he'd never seen the witch.'

'Like I said, you don't want to believe all that crazy old man says. He's seen her plenty. He's probably told you that to throw you off, otherwise you'd be asking him a load more questions. He can deny everything and just seem like a fanatical historian or something. We don't need to find her; we need to find evidence of her.'

'And then what?'

Yannick shrugged in his way. 'I don't know. Again, it's above me.'

'And have you had more activity since we moved in?'

'Yes. A lot more. We can compare our sensors to baselines when nobody is living in the house – Idris will have told you how nobody stays there for long. And these are quite high. She's active.'

'Is that your evidence that you need?'

'Apparently it's still not enough.'

'Need a close encounter of the witchy kind, do you?'

Yannick snorted on his coffee and smiled. 'Yes! Something like that.'

∞ ∞ ∞

Yannick stood at the door watching Hooper turn the car around on the narrow ledge outside the cottage. They seemed a nice couple, and he was genuinely concerned about what might happen to them. About how they were being pawns in a wider game. As Hooper completed his manoeuvre, beeped the horn and slowly set off down the steep lane, Yannick's phone chirped in his pocket. Pulling the phone out he looked at a summary of the text message glowing on the screen.

London: Green Light

∞ ∞ ∞

Gabe stirred in bed, a dream at the edge of his recollection but no nearer. He moved his leg – the ankle feeling stiff under the weight of the bedclothes. He felt her small hand stroking him down below, occasionally, playfully drawing her fingernails along his member with great care. He murmured with appreciation. Her hand delved deeper, encircling his balls, the skin contracting at her touch, showing the first signs of his arousal. She stroked upwards again and grasped him, and he continued to grow in her grip. Her hand began to move up and down, slowly at first, making him start to rock his hips back and forth in response, but then faster, with greater urgency.

Suddenly she was astride him, lowering herself down, taking him all the way inside her, grinding her hips hard down against his, beginning a rhythm that rapidly increased in speed and urgency. She reached back and down, fingers encircling his balls once more, fingernails gently pressing against his flesh. Her other hand took one of his, and held it firm against her breast as she rode him harder, his breath catching in his throat as his arousal reached its peak. He was almost at the point of no return when he felt her fingernails dig into his delicate flesh. There was sharp pain, but he let it go, not wanting to spoil the moment – he'd discuss her newly discovered *50 Shades* tendencies with her later. He threw his head back on the pillow as the waves of pleasure rolled over him and her fingernails dug in hard, penetrating through the skin, scissoring left and right, opening up deep wounds within his flesh. He screamed in pain and she rode him even harder, his cock undiminished as it approached the finish line. She dug one final time and as his balls contracted, as his manhood spasmed inside her she twisted her claw like hand and ripped the sack away from his perineum. The pain was unbearable and he opened his eyes for the first time to see, in the gloom of the moonlight, not his wife astride him once again, but a wizened hag with papery skin and thinning wisps of hair, sagging breasts and a wicked sneer on her face. She brought her hand round, the hand holding his severed testicles, still twitching from their final spurt, allowing the blood to cascade from them down onto her sagging chest and abdomen. She leaned forward and screeched at him as she brought her hand to her mouth and kept eye contact as she ate his balls.

∞ ∞ ∞

He woke with a start and a gasp, his body drenched in sweat, the same pale moonlight peering in through a gap in the curtains. Tor lay still beside him, turned on her side, breathing softly. Instinctively he reached down to check his nether regions - all was present and correct. And working okay it seemed he thought, somewhat ashamed as he felt his dwindling erection, but nothing else this time.

CHAPTER 33

YOU THINK YOU KNOW SOMEONE

Gabe pulled on the handbrake and turned off the engine, looking through the windscreen at Idris' dilapidated bungalow, noticing a thin wooden trellis hanging off the wall, with a long-dead climber helping it to resist Isaac Newton's discovery. By the time he was halfway to the door, the old man was standing waiting for him. Today Idris hadn't even bothered with a shirt, and his brown elastic braces were stretched across a string vest.

'I put the kettle on, Mr Hooper,' he said, genially.

'Thank you. A cuppa would be nice.' Gabe smiled as he was invited in, hanging his jacket on the coat stand.

'Mrs Hooper, okay?' Gabe had become used to the old man's mutterings but this one was so quiet that he wondered for a moment if he'd spoken at all, or had rather projected his thoughts.

'Well, that's one of the reasons why I'm here.' Gabe sat in familiar position at the breakfast bar as Idris pottered around the kitchen making their tea.

'Oh?' Idris replied absently as he poured water into the pot, making the tea bags float.

'She's not been herself.'

'Under the weather, eh? Bugs going around in the village so they say. Andy Thomas, the butcher, said his wife coughed so hard the other day she nearly shi–'

'She's not ill.'

'I thought you said she had been.' Idris looked confused as he hefted the china teapot.

'No, she's not been herself – ever since we've been here, really. We'd only been here a couple of days and went for a walk. We saw this woman in a white dress.'

'The witch,' Idris replied with a nod.

'So, it is her?' Gabe sipped his tea, eyes widening slightly at the matter-of-fact way they'd decided it was the witch.

'I would imagine so. There've been reports of a girl in a white dress, and she was known to wear one round here… back then.'

'Tor bought a dress just like it.' Gabe said, watching Idris for a reaction. Something wasn't quite right. He couldn't put his finger on it, but the old man was being strange with him. 'She hardly seems to take it off.' The old man looked up, only briefly, but it was enough to make Gabe push harder. 'She wears it to go off into the woods, every day, to find her, to walk with her.'

'With Morvith.' Idris nodded. It wasn't a question.

'Yes.'

'Hmmph.' Idris snorted.

'Does that strike you as odd?' Gabe raised his eyebrows.

'It does and it doesn't.' The shoulders beneath the string vest shrugged and looked oddly to Gabe like onions in a net bag.

Exasperated by the straight bat that Idris was playing, Gabe decided to change tack. 'I saw a fire on the other side of the lake, the night before last.'

'Oh?' Idris poured the tea into two mugs, as if he were barely aware of the conversation.

'I drove round to investigate.'

'Uh-huh.' He slid a mug across the counter.

'Did you know?'

'Know what?' Idris looked up with a scowl.

'Did you know that I'd gone there?'

'Why would I do that?'

Gabe shook his head. 'Here's what I think. I think it was you and your cronies up at the clearing the night before last, doing whatever, lighting a fire, toasting marshmallows for all I know. And I suspect that you know I was up there. When I drove by the place to see Yannick yesterday, the gate that led to the woods was shut, and I was the last person to leave. So, someone closed that gate. And then Yannick told me all about you. All the things you didn't mention.'

The old man pursed his lips, took a sip of his tea and pulled a face, appearing to make a decision. 'A few of us go up to that clearing – it's as near as we can fathom to where she hides away.'

'A few of you?'

'Yes. Why?'

'There were at least a dozen places where the grass was flattened and people had been sat – more if they'd been in couples. That's a lot more than a few of you.' Gabe's anger was palpable.

'Sounds about right.' Idris smiled back at him.

'So why say a few?' Gabe looked exasperated.

'Because why should I give it all to you on a plate. Work it out for yourself.' Idris folded his arms across his chest, shutting up shop. 'You seem to be coming up with some answers yourself.'

'So, she's a real thing then?'

'What?'

'You said you went to that place because it was as near as you could get to where you think she hides away.'

'Yes, that's right.'

'So, she's a real thing then, not a ghost or a spirit, or something that you've never seen.'

'I still haven't seen her – that's the truth.'

'But others have.'

'Enough, yes.'

'How is it you all believe in her?'

'Self-preservation.'

'Now I don't follow.'

'We want to appease her, keep in her good books, so we worship her once in a while. Pay deference.'

'But why do you need to do that, you don't live at the house?'

'Do you think a spirit as powerful as her, can only cast it over the Lake House? She could come for any of us, she could just as easily visit me or anyone in the village.' Idris' eyes were on fire with fear and passion.

'So, you keep her onside?'

'Something like that, yes.'

'And it's practically the whole bloody village up there? All those people that chided you in the pub for mentioning her are up there in your little circle.'

'Most of us believe and know what we have to do.'

'And you play your games for the strangers, the new people and whomever, playing coy and dumb so you're the only crazy one.'

'They didn't like it when I mentioned her to you on that first night. But you seemed like nice people and I thought it only fair to give you a warning.'

'Well, I suppose I should say thanks. And it's the same folk, the people of this valley that keep her secret.' Gabe wasn't asking – he shook his head and smiled.

'Sometimes we get others visiting us.' Idris spoke quietly, as if to himself. Gabe wondered if he raised his voice any more, someone might hear.

'Visitors? As in, visitors who know why they are coming?'

'Yes.'

'Didn't find you on Trip Advisor?'

'I don't know what that is.' Idris pursed his lips and gave a small shake of the head.

'How do they know? How do people find you?'

'It's all on the web – I only do it a bit myself.' He shrugged as if he was disconnected from the whole process.

'What's on the web – you're not advertising as a holiday destination?'

'Clues. Facts. Stories. There are plenty of people out there in'erested in ghosts and witches – paranormal things. They do their research, they look around, they put together the evidence – there are a lot of pieces by all accounts, and sometimes they get as far as the witch. They dig a little deeper, find out more about what power she had, who she is and where, and then the folks turn up.'

'Why would they? What would attract them about her power?'

'There are some who are a bit crazy – modern witch hunters, I spose. They kick around for a bit then leave.'

'And what about the rest?'

'They come because they might want healing – to see if she could help.' Idris looked up and made eye-contact with Gabe, for the first time since they had been talking about the clearing.

'They think that the witch might not only find them but heal them as well? And all this is online?' Gabe was incredulous, shaking his head.

'Like I say it's hidden, but if you are used to researching this stuff, and you follow the clues… We get a few people a year.'

'And has she… healed them, I mean?'

'Not that I know of, no.'

'I can't believe people come to try to get help from a dead witch.'

'Be careful what you say, Mr Hooper,' said Idris, his voice stern. 'People do this because they are desperate. They've exhausted every avenue, but maybe there might be one more option they can try. Just maybe.'

'Do you think she would, you know, potentially help people?'

'I dunno. You're asking the wrong person. But they don't just come wanting to be healed. Sometimes they want… other things.' He hissed the last few words as a whisper through gritted teeth, keeping his voice quieter still, so Gabe had to strain to hear him.

'What other things?' Gabe asked, fear starting to creep over him, as if his adrenal glands knew something he didn't. He was coming out in a cold sweat.

'If you've found out enough about her – like the stuff in my chest – then you know what she can do. Sometimes they want… darker things.' The old man's chin was on his chest, his breathing slow and rasping. It was almost as if he was talking to himself, narrating an episode of *Quincy* or *Murder She Wrote*.

Gabe's heart was beating faster and getting tighter in his chest, but he couldn't for the life of him work out why. 'I don't know what you mean about darker things – black magic or curses or something?' Gabe looked intently at the old man, seeing him almost shrivel before his eyes, become older and more bent, before he finally lifted his head from his chest, his eyes mournful, on the edge of tears.

'Like bringing back the dead,' he said, and lowered his head once more. Gabe heard him, of course, processed and understood what Idris meant. But then slowly, as the icy tendrils of fear climbed up his arms and circled down across his abdomen, squeezing around to caress his balls with their chill fingers, he began to realise.

'You're not talking about…' Gabe's mouth was quivering and it was his turn to have tears in his eyes. The old man didn't look up, his nod almost imperceptible.

'She came to me,' he said quietly.

'When?' Gabe's voice was cracking.

'About three months before you arrived. She knew as much as anyone outside of this valley. Knew what Morvith's power was.'

'And you told her more?' His voice grew more shrill.

'I answered her questions, Mr Hooper, that's all. If someone is just curious – a flight of fancy – then there won't be enough answers here for them. But if they un'erstand, if they know who she is, can appreciate the…'

'Psychology?' Gabe offered.

'Aye, that. If they know all of those things, then they will know the right questions to ask. I guess I helped make up her mind.'

'Jesus, you think you know someone.' Gabe got up, rushing from the room, pausing at the door to take one more look at the wizened old man crumpled in his chair, before racing for the car. He reversed down the loose gravel, spinning the car into a U-turn and engaging first to roar away, like in a movie. Barely pausing at the bottom of the lane to bounce onto the main road, Gabe floored the accelerator, the chassis and body panels of the car groaning as he wrestled the wheel round – trees rushing by in front of him, seemingly right in front of his face as he turned the car onto the tarmac, the back end managing to hang on and then roar up the road, gathering speed. Gabe threw the car left and right around corners, changing gear like a racing driver to get back on the power again and keep his speed. The car screeched around the corner and almost took off on the tree-trunk dip, the whining tyres gaining some modicum of traction, blue smoke coming from the nearside front as it fought to hold on to the loose tarmac at the edge of the road, Gabe struggling with the wheel, spinning it as he overcorrected coming out of the corner. Changing down he gunned the engine, their driveway entrance in sight, maintaining his speed and only braking at the last moment, hand on the handbrake in case he couldn't get around, the heel of his hand spinning the wheel, for a moment sliding the car sideways, wondering if his car would slide or roll if he pushed it too hard, before the tyres gripped and he roared down the gravel of the lane. The noise inside was deafening as chippings scatter-gunned the underside of the body work, dashing chips of paint off on both sides. Drifting round the bends, he skidded to a stop in a hail of gravel, dust and smoke from the brakes. Gabe barely registered the smell of burning brake shoes as he rushed into the house. By the time he reached the bedroom, he knew Tor wasn't home, the white dress, permanently hanging on their wardrobe, was gone so he knew she must be out.

In the spare room, he pulled out a concertina file containing their house paperwork from the shelving unit and started rifling through the sections. The back half of the file was all about the house, the survey, the searches, land registry, solicitors and estate agent's letters. He flicked through the compartments, further and further back. In the last one he found printouts from the internet. Names and lists of 'cunning folk', stories and biographies of some, printouts from websites detailing the history of several witches. But the majority of the information was about their witch.

She knew all along.

She'd come here to find the witch. And it seemed in all likelihood, to see if she could bring Mikey back. And now she was out there, looking for her.

CHAPTER 34
– THEN –
PROPOSAL

Morvith took to attending at Ty Llyn on a daily basis, checking and re-applying treatments, monitoring the boy's response and watching the Master's despair, yet still dragging him into the bedroom after applying whatever herbs she thought of to the boy. After a week of no improvement the Master asked her to accompany him in a walk on the beach.

'He is no better,' the Master stated simply – an unavoidable truth.

'No.' Morvith walked with head bowed.

'The herbs have never worked for him. We must try something else.'

'There is nothing I know, Master,' she said, contritely.

'Yes, there is,' he said quietly, almost to himself, his hands shoved deep into the pockets of his maroon jacket.

'Master?'

He turned on her, pushed her against the toad rock by the shore, his hands on her shoulders, pressing her against the cold damp stone. 'You are one of the cunning folk, are you not? Not a woman versed in herbs or remedies, but a user of… darker things.' His hand slid around her throat and squeezed. She said nothing. 'Can you use darker powers to help him?' Fingers tightened on her windpipe.

'Yes.' The tightness of his fingers eased, but his angry face was still close to hers. 'But it is not allowed.'

'What isn't?'

'The things you ask, Master.' He grabbed her dress in his other hand and yanked her towards him, dragging her back up the beach toward the house, her feet scrabbling to get any purchase on the shingle. Pulling her up the stone steps that climbed from the beach and scrub and gorse that held the forest back, long before the decking overlooked the water, they burst in through the door, the Master releasing Morvith and walked briskly across the kitchen to the dresser. He picked something up from the counter top and tossed it between his hands.

'Perhaps you can explain this. My housekeeper found it whilst changing my bed.' He flicked his wrist and the object he'd been playing with flew through the air and skidded across the table, sliding toward the girl. She looked down and saw it was a crude figurine, with arms stretched wide and legs together, looking a little like a crucifix. The figure was red because it was wrapped in the cloth that had mopped up the master's nose bleed the previous week. It was very obviously a charm, and the master had found it tucked under his mattress. 'She found a split in the mattress, and was about to effect a repair when she found something hard tucked inside. This… magic.' Morvith stared at him, head slightly bowed, watching him, mouth curled into a thin, knowing smile. 'Morgan continues to get worse. His heart hammers in his chest. His body wastes – his skin stretches across his bones like a drum. And while he lay stricken, all you were interested in was having your way with me. You 'charmed' your way into my bed.' The master shook his head, tears in his eyes.

'You did not seem to object at the time, as I recall, my Lord.' The smile still played at the corner of her lips, giving a mocking curtsey. Then her head tilted to one side, as if she were a bird of prey eyeing a mouse. 'My charm is but a guide – a map to steer the lost – it does not have the power to force someone to do something they do not wish to do.'

'Yesterday, I received a visit from Eiddwen – a friend of yours. She was troubled by something and needed to unburden herself.'

Morvith didn't reply.

'She told me that it was you that were the cause of his illness. That… somehow you made Morgan ill to get close to me.'

'And did it not work, Lord? Have we not been… close?' Her smile broadened, seemingly unconcerned about the accusations he was levelling at her.

'This charm, these actions, girl, are your death warrant – you know what a magistrate will do. So, once where I was yours, now you are mine.'

It was only then that Morvith realised that Griffiths, the carriage driver, was standing immediately behind her. With a nod from the Master, he grasped her upper arms firmly in his big hands. 'Restrain her in the cellar,' the master said. 'You will find a table down there, with your equipment, where you may continue to work to cure my son. You will remain there until Morgan has recovered.' The master, at times broken with despair over his son, or meekly subservient to her charms, was hard and firm now. He nodded to his man once again who picked Morvith up, tucking her under one arm and carried her down the wooden steps into the cellar. A table had indeed been prepared along one wall – the storage larder of cured meat, cheese and bread now moved to the other side – in days before it was a coal bunker. A chain was bolted to the wall in the corner, attached to a metal collar, and, holding the struggling woman, Griffiths attached it around her neck. He stepped back as she came at him, all nails and teeth, and she reached out to slash at his face and arms, the chain tightening, jerking her head back, so he remained safely out of her reach.

'Oh, you're a nice one,' he said, then turned and left her there as he climbed the steps, shutting out all the light when he closed the door at the top.

∞ ∞ ∞

The Master returned for her the next morning. Steadily descending the steps to avoid a fall and finding Morvith huddled in the corner, her dress filthy and ripped in places.

'I trust you had a pleasant evening?' he asked, a look of distaste on his face. She glowered at him from the corner. Freeing her from her restraints, he gently assisting her up the steps, seating her at the traditional farmhouse table and offered bread and cheese to eat. 'Have you given my request some consideration?' he asked, brightly, as if he hadn't kept her captive overnight in a cellar.

'I have, Master,' she emphasised this to sound particularly deferent. 'But I have two conditions.'

'I am not sure you are in a position to strike bargains, but, do go on.' He frowned and folded his arms.

'If I cure the boy, no more will be said about this, and I will be free to go.' It wasn't a question.

The Master stared at her, lips pressed together in a thin line, considering her proposal, then nodded.

CHAPTER 35

THE MASTER OF TY LLYN

As the afternoon wore on, Gabe grew increasingly frustrated and annoyed. He wanted Tor to get back so he could have it out with her. She had betrayed him, planning to move here all along – maybe even waiting for it to come onto the market before she 'found' the place and showing it to him. And when it was all new and exciting and video viewings on estate agents websites, and doing research on the local area to find out what was around, Gabe was sucked into the beauty, the tranquillity, how it might help them start again, and move on with all the right memories of Mikey, when, in reality, it was all arranged for her to try and bring Mikey back from the dead with the help of the witch. From pacing around the house, Gabe decided to move outside, marching across the driveway, trampling the ferns at the edge of the forest and then on through the trees, eyes scanning as far ahead as he could, as low cloud and mist rolled in off the lake, dropping the temperature. Between the trees up ahead, he saw a figure. Not like when they'd first encountered Morvith in the woods and she darted between the trees in her dress. This was in the distance, at the edge of the gloom, like some old cine footage of bigfoot that you can barely distinguish. But there he was, a little boy, walking stiffly through the trees, awkwardly scrambling over rotting tree trunks like he had no joints in his arms or legs, an unruly mop of dark hair plonked on his head. The gloom seemed to close around him like he'd been wrapped up in a dark blanket – the light was fading fast, and soon he'd be crashing around in the dark. And then, just like that, the boy was gone – gobbled up by the encroaching darkness, swallowed by the fingers of the night.

Gabe froze.

As if he'd seen a magic trick of someone disappearing, now he needed to see them reappear, to check they were okay, and that something bad hadn't happened. Let someone have their 'ta-da!' moment, but bring the boy back. He took a couple of steps forward, but stumbled over a tree root, unseen in the dark, jarring his ankle in the boot, and reached out to get the support of a bark-covered neighbour. There was no sense in going any further. With a final look, he turned back for the house, the security lights illuminating a safe and welcoming circle around their house. Tor was still out there, unless they'd missed each other and she was already at home. But what to say to her?

Emerging from the treeline, he turned to look back into the woods, expecting a wall of darkness. Mist hung between the trees like a cotton wool curtain. It should've been pitch black but there was some light coming from somewhere – was the moon out, shining a watery light down, or was it the fog itself emitting a phosphorescent glow? Either way the lights from the house weren't the only thing cutting through the darkness tonight. He heard a noise up ahead – a hard sound, like metal on metal, and it seemed to be getting closer.

The witch appeared out of the gloom, the mist parting as if on cue for her to scuttle through, from out of the undergrowth, legs twisted so that she walked sideways like a crab, upper body arched backwards and up, raising her head up to his eye level.

'It's a pleasure to see you again, Master.' She tilted her head on an angle, rotted flesh of her face unable to contain the eye which once again fell out onto her cheek, with a degree of gruesome familiarity. Her wild hair jutting out in crazed angles like matted dreadlocks.

'I'm not your Master. We don't know each other.' Gabe replied, trying to stay calm, the creature just ten feet away from him.

'You are the Master of Ty Llyn, yes?' she asked, fire in her one eye.

'I'm the owner, yes.'

'Then you are the Master.'

'What do you want?' Gabe raised his arms out to the sides in anger and exasperation. She gradually inched closer on her crab legs, her head moving sideways like a hawk. With a sucking and squelch of tissue, her neck started to stretch, growing longer as skin was pulled taught and joints popped as it grew, her head slowly pulling away from her body assessing her prey from a higher vantage point. The Witch's head teetered on top and stared down it's nose at Gabe who returned her gaze, horror struck.

'The Master of Ty Llyn,' she said, her head sometimes lolling backwards almost comically on her neck, as if the overstretched sinews and muscles could no longer control it, blue-grey tongue hanging grotesquely out of her mouth. Looking like someone starting to fall asleep on their couch, their head dropping and catching again as they started to wake, before repeating the process.

'What?' Gabe said, not needing to shout now she was so close.

'I want, the Master of Ty Llyn… in exchange for his boy.'

'What boy? Mikey? This is a fantasy you've spun my wife to, fucking, brainwash her or something. It's not possible. Mikey is… dead.' The last word caught in his throat, and his voice cracked as he spat the word at her with as much venom as he could muster.

'You look… spellbound.' The witch enjoyed her little joke, face cracking into a semblance of a smile which faded as quickly as it had come. 'I brought him back. I found him – I know how to find people between this world and the next. You get to know how over… time.' Her voice was the sound of granite scraping across granite – ancient, the words came but it was as if he'd always known them. 'He's here. He can live.'

'This isn't Pet fucking Sematary! He's dead.' Gabe turned his back on her, meaning to go back to the house, to shut the witch out and somehow hope that Tor could come to her senses and return home. There'd be no point trying to look for her if the witch didn't want him to.

'He's here.' The voice was soft and almost gentle now, echoing through the trees – none of the harsh screech of before. 'Want to see?' Gabe stopped, still facing the house. Part of him wanted to carry on walking, not wanting to see what trickery this was, to refuse to take part in her games. But part of him had to see. His heart beating wildly in his chest. This could be that moment, that one defining point in his life where he would always think, *what if*? He wrestled with his thoughts for the eternity that was a few seconds then turned back to face her again. The little boy he'd seen from a distance in the woods was standing next to the witch, with Tor on the other side, both holding his hands. Gabe stared at him.

It's not Mikey.

He was wearing the same red coat he always did when they went out in the woods.

It's not Mikey.

Blue wellington boots he always splashed around in in puddles in the back yard.

It's not Mikey.

The shock of unruly, dark curly hair on his head that may well be able to accommodate the birds should they wish to nest in it again next year.

It's not Mikey.

The little face turned up towards him, big blue eyes like saucers, as they so often were in wonder and surprise at the world around him – the intricacy of a snail shell, birds flying in tight formation, how all the leaves knew to fall at the same time in exquisite team work.

It's Mikey.

He bent and looked more closely at the boy. His skin was a somewhat pale grey-brown – the skin of a boy with terminal cancer. Except it wasn't skin, it was rutted and grooved, lined with cracks and whorls. Mikey's face was made of bark. All contoured and curved to look like a jigsaw of a human face – Mikey's face, with every freckle in place – but bark all the same. The same silver grey as the Dead Tree – the seat of power for the witch – and Gabe wondered if it was bark from that tree that had 'made' him. His birds nest hair really was a birds nest, twigs and moss and feathers and straw all interwoven – not intricately like some nests, but haphazardly, disorganised, thrown together to see what stuck and then plonked on his head like the worst fitting toupee in history.

Gabe's eyes had grown accustomed to the darkness, and he could see the boy better, his big blue eyes were expressionless – glazed over with nobody home – his body slightly slumped and arms hanging limp at his sides, like a puppet whose strings have become slack. Now, having decided that this figure – despite being obviously built from the very forest around them – was his long dead son, somehow Gabe didn't notice these things, glossed over them, seeing all the things that were his son, not all the things that weren't, or that had changed.

'Mikey?' He took a step forward, forehead furrowed with a frown, his face a mass of confusion, reaching out a hand toward the boy that looked like his son.

The boy that looked like him? What the hell was that about – it either was or it wasn't.

Mikey stared straight ahead, not offering any acknowledgement.

'Mikey. It's… Dad.' Gabe's eyes filled with tears that spilled over and rolled down his face, barely stopping at his jaw before jumping off into thin air. Tor, her white dress muddy at the bottom, smiled and looked on. Mikey did turn towards him, but his eyes were vacant, glass like a doll's – empty and devoid of anything like joy or humanity or hope. His mouth opened – not a voluntary movement, but it fell, crooked to one side, saliva drooling out down his chin and onto his jacket lapel. Tears pouring down his cheeks, Gabe had to stop himself from reaching forward to wipe it away. Like any dad would.

CHAPTER 36

NOT TAKING NO FOR AN ANSWER

23rd November 2019

Gabe's eyes opened and he took a minute. The room came back to him along with the reality of who he was. Reaching up to rub his eyes, his fingers touched wet traces on his cheeks and he realised he'd been crying. The bedroom was still and quiet – moonlight seeping through the curtains creating a familiar glow. At first, he was relieved that he didn't have a hag in a white dress riding him and about to rip his balls off. *Yes. Always a relief to find that when you wake up.* Then he remembered the dream, remembered the witch and Mikey's face, shuddering at the reality of it all. But more particularly, he didn't remember going to bed that night. He and Tor had argued – Morvith and Mikey had melted off into the forest, leaving the two of them. Tor was covered in mud and scratches, being non-committal about her whereabouts or activities. He hadn't wanted to push her. Despite the strangeness of the witch or haunting or whatever it was that was happening to them, they'd been getting on better than they had since… And he despite her weird behaviour, he didn't want to spoil anything else – didn't want the wheels to come off (again), so he hadn't pushed her. And he hadn't pushed her about Mikey, either. That was for tomorrow. A new day. A normal day. One where kids made of bark didn't come back from the dead. It wasn't for darkness and foreboding and a pitch-black forest.

He gradually became aware of tension and discomfort in his lower belly – he needed the bathroom. Cursing the extra couple of glasses of wine before bed, although certainly useful for calming the nerves, he shook his head and slowly swung his legs over the side of the mattress. Perhaps this was the shape of things to come, approaching middle age and old man's bladder. As quietly as a creaking bed and a half-asleep man can muster, he padded off down the hallway into the bathroom to void the remains of the cabernet sauvignon.

Never one to concern himself with aim in the middle of the night, he sat and emptied his bladder. And whilst his ability to understand the physics of fluid dynamics, trajectories, and the parabolic curves from dick to toilet bowl were not at their zenith at 3a.m., his brain was perfectly capable of wondering, going off for a wander around the loft that was the back of his mind, kicking over some boxes and dusting off some cobwebs.

Until it found, Mikey. The kid did like to play in his brain-loft these days. It was disconcerting – upsetting even – having him there, doing his own thing, building the final stages of 'Mousetrap', which he loved, or putting together the wooden train set they so painstakingly used to build on the living room floor, to then not be played with, gather dust and be tripped over repeatedly until Tor made them put it away a few days later. It was the *building*, you see, not the playing with. Like Lego.

Don't mention Lego, however, or that will be the rest of the day gone.

But Mikey was there, as he always was, and, as hard as it was, Gabe wanted him to stay. At least he knew where he was and could shut down and go and see him whenever he wanted. He kept him here where he was safe, close by so he never had to let him go. It wasn't like his brain was this idyllic playroom, full of all the toys in the world, where every day was Christmas and where Mikey was joyfully playing with puppies and chasing balloons around. It was the loft from the old house. A dusty, dark attic only illuminated by a bare lightbulb at one end, and a Velux window at the other. The central part was boarded out and all of Mikey's toys and games were there – that's where they played. They'd done it once in real life – Mikey loved to go up into the loft with Gabe, eyes like dinner plates at the wonder and excitement of it all – pipes, and loft insulation, old cardboard boxes for telly's that had long since gone caput, and a set of golf clubs that every loft in the country seems to have, but with no real knowledge of how they got there. He'd found all his old stuff that one time, and sat on the floor playing with Duplo and Bob the Builder toys. Gabe had told Tor that he'd taken all Mikey's toys to the dump, but he hadn't, he'd just put them up there, to go and visit whenever he wanted to, that Tor would never find as she never came up here. It was like an illicit porn collection. In the brain loft he had access to everything he'd ever owned. But there were other things here as well. Things sat in the corner, in the dark, as hidden from the lightbulb or window as they could be, but lurking in the shadows, ready to pounce, to reach out and grab and never let go. In the far corner was the cancer monster, a hideous Michelin-man type thing, sat hiding, wedged between the floor and slope of the roof. It was bigger every time he looked, and it never took its eyes off Mikey; drool dripping onto the rolls of fatty tissue that was its body. In another was a hole, a spinning, turning black hole, drawing in every element of hope, joy and light that there might be in that place – the fulcrum of his grief. There were days when he went there specifically to feel it – a need, a masochistic desire to have that pain in his heart, to feel himself dropping. The despair would wash over him, like he was drowning, giving him the darkest thoughts he could have. The ones where he wrapped the car around a tree, or drove it off a cliff, descending into a pit that he somehow always managed to drag himself out of. He didn't know why he went there – it certainly wasn't his happy place, and it was something that always wrenched at him, sent him spiralling, sucking him toward that black hole. But that was where Mikey was, and that was all that mattered.

Mikey.

What was he to think about that? She'd clearly bought this house in the misguided view that this witch, this ancient spirit had enough magical power – *am I even thinking this,* he thought – to bring him back. Perhaps it was *Pet Sematary* for humans. But he'd seen him. He'd seen a boy of Mikey's age, that looked just like Mikey, and dressed like Mikey. But it definitely wasn't Mikey. He suddenly thought of the Frankenstein story and the myth of it – that you could bring someone back bodily in some way or another, but you couldn't bring back the essence of who they were. Their spirit. *Their soul.* Was he really thinking about the version of Mikey he'd seen as something out of Frankenstein? His own son – regardless of how much of a bastardised version of him that it was – it was unmistakably Mikey.

But Mikey was dead.

And not just dead, but long dead. Dead and gone, burned away to ashes and stored on their mantel piece. In his mind, his boy was close to him, but in reality he was too, in the little urn in which they'd brought him home from the crematorium. The one that stayed with them, that their friends thought was a bit odd, and why don't they go and scatter them – scatter *him* – somewhere nice, like at the park or the beach or somewhere? But then they wouldn't have him, he wouldn't be near to them, and now that they'd moved, he would be miles away and they couldn't be close to him again. Gabe realised, for the first time, just how absolute – how all-consuming – his grief was. The Michelin blob was in his head, not Mikey's, and was eating away at him – not in the same way, but it still was – hollowing him out. For Tor, it had been external, obvious how she'd struggled. It had been almost impossible to support her, to get her through and, whether it was a good idea or not, he had internalised all his feelings. Tor had thought him cold or unfeeling, but it was never that. He couldn't afford to let go, to run outside and scream, scream until he was hoarse at the injustice of it all. He couldn't let Tor see that because he had to be strong for her. But because of that, he couldn't let Mikey go. He had to have him – to cradle him, like he did when he was a little baby, to cradle him when he died. And now maybe they could think about letting him go. Maybe they would, now they were here, scatter him down by the water's edge or in the woods. He was too precious to not get this decision right – Tor had said it herself, they had to keep him, they had to…

Oh no.

He stood up from the toilet, bringing his shorts up with him in one movement, ignoring the pins and needles that were forming in his legs from being sat there for too long, thinking. He stepped out of the bathroom *don't flush if it's only a pee*, ignoring the bedroom, rushing down the stairs, through the kitchen to the lounge. The windows allowed the brightness of the moonlight to illuminate his way through the house. His bootless ankle causing him some pain with every step but not that much, and not enough to stop him. He saw the small urn that contained Mikey's ashes on the thick wooden window ledge in the lounge, looking out over the lake. It looked like an old piece of oak or something, just cut from a tree and fixed there in some way. The little urn looked almost out of place sat on top of it, off to one side like it was hiding, hoping nobody would notice. Even in death, Mikey was shy. Gabe reached for it, hesitating at the last minute, feeling a sudden chill in the room, but also a viscosity, as if someone had added cornflour to the very air itself to make it thicken up. His hand pushed through the treacle that surrounded the small urn, having to strain to push against it, like bench-pressing in the gym, until his fingers curled around the cool stone. Slowly lifting it, he turned the small vessel in his hand, so it became illuminated by the outside so he could see what he was doing. He hoped Tor didn't wake up and catch him, because what he was doing was crazy, it meant he had crossed the line as much as her. Not only was he believing in the witch, but he was considering her as an entity, a threat, of someone with power.

Someone?

Something?

Regardless. She had power. Power to hurt them, power *over* them, and power of an unknown limit so that he didn't know what she might, ultimately, be capable of. He'd heard Yannick and Idris, and knew of the government interest and involvement. Clearly, they wouldn't be involved if she wasn't a thing of interest to them, but it didn't necessarily mean she was powerful, did it? Just different. Surely if she had that much power, they wouldn't have retired Yannick down here with a computer and a few sensors to monitor her, they'd have come in all guns blazing – not taking no for an answer.

CHAPTER 37
-\/-
THE MAYOR OF CRAZY TOWN

Lifting the lid off the little blue-grey jar and putting it on the window ledge, he slowly started to tilt the urn, tipping it so the open end would pour into his other hand. He really didn't want to be doing this to what was left of Mikey, to potentially spill his son all over the wooden floor and needing to resort to sweeping him up again with the dustpan and brush, leaving small specks of him between the gaps in the floorboards. But that was the crazy time he was living in, and he had to know. The pot continued to tilt, way beyond the horizontal, with no sign of (*life*) the dust he expected to see. Eventually the urn was completely upside down, and just the faintest trickle of dust and ash dropped into his other palm.

She'd taken Mikey. Taken his ashes, taken *him* to the witch. Used his remains so she could… reanimate him in some way.

Gabe, mate, not only have you taken the bus to crazy town, but you've bought property there and are about to move in.

But that was it, right? That's all it could be. The witch must need some kind of link to what was him – she can't have his body, but she could have the next best thing. Probably took the clothes Tor'd kept too. Gabe had thought her a little overly-sentimental about keeping them, but he hadn't pushed her – they'd both needed to get over his death in their own way. After all, he'd kept his toys and games, so giving her a hard time and making her give up any of Mikey's things just because *he* didn't think it was helpful was really not the way to go. And so, he hadn't. Tor kept what she wanted, and she'd hid them away in a 'treasure box' as something to remember him by. But not as something to reanimate him with.

There goes that word again. Crazy town is nice this time of year, but you do need a jacket – one that fastens up the back.

But regardless, Mikey's ashes weren't here. Even if she'd dropped the urn and spilled them by some accident, he wasn't here, and that in itself was worth a discussion. What had happened to Mikey?

Carefully cupping his palm to form a funnel, he poured the few remaining flecks of ash back into the top of the urn, replaced the lid and set it back on the windowsill. His brain working overtime, he slowly climbed back up the stairs, each one creaking like the rigging on a boat, not even noticing the discomfort in his ankle. Distracted with his thoughts as he entered the bedroom, it took him a moment to spot the difference between the two pictures of when he'd left and now. It wasn't hard though, the curtains were drawn back, billowing softly in the breeze. The wind blowing in through the wide-open window. A minute before, when he'd left, both window and curtains had been closed. Watery moonlight illuminated half of the room and the room was now icy cold. He glanced across to the bed and saw a hump under the duvet on Tor's side, which was reassuring. The last thing he needed was for her to be behaving even more strangely and going off to find the witch at night. It was bad enough during the day. But what the hell had opened the window. An image of Dracula entered his head from some gothic Hammer tale – a fanciful notion, but then one that burrowed into his brain, wondering if the witch could open windows like an ancient fictional character.

He noticed something on the floor, under the bed – a small object on the polished wooden floor just below his side, as if it was something that had fallen out of a pocket during the night. Bending awkwardly, he picked it up, laying it in his palm, and walked across to the window so he could examine it better. It was like a crude figurine shaped from twigs or other thin bits of wood, in a similar shape to a crucifix with arms outstretched, and legs together. Some kind of material was stretched across the frame and tied with twine to give the figurine more substance – appearing dark and almost black in the moonlight, with darker patches in places – what was it? He untied the twine and pulled the material away, holding up one of his handkerchiefs, still white at the corners, but dyed across the rest.

Then it dawned on him.

This was what Tor had used to blot his head wound when he'd fallen over the dishwasher after seeing the witch in their kitchen. She'd used a clean handkerchief to mop up the blood, which, at the time, had seemed a little odd when she could've used kitchen roll, but he was in no fit state to comment. Perhaps she'd just grabbed the nearest thing, he'd thought. And now here it was, a charm fashioned under Morvith's guidance, no doubt, to summon the witch to their bed to have her way with the Master of Ty Llyn once more.

Shocked at another revelation about his wife, about the level of both deceit and involvement with Morvith, he shook his head, looking up from the twigs in his palm, through the window and out across the lake, reflecting the cloudless sky in its mirrored surface, movement caught his eye at the edge of the trees down to the left. He looked across the drive, beyond the car and saw a woman in a simple white dress – standing next to a fallen tree. His eyes adjusted to the light and he continued to watch as she moved around the edge of the clearing.

What was she doing?

There was a certain familiarity to her movements but his half-awake brain couldn't place what it was. She moved with elegance and purpose - reminding him of Tor in her grace, and finally he saw what she was doing. She'd been tying a rope to something on the ground and now, complete, she picked up the remaining coil of rope and threw it up and over the long horizontal branch of the big oak. Morgan's oak, where the boy was buried. The rope uncoiled as it flew over the limb, dropping down on the other side revealing the noose at the end. She took one step up onto the trunk of the fallen tree, bringing her head up to the level of the noose which brushed against her hair. She tossed her head to move the hair from her eyes – just like Tor, then reached up and pulled the noose over her head.

Just like Tor.

He turned back to look at the bed and went over to check on his wife. But there was something wrong, the lump looked wrong, out of place, like it wasn't–

He yanked the covers back and saw the two pillows laid at right angles to each other to simulate a person in a foetal position. *Idiot.*

'Tor!' He screamed and sprinted to the window, his ankle, having grudgingly improved to allow him to walk around without too much protest, now started waving banners and opened a *Just Giving* page. Without thinking, he hurdled the low sill, landing with his good foot on the steep slope of the roof, which immediately slipped out in front of him and causing him to land heavily this time on his backside, momentum causing him to continue to slide down the roof. Slates slipped and skidded away as he scrabbled to arrest his descent, grasping at the sharp edges of the roof tiles and the nails holding them in place, shredding his fingers, but finding no clear purchase. He accelerated toward the edge of the roof, flying off into mid-air, his eyes fixed on his wife who had tightened the rope round her neck and was now holding something in front of her that glinted in the moonlight.

The sharpest knife in England.

CHAPTER 38
-\/-
THE SUN AND THE MOON

Focusing on Tor meant Gabe couldn't pick his landing and the ground came up to meet him far too quickly, ten feet below. He landed on both feet just beyond the decking, and for a second he thought he'd nailed it – like a gymnast, bending their knees and wobbling before standing up straight, arms out wide to impress the judges. But his momentum was too great and his weak ankle succumbed – once more going over to the side, twisting under him with a crack, and he collapsed in the dirt. Crying out in pain, a scream like a gunshot, jolting Tor from her reverie – looking up from whatever ceremony was taking place in her mind. She paused with the knife held across her opposite forearm and wrist.

'Tor!' Gabe cried, scrabbling round in the dirt, propping himself on an elbow and reaching his bloodied hand in her direction. 'Wait!' He tried to lever himself up from the floor, putting his injured foot under him to take some weight, but it jolted him with pain and he sucked air in through his teeth. Looking down, the ankle was already swelling heavily and he knew he must've really done it this time – not like the ligament injury, this felt so much worse, like he'd broken it. Once again, he tried to lever himself into a standing position, managing to get his good leg underneath, and put all his strength and power through it to get him upright, gingerly putting his injured foot to the floor. He took his eyes off Tor for a second, ensuring he planted the foot flat on the ground before putting weight onto it. More searing pain shot up his leg – a red hot arrow going as far as his knee, making him shout once again. He quickly limped off his foot onto his good one, hobbling as fast as he could toward Tor.

He looked up in time to see his wife raise her hands in the air, above her head, and slowly draw the knife in a downward angle across her wrist and forearm, finishing with a flick that nearly took the knife into her head. Blood, appearing black in the moonlight, spattered across the front of her dress and onto the floor in front, with more starting to run down toward her elbow. She calmly swapped the knife to her other hand, blood coursing from her open wound down across the handle to drip on the floor. Morvith had appeared by her side, out of nowhere like the shopkeeper in *Mr Ben*. She was holding Mikey's hand and looking up to the raised log on which Tor stood, clearly whispering something – smiling, encouraging. She raised her hands once again, the knife poised, a mirror of the ceremonial position she'd used to slash her other wrist.

'No, Tor,' Gabe called, limping heavily but almost at running pace, half hopping and half dragging his leg. She stared down at him, eyes unwavering, and he was certain she was about to cut herself again.

'Wait. Tor,' he said, each step taking him closer to her – ten yards away now – mind working overtime. 'Remember,' he gasped at the extraordinary pain coming from his foot. 'Remember Ellham? Remember our little house and having that solid fuel boiler and what a fucking pain in the arse it was?' Tears rolled down his cheeks. 'Remember how one night we'd got a bit pissed after having a takeaway, and we were both sat next to each other on the floor and you said, "Life is the sun and love is the moon and neither the sun nor the moon can pull us apart." Do you remember?' He reached out to his wife, who still maintained the pose and was about to slit her other wrist, but she was concentrating on him now, seemingly transfixed as the distance closed between them. 'And that's always been it for us; the sun and the moon. And now I will not let the moon take you away. Not now, not ever.'

'Nice speech, Englishman.' Gabe looked to his left, in the direction of the familiar voice. A movement caught his eye and he turned round. A man was standing twenty yards away in a dark brown robe, old and threadbare, making him look like a giant Jawa. Behind him was a beaten-up old Jeep Wrangler, it's headlights on full, adding to the moonlight. He carried a long flaming torch, and now, either side of him, other torches burst into flames, until there was a line of twelve of them. Idris threw off his hood. There were other cars behind the Twelve that he recognised from around the village – ones that he'd seen parked on the main street or in the supermarket car park. It dawned on Gabe that the witch was the business of everyone in Cwm Cysgod and not just the obsession of one or two crazy old men. This wasn't about Idris versus Yannick in a pissing contest of obsession pitched against science. It was like Idris had been talking about, it was the story of every fanatic and crank that had gathered to become disciples of the witch – one of the Twelve. And now Tor was the queen of them all.

Looking back at his wife, he saw Morvith step up next to her on the fallen trunk, helping the Mikey-golem scramble up awkwardly to join them. She took the knife from Tor's hand and held the blade firmly against the skin of Tor's throat. As close as he was, he could see the skin indent around the cold steel, still glistening with her own blood. The knife in place where she wanted it, the witch looked back at Gabe.

'The Master of Ty Llyn,' she said in her granite voice, and sneered at him, looking back to the knife, licking her lips in the most basic, suggestive manner, her purple snake-tongue, huge and grotesque, looking like it could lick Tor's whole face before slithering back into her maw. She turned back to him, eyes boring into his, but then looked over his shoulder, beyond him, back to the house. Gabe stared at her, stealing a glance back over his shoulder and back to the witch again.

Tor said she wanted me dead. I'm the 'Master' of Ty Llyn. And she wants the Master dead. And that's how she gets Mikey back.

'And now I see where this is going.' Gabe said, grimly, to no one in particular, but enough for Idris to hear. 'Why, Idris? Why do you do this?'

'We have to protect her, to protect the idea of her – she does the rest.'

'You are curators of a museum piece, that's all she is.'

'She's far too powerful to stop – I've told you before.'

'So, when you said before that people come from all over to see her, to live near her in the hope of seeing her, you neglected to mention that they, you, serve her.'

'We all serve her. We are the community of the witch.'

Gabe shook his head, at the madness before him. Tor seemed to be in some kind of trance, oblivious to the blade pressing against her skin. The witch held court, her cronies in their robes, her apprentice – or whatever Tor was becoming – by her side, and then Mikey.

'One of you dies,' she hissed at him, pressing the cold knife blade even harder against Tor, piercing the flesh, a droplet of blood slowly oozing out and running down her throat to collect in the hollow of her collar bone.

'Why?' Gabe stood defiantly, staring the witch down. Her face hardened – he suspected that she wasn't used to being questioned. The air seemed to change around him, becoming charged, bursting with electricity, and he expected to see a lightning bolt at any moment – maybe even coming from her hands. The wind rose up from nowhere, bursting through the trees and racing around between them and the house, like riders on a wall of death, whipping by the group of people in the middle. Gabe remembered he was just wearing boxers and a t-shirt, and Tor's comment popped into his head when he'd been stood outside on the decking the other day, a thousand years or so ago, about not wanting to meet any of their new neighbours dressed like that. And now here he was in front of all of them. The thought took his mind away from how cold he was getting as the wind buffeted him.

'To bring a soul back, I have to send one,' she sneered now. 'Is it her, or is it you?'

'I'm the Master of Ty Llyn.'

'Yes. You are.' The witch's eyes widened, her voice hissing and snake-like. She smiled at the thought.

'And you want me dead.' That's what Tor had said just after the witch had passed through her. *She wants you dead.*

'Yes. The Master of Ty Llyn will die, and I will be free.'

'So, you are cursed to stay around here, just for revenge?'

'No curse. I'm from here – it's my home. It was more my home than anyone else's – any of you. And you took it away.' She pointed at the Master of Ty Llyn, and there was no point arguing with her madness. Her spite and anger and thirst for revenge had made her blind to any logic.

'What if I let her die.' Gabe pointed at his wife and shrugged. 'You haven't killed the master of the house then.'

'No. But I'll come after you until I have. You *will* die.' She cackled at him, screeching on the wind like a thousand seagulls. Gabe nodded, realising the likelihood of what was about to happen. He could either give in to the inevitability of the witch and her followers surrounding him, or he could–

CHAPTER 39

THE HEART OF ALL THINGS

Gabe looked at the distance between him and the fallen trunk – about ten feet. An old tree stump sat about halfway between. A plan formed in his head, a plan to finish this, to put an end to the possession of Ty Llyn, his wife, to put an end to the witch. Without any further delay, as if by thinking it his thoughts would betray him to everyone else in the clearing, he took a step forward on his injured leg. He'd planned this and knew it was the riskiest moment – whether his ankle would stand up to the next part. Planting the foot, the pain exploded like a bomb, sending a shockwave up to his knee, causing him to cry out. But he'd expected it, and so it was right, the next part of the plan, a necessary evil which made it bearable and something to tick off the list. And the ankle held. Wobbling and threatening to collapse, like the last remaining upright timber in a burning house, that has almost burnt completely through, but somehow still does its job. It allowed him to propel himself forward up onto the tree stump with his good leg, and to drive off from it, pushing down as hard as he could, launching himself at both Tor and the witch, airborne, his plan evolving in the time he hung in the air.

Morvith saw him coming and flicked a glance at Idris. Gabe landed on the fallen trunk and wrapped his arms around Tor, who seemed limp and unresponsive – but to have got this far, from having looked out of the bedroom window to see her with a noose round her neck and a knife in her hand, he felt triumphant to feel her warm body in his arms. He spotted movement out of the corner of his eye – robed figures rushing towards him – but his bigger concern was the knife that Morvith still held at Tor's throat. With her distracted for a split second to summon her followers, he quickly managed to slide his fingers between the point of the blade and Tor's tender flesh, pushing her head backwards to create a gap, feeling the metal cut into him, the skin being broken as the witch fought against him, his blood – black in the moonlight running down his hand and arm. He curled his fingers around the blade, gripping it hard, squeezing against the cold steel, relishing the pain, taking his mind away from his ankle as this reached another level. Releasing Tor so he could use both hands to struggle against the undead witch, he pulled the knife away from his wife, even as he felt some of the Twelve reach him and start to grab at his legs and shorts, to try to pull him away. With his other hand he grasped the handle of the knife, prising it away from the witch's fingers, looking straight down her arm, and she cackled. Laughing as if he'd said the funniest thing in history, but her laugh very much at him, not with. He held the knife but all of a sudden found himself airborne, suspended a couple of feet above the trunk, his ankle no longer in pain because it wasn't weight-bearing, the witch holding her hands in open claws in his direction, lifting him with her dark magic. He knew then of what she was capable, knew her power, and felt like he had lost.

'Tonight, is the end of the Master of Ty Llyn. Tonight, is the 23rd of November,' she hissed and looked in the direction of the house. Gabe turned in her grasp and, through the open front door, saw fire break out in the lounge and kitchen. 'Go and they live,' she said, although the voice was largely in his head. He stared at the witch, their faces just three feet apart, her eyes glittering, like they were on fire. It was as if she were playing a game with him, challenging, daring him to take her on, wanting to see if he had the fight inside him. Their eyes were locked for an eternity, testing each other, pushing, two gunslingers facing each other in a dusty street, hands ready to draw their weapons and unload into their enemy. Finally, Gabe nodded, knowing when he was beaten, knowing that Tor and Mikey were the priority, and he was secondary to them. The witch nodded back and slowly lowered him into the waiting arms of the Twelve. Gabe felt hands reach up and start to pull him in, consigning him to his fate, but he still had the knife. Before he was engulfed, he flipped it around in his hand, grasping the handle in both hands, and suddenly sat forwards, jerking against the hands holding him, raising both arms above his head and with a loud cry plunged the cold steel with all his might into the witch's chest. The blade penetrated her ribcage, disappearing inside, sliding between the bones as it sought out any remaining soft tissue of importance inside the hag in front of him. She screeched as the knife was shoved inside her – maybe she was feeling pain for the first time in hundreds of years, maybe it was surprise that he'd got to her, broken through her defences – but then she sagged as if the blade had robbed her of strength, energy and fight.

'No!' exclaimed Idris somewhere below him, and he felt the hands suddenly pulling more insistently, dragging him to them. Still gripping the knife, he gave a last twist of the blade, wrenching it as hard as he could, waggling the handle so the business end would slice back and forth against anything of value inside her, the blade butting against bone. The witch screamed again, this more guttural, growing to a deafening animalistic roar that whipped up the wind even more, swirling around them, her head flew back and her back arched, shaking and twitching. The Disciples of the Witch gathered around her, cradling her body, holding her upright as energy crackled around – the air itself charged and angry. The guttural cry turned into a howl of the wind, which seemed to explode out of Morvith – from her mouth at first and then, very gradually, as fast flowing water erodes the banks of a river, it pulled her face apart, ripping away at mouth and nose, and then her head was just a faucet for the most powerful shower in history, wind and lightning ripping out of the witch's body.

'You've pierced her heart! Look what you've done.' Idris cried, turning from the stricken sorceress.

'How's she got a *heart*? She's been dead for hundreds of years,' Gabe replied, having to shout to be heard over the maelstrom.

'It's the centre of her, where she stores her power, like a battery of energy encapsulated to hold it within, that she can control as she wants, and you've let it lose! The power will be uncontrollable!'

'Oh, I'm sorry, I thought she was going to kill my wife and my son who's now a tree! Fuck you, Idris, and fuck you for protecting her.'

The wind circled and buffeted around the clearing, hammering against the trees, ripping away branches and uprooting saplings at the edge of the treeline. Like the swirling storm of a hurricane, the windspeed grew, catching more and more debris, whipping up the forest floor, turning pine cones and broken branches into hundred mile-an-hour weapons, a deadly forcefield surrounding the calm eye of the storm in the centre – centred around the witch.

Cloud had rolled in across the lake at breakneck speed – racing over the water as if it was late for a meeting, and now it circled around above their heads, a clear gap in the middle above Morvith as the clouds deepened, climbing higher and higher into the stratosphere, becoming like the storm clouds in tornado movies, just waiting for a tube to drop down and suck them up like Dorothy in Kansas. Electricity flickered across the cloud surface, lighting them up, giant sparks flying across the highly charged atmosphere. The first bolt of lightning crashed down, sizzling on the ground a few feet away, dead leaves and twigs exploding everywhere like someone had thrown a grenade. It made landfall again, striking the edge of the fallen trunk on which Tor was standing. As if having tried a couple of sighters, to get its eye in, to make sure its aim was true, the sky blasted down once more, striking the witch in the throat – there was little left of her head now as the power ripped out of her and escaped into the surroundings – but this was no momentary blast, this bolt of lightning continued, jerking and moving, swaying as it came down from the heavens, but remaining like a light that no one remembered to turn off. Small forks came off the main bolt, striking trees and singeing the brows of some of the Disciples, some reflecting back off the witch's body and arcing onto the ground or stinging one of the Twelve, hungrily seeking out a victim like the electricity in a plasma ball. One arc came off and headed toward Tor, flying over Gabe's head, bending with the strain, sounding like overstretched elastic in a *Tom and Jerry* cartoon, the incredible searing heat scorching his face as it flashed past him, seeking out Tor like a flame to a moth, the bolt striking her hard in the mouth.

'No!' Gabe called, fighting off Mal the pub landlord and Bobby the cricketer to try to get to his wife as the lightning hit. For a second, he thought she might explode, such was the energy and power in the lightning, but her body held as the beam forced itself inside her, lighting her up from inside like some kind of x-ray machine, her arms blasted outwards, hands and fingers glowing yellow then slowly turning white, blurring with the heat coming off them. She was shuddering, as if she was being electrocuted – maybe she was – maybe it was killing her with the current and not the heat, her body shaking as if a giant hand had hold of her and was throwing her around like a rag doll. Surely, she must burn up, surely it wasn't possible for living tissue to sustain this onslaught? Wondering when it might stop, he looked back at the witch, who was sagging as the lightning drained her. Her long-dead body collapsing in on itself, the skin, gone from the alabaster pale of the girl in the dress, to the shiny grey of the old hag, was now stretching tighter and tighter across the old bones as the muscles and sinew beneath eroded away, becoming tissue paper thin as it was stretched impossibly, beyond the strain any skin had ever been placed upon before, dead or not. For a moment the witch's body – the dead carcass of the last of the cunning folk – tensed and quivered, barely held together. But there was only so much that it could take, and the tissue gave, seemingly every cell finally giving up the ghost simultaneously, the bone beneath shattering too and where there was once the contorted body of the all-powerful Morvith, now there was an explosion of dust and ash and evil that disappeared on the wind. Being taken up and around, whipped up into the clouds to become one with the surroundings that she had never left.

And just like that, she was gone. A silence enveloped them as the roar of the wind faded, seemingly blowing itself out now that its favourite cheerleader wasn't there. Gabe watched as the lightning stopped, sparks and bursts of energy racing across the floor, disappearing into the earth. He traced the last arc of brilliant white energy as it flew over his head and into Tor, before it suddenly stopped, like switching off a light. With this final burst, Tor jerked once more and collapsed on the floor.

CHAPTER 40

-\/-

LONG LIVE THE WITCH

The brightness of the lightning storm now gone; Gabe's eyes had to adjust to the dark once more, still seeing yellow trails imprinted on his retina. The only light coming from the house behind him and the torches that some of the twelve still held. He limped across to Tor, who was stirring, pushing herself up on one arm, smoke and steam rising from all over her body, sparks crackling and fizzing over her skin – igniting and racing along her arms and legs like pure white spiders, before colliding and exploding like tiny fireworks. Slowly, she levered herself up onto her feet, ratcheting up into a standing position. Cracks and pops came from the joints in her spine and ribs, as if she were manipulating her bones back together – needing to rebuild herself like the car in *Christine* – body jerking grotesquely as it righted itself. Raising her head, she looked straight at him, or through him, it seemed – there was no immediate recognition. And then, as her operating system rebooted, her eyes cleared and settled on him for the first time – a camera regaining focus. Staring unmoved for an age, Gabe thought he would try to rouse her from her reverie.

'Tor?' he asked quietly, reaching his hand out, closing half the distance between them. She tilted her head to one side as she regarded him, curiously, like a cat looking at a mouse, and Gabe felt small, regressing back to being a young child looking up at an adult or a teacher when he had done wrong. She slowly turned her head to look across at the Twelve, who'd stepped back from Gabe and gathered around the dusty rags that was all that remained of Morvith. Suddenly, her eyes lit up, becoming balls of yellow fire, the concentrated energy of the lightning still inside her. Opening her mouth with her head lolling on one side, for a moment she was a zombie from any cheap 80s horror movie, but then she roared. It was the roar of a thousand lions, the biggest hurricane, a giant wave crashing onto the shore. Her voice changed the air, stopped the wind from circling round the trees and directed it towards them, a fearsome blast as if they'd stepped out into the middle of a storm, jerking the Twelve away from their grief at the loss of their mistress. *Dr Who* had regenerated. Confused, Gabe stared at his wife. Suddenly she was showing signs of being possessed by immense power, of harnessing electricity or lightning or something and being able to hold it within herself. But he saw how the Twelve gazed upon her – they were enraptured.

'The witch is dead, long live the witch!' One of them cried out. There was a murmur in the group and a few others joined in, repeating the phrase, not in time with each other. By the third and fourth time they were all chanting, and it was a mantra that they repeated as Tor looked upon them. Beyond the Twelve, Gabe saw something move, passed the line of cars, it could've been a shadow, barely illuminated by the glow of the house lights. After watching it for a few moments, he realised it was someone pacing up and down, bent forward in silhouette, markedly so toward the top of the spine, and their head looked like it grew out of their chest. Gabe thought it looked like some kind of shadow animal you made with your hands to project on a wall. From what he could make out, it looked like Yannick had his hand pressed against his head, probably talking on his phone. Whatever he was doing he appeared agitated, quickly turning this way and that, gesticulating with his other hand.

As the chanting continued, Tor turned to face the house, staring at it, as if transfixed. She took it all in, and then slowly raised her hands in front of her, and roared again. Tiny balls of light appeared in the palms of her hands, spinning and crackling with energy, quickly growing so they were bigger than her hands, arms shaking with the control required to hold their power. Her roar grew in pitch and intensity, rising to a screech, and, with a flick of her fingers, the lightning balls flew away from her. Free of the metaphysical restraints which had created them, they accelerated away, flying past Gabe so fast that he barely saw them and would've had no time to dodge out of the way if they had been directly aimed. Still, their shockwave threw him to the ground, landing hard on his side, his painful ankle mercifully out of the way. They were flying straight for the house, like two rockets fired from a plane, course plotted and aim unerring, smoke billowing behind them like vapour trails. The lightning balls smashed into the front door together, the wood exploding into a million splinters and taking the doorframe and some of the front of the house with it. Whatever they were made up of spewed out along the hallway and all through the downstairs, a trail of flames springing up, like a giant petrol bomb. Looking into the giant maw that had been the front of his house, Gabe could see the flames joining those of the fire Morvith had already started, and spreading up the stairs. He levered himself to his feet and turned to look back at Tor.

Go inside. Her voice inside his head. Unmistakeably Tor.

'In the house?' Gabe asked, incredulous.

Yes. Tor's expression was firm, her jaw hard and unyielding. Her head tilted on one side.

'But it's burning down!' Gabe exclaimed – pointing, as if further emphasis was needed, in the general direction of the house.

Yes.

'You want me to go into the burning house?'

Yes.

'Why?'

You are the Master of Ty Llyn.

'But I'm not.'

Yes, you are. And it is you… or us. Tor pulled Mikey to her, sparks jumping around her skin, singeing the boy's birds nest as she slowly slid her palm under his chin. She held her other hand under her own face, skin aglow with the yellow and orange flames that were leaping from her fingers. The threat was very obvious. He needed to sacrifice himself – the last master of Ty Llyn, the last wish of Morvith the witch. And if he didn't? Morvith, or the spirit of Morvith or whatever it was that was inside Tor, was going to kill them both. Checkmate. Out of the corner of his eye, he noticed the Twelve moving closer toward them, the torches slowly spreading out into a line, stopping any idea he might have of escaping to the car. But that wasn't what he was thinking. He was thinking of any other way of reasoning with her, reasoning with the witch, trying to make her see that he wasn't the old master, the one that was to blame for what happened to her, for putting her to death four-hundred-years ago to the very day. But her mind had clearly become crazed and twisted over the years – one couldn't blame her for going mad, from being isolated, living in a cave by the lake, with only generations of these disciples for company. And now what choice did he have? Let Morvith kill them so he can walk away, or let Tor and Mikey live, in whatever state they are both in – Tor, his love, his life, with whom he'd been through things that no one should ever have to endure. Something that had almost finished them. The irony, of course, was that the move that was meant to save them had done the opposite. Just as Tor had planned. And then there was Mikey, a caricature of his son, taken from them and brought back by who-knows-what magic but, regardless, even if it was just some of Mikey, ten percent of him, maybe, it was worth it. Another day with him, even just a fraction of him, it had to be worth it.

Right?

Tears rolling down his face, Gabe nodded at his wife and son one last time and turned to walk purposefully toward the house, the second step landing on his painful ankle, which he'd forgotten about, making him wince and stumble. Pausing he bent double and caught his breath, before continuing on, limping toward the flames, the Twelve forming a semi-circle walking slowly behind, as if he couldn't work out where he needed to be.

I'm being herded, he thought, looking over his shoulder.

The pain in his ankle hadn't gone, but it seemed further away, more distant. And after all, it didn't matter anymore – it was an irrelevance. As he grew closer, the heat from all the fires downstairs was intense, he could feel it picking at his skin already – all he needed was some olive oil and seasoning and he'd be ready for the oven. An oven that, with one last look behind him, beyond the Twelve, to what remained of his family, he stepped inside.

CHAPTER 41

-\/-

TO RUN AND PLAY AND LIVE AND LOVE

Their home, their beautiful retreat by the lake – or at least what could've been if they'd been allowed to live in it for more than a few weeks – was ablaze. It wasn't a series of fires anymore but one huge inferno that had engulfed the kitchen units, the sofas in the lounge which were just carcasses dressed in flames. The bookcases and shelves had easily collapsed and were starting to ignite the polished wooden floor – the last to take. Taken aback by the scene, and momentarily frozen by a desire to try and save the place, Gabe considered the fire extinguisher beneath the sink or the hosepipe outside that he had yet to rig up and was on an ever-growing list of jobs he needed to do that, now, wouldn't ever be done. He remembered what he must do, remembered the deal, and smiled grimly as he abandoned his natural instincts. Turning to climb the wooden staircase – which had seemingly escaped the effect of the fire – he grasped the banister rail, then cried out in pain as the heat from it singed his skin. *That will leave a blister*, he thought. As he climbed higher, the step below would burst into flame in time, herding him again, exactly where she wanted him. For a brief moment there was respite in the upstairs hallway – seemingly almost cool with no flames having reached this far. Their bedroom, too was unblemished – despite it filling with smoke which poured out through the still open window he had slid out of an age ago, back when the world was a little less insane than it was now, although it was all relative. The room was cooler, and he felt he could draw breath in spite of the smoke, his lungs not being seared by the heat of downstairs. Somehow knowing that Tor wanted to see him, he moved to the corner window. Through the smoke, through the shimmering heat haze, through his own watering eyes mixed with the tears he had for his family and his life, he could see her, holding Mikey's hand, staring back at him. With her free hand she made a simple gesture, lifting it up a little as if she were holding her palm out to check if it was raining. But it wasn't that kind of sign, it was a command to turn the burners up. The low rumble of the fire downstairs, suddenly became a roar, and Gabe could immediately feel the heat through the floor, through his bare feet.

You've just been outside in the cold with nothing on your feet – you'll catch your death.

The downstairs windows bowed outwards under the onslaught, as if under the manipulation of a master glass blower, before exploding – shattered glass landing with a tinkling sound, like Christmas bells, all over the decking. Flames shot out of the now empty windows, curling up around the wood cladding, licking up all around their bedroom – like a lascivious lover, teasing with their tongue. Yes, their bedroom. Gabe watched the beauty of the flames crawling up and over the glass, waves of colour, searching for imperfections, holes, places where it could get in. The creeping monster in blistering yellow and orange and red found a better way and poked its head around their bedroom door before rushing in, consuming the chest of drawers, and melting the bed linen before leaping up to dance along the curtains like molten liquid gold.

Gabe's t-shirt was smoking, and his shorts were already on fire, the soles of his feet burning. Flames crawled up above his waist until the shirt gave up its resistance, and it, too, was ablaze, setting his hair on fire as well. He maintained eye contact with Tor, his entire focus on her, and his thoughts of Mikey. Not this Mikey, not the one that would inhabit the forest with Tor for all eternity, which was okay because it was Mikey in some form, just not the one he knew. Not *his* Mikey. He blocked out the flames, blocked out his breathing or lack of as his mouth and lungs were scalded beyond any viable use, blocked out the pain of the fire which totally surrounded him, despite somewhere within, his body was screaming for mercy. He blocked it all out as he thought of his wife and son, of better days, of holding hands in a perfect world where they could live happily away from everything that could threaten them. Like a photograph, the image of his family – the last thing he saw and experienced – was burnt onto his brain as he collapsed into the inferno of the bedroom, the rampaging flames hungrily consuming him.

∞ ∞ ∞

Tor watched impassively as Gabe fell, disappearing from view, the flames filling the bedroom. From below came a groan and the whole building seemed to shudder, shaking on its foundations. Behind the house, the oil tank went up with a mighty explosion that rocked it from the rear – the top of the tank propelled like a rocket straight up and above the roof before clattering down in the drive. The wooden front – which had stood for all those years, and yes had been replaced and replaced like Trigger's brush, with no original parts left – could no longer support the weight of the house. Beams buckled and twisted, cross-members snapped or burnt through – vaporising in the heat – and in one moment, as if the combined timbers of Ty Llyn had rehearsed their simultaneous demise – they failed as one.

The front collapsed down, taking half of the roof with it, pulling on the other half, and collapsing this down into the lounge, the other walls folding in on themselves – a giant house of cards, falling into the ever hungrier inferno, eager for more timber to feed its insatiable appetite. The final part of the roof took the last wall down and somewhere in what used to be the kitchen there was an explosion of heat and who knows what else, but it was as if the rest of the house ignited so intensely that it only took a few seconds to burn completely through before the flames started to fade. Receding – dying away. Like people at a party that's ended prematurely, the flames quietly left, going their own separate ways over the now black timbers of the main roof beams which were scattered by the front door – or where it had been. Suddenly there was quiet, save for some cracks and pops, some spitting wood. A partition wall – the last one standing – creaked and collapsed into the remains of the lounge, showering sparks into the air – fireflies being given their freedom to tell of the great fire of Ty Llyn.

The house would smoulder for days, turning the final remaining timbers to ash, and despite the eye witness reports, the fire and rescue teams would never find Gabe's body.

The Twelve gradually melted away – dumped their robes in the back of their cars, dropping their torches that someone would collect again, and drove away into the night. Returning to their dilapidated cottage, the pub, the vicarage, their house next to the cricket club, and all the other homes from where they worshipped the witch. They would meet the next day in the pub to discuss what had happened – and there was plenty to discuss.

Tor turned back to the forest, taking Mikey's wooden hand in hers, and led him off into the trees, happily skipping away from the house, now that the Man was gone. The Master, the monster that had made Morvith what she was. And this was Tor's gift back to her – to ease her pain, and let her rest easily inside her. They would run and play and live and love in these woods forever more. Free and together, unburdened by convention and requirements, rules and demands. They would please themselves, and no one else.

She looked down at the boy whose eyes were now bright with wonder and recognition – the lights were on and now somebody was at home. Morvith had been right, she needed to exchange one soul for another.

∞ ∞ ∞

As they kicked happily through the dead leaves and ran through the trees hand-in-hand, the moon swept along the surface of the lake. Except it wasn't the moon, but the searchlight of a helicopter, swooping low over the water, whipping up clouds of spray behind it, followed immediately by another, skimming over the tops of the trees then dropping down, weaving left and right like dragonflies on a summer evening, heading for the wisps of smoke slowly drifting up from Lake House and the bright red flare that Yannick had lit on the beach below. He waved another flare in his hand, guiding them in like ground crew at an airport. The wind rose again, but this time whipped up by the rotor blades, skidding off the water surface to deal an icy blast to his face. Both choppers swooped in, pulling their noses up at the last moment to stop their forward momentum, and settled their skids on the gravel beach. Soon there would be boots on the ground, the containment device readied, and the final hunt for the witch would be on.

The End

Mark Brownless
Carmarthen
August 2021

AUTHOR'S NOTE

I set my first novel, *The Hand of an Angel*, in a fictional city, that, very deliberately, could've been anywhere. *The Shadow Man* was set in a fictional version of my home village in Lincolnshire, paying homage to the memories of my childhood. So, it has taken until now to be able to set a story in my adopted home of West Wales. Once again, it's a fictional village, and this was where I ran into a problem. I wanted a Welsh name for the village, but lacked the necessary language skills to come up with one. My thanks, then, go to the Seymour family and the rest of the 'Aberaeron caravan crew' for selflessly staying up to all hours of the night to come up with not only the brilliant village name of Cwm Cysgod – Shadow Valley – but that of the region of Cwmgwrach – Witch's valley. Thanks guys!

In putting Witch in your hands, there are a number of people to thank. First and foremost, my publisher, SpellBound Books, and the ever-expanding team of Nikki East, Sumaira Wilson, Zoé-Lee O'Farrell and Dee Groocock.

As always, Sam Missingham and Dale L Roberts are always there for me and are about as close to an agent as I have. Thank you both, and I hope you'll always have my back.

Chucking some words down on a page might not seem that challenging, but, at least for me, wrangling them into something resembling a coherent story isn't that easy. So, I'd like to thank all those folks who've provided some support, encouragement, advice, pep-talks, bollockings (sorry!), words of wisdom, or generally given me something that meant something at the time. And they are, in no particular order; Keith Wheeler, Joel Hames-Clarke, Andy Hill, Warren Dudley, Fenella Ashworth, Mark Stay, Donna Morfett, Kevin Maguire, Jim Ody, Claire Sheehy, Gary Twigg, Stu Turton and Caz Tudor.

And, finally, to you, dear reader. Thank you so much for reading, for getting this far, and I do hope you liked Gabe and Tor's story. I hope it won't take as long to share the next one with you.

MB

www.markbrownless.com

www.facebook.com/markbrownlessauthor/

twitter.com/MarkBrownless

Printed in Great Britain
by Amazon

71676382R00200